SMEG

DIANE WISHART

This book is a work of fiction. Any references to historical events, real people, or real places are used fictitiously. Other names, characters, places, and events are products of the author's imagination, and any resemblance to actual events, places, names, or persons, is entirely coincidental.

Distributed by Simon & Schuster

ISBN: 978-1-998672-12-7
Ebook: 978-1-998672-13-4

FIC022020 **FICTION** / Mystery & Detective / Police Procedural
FIC022070 **FICTION** / Mystery & Detective / Cozy / General
FIC090000 **FICTION** / World Literature / Canada / General

#SmegBook

Follow Rising Action on our socials!
Twitter: @RAPubCollective
Instagram: @risingactionpublishingco
Tiktok: @risingactionpublishingco

To my family

SMEG

The First Detective Smeg Mystery

Chapter One

Chamberlain Smeg, Charlie to his few friends, unfolded the *Edmonton Journal* in a ritual as familiar as putting on socks. He leaned his ample frame forward on his elbows and peered through drugstore reading glasses at the print that faded with each passing year. He longed for the time when newspapers hadn't cheaped out on ink. The headlines reported the same news as every day that week but he was compelled to read on. It wasn't the need to stay up-to-date to engage in water cooler chat; he was never one for that, and now with the job behind him, the only water cooler he saw was attached to his fridge. Paul Galloway, his twenty-two-year-old stepson, stood rooted in front of it, his legs unnaturally wide apart like he needed to scare off a large animal. Paul opened and closed the fridge door multiple times, either because he also needed glasses or was hoping for a different result; maybe some leftover sausages or an egg he didn't have to fry himself.

The furnace moaned, trying to reach the temperature Paul had jacked the thermostat up to. Charlie had a right to say something about the heat as the guy who paid the bills, but would have to wait until the earbuds were removed from Paul's ears. Charlie set his glasses down on the table as Paul grabbed a four-litre plastic jug of milk, poured liberally over his Honey Nut Cheerios and over the side of the bowl onto the counter. What was still in the jug made it back into the fridge for once. Paul padded across the room on bare feet, his sports shorts hung low over his hips, the only nod to winter a heavy black hoodie with a PlayStation logo on the front.

The house, typical of the period homes in the neighbourhood, had a large kitchen, the kind meant for boisterous chatter, filled with the hominess of bread baking and mounds of potatoes being peeled. It spoke to a time when children built snow forts, careened down hills on toboggans, and moved out when they turned eighteen. In Charlie's day, becoming an adult was a rite of passage, an accomplishment, a chance to show what you were made of. After scraping a chair over the tile floor, Paul landed the bowl of cereal safely on the table and sat down. Some days, Charlie wondered what Paul was made of. The young man pulled one earbud from its nest and croaked a good morning. His face lit up to reveal tiny crow's feet around his eyes. Charlie caught a glimpse of the boy he used to take to the park.

"You're up early," Charlie said. His time to chat was limited before the earbud went back in.

Paul's head bobbed up and down vigorously, his black hair sweeping his face like the back end of a street cleaning truck. "I wanna catch a podcast on writing a novel."

Charlie choked on his coffee, although by now he shouldn't be surprised at the whims of his stepson. He peered at him over the large blue and grey clay bowl in the middle of the vintage table, which housed two blackened bananas and a wrinkled apple. Both the bowl and the table were additions Nancy added to the room. The bowl had always been filled with fresh fruit—oranges, grapefruits, kiwi—in colours that changed like the northern lights. The boys knew they were expected to eat it. The table abutted the kitchen window, which faced north into a snow-filled backyard shaded from the sun that crept slowly above the horizon. Light found its way through the stained glass of the front door, splashing up the hardwood floors to display an array of paint samples over the wall that needed restoration. In fact, the entire kitchen had been neglected since Nancy died.

Charlie reached for his forgotten peanut butter toast and took a bite. He slurped it down with coffee, this time with more success. "You're writing a novel?"

"Yeah, I can express myself so much better in writing, you know? Like when I write an email, I can get all my thoughts down way better than when I'm talking. I'm just not a gifted talker like you." He shovelled in two heaping spoonfuls of Cheerios in quick succession.

Charlie didn't consider himself a gifted speaker, maybe because he lacked interest in communicating with people. Paul, on the other hand, was loquacious, and a mouthful of cereal didn't usually stop him. It was Charlie's assumption that he was talking about games when he chattered on about dark fantasy worlds and romantic landscapes; it seemed unlikely the boy had an imagination. But still, the content of his soliloquies could be the stuff of stories.

"I suspect there's a lot more to writing fiction." Charlie wasn't keen on encouraging this latest distraction of Paul's.

"I didn't expect you to understand, but I've got to do something with my life," Paul said, his chin pointed in Charlie's direction.

Charlie didn't appreciate hearing his own words parroted back to him. He'd meant a job with a paycheck. He glanced down at the sports section. The player grades from last night's hockey game were dismal.

"What are you writing about?" he asked, without looking up.

"It's not *about*, man. You write from within, your emotions, not looking down at it. No sage on the stage. That shit's not gonna work."

Charlie had no idea what response was expected from him. He lifted his gaze and stared at Paul, and tried to figure it out.

"Sorry. Likely never mentioned, I've been writing rap for quite some time now. Poetry, I guess you'd call it."

It didn't matter to Charlie what it was called. The longer he and Paul lived together under one roof, the farther apart they drifted. Charlie blamed himself. Nancy's illness had consumed him; he wanted so much to ease her pain that he didn't notice Paul's. He had managed to connect with the twelve-year-old who walked into his life, but reconnecting with the teenager was a whole different thing, and the man sitting in front of him was still a riddle. Now he wondered about the emails Paul had started to send him—mostly musings about dinner. Charlie thought it likely Paul didn't want to get off the couch in the basement and walk upstairs to have a conversation. But maybe there was more to it.

"Can I read your poems?" he asked and hoped that the answer would be no. Then he'd have to respond intelligently.

Paul tipped his bowl and drained the remaining milk. "Sure, but I don't know if you'll get it. I could give you some books to read to give you a sense of the genre, you know, like Tupac?"

"Isn't rap associated with violence and the glorification of criminal lifestyles? I'm not sure you have the experience to write authentically about it." Paul had grown physically into a man, but emotionally, he wasn't much beyond that boy Charlie used to guide through the Toys R Us parking lot. Street smart, he was not.

"That's a stereotype. You should learn more about it before you criticize."

"Okay," Charlie said, knowing it was going to be a stretch for him to meet his stepson where he was at. Wherever that was.

"Anyway, I have to go. My podcast is starting." He dropped the bowl in the sink.

"Pretty sure you can listen to those any time." Charlie opted to ignore the bowl that hadn't been put in the dishwasher.

"They're posted at set times. This one just came out," he said, and stuck his earbud back in place. "I want to get started on my book." His receding footsteps echoed the still bouncing bowl.

Charlie, book in hand, was engulfed in the mission to track the murderous Kelso brothers when he was pulled off course by the chime of his wired doorbell, one of the original features of the house. He'd consciously not updated it, as opposed to not getting around to replacing. He cherished the early twentieth-century brick house with its low-pitched roof, dormer windows, and large front veranda, much like he did his grandmother, who had raised him in it. As the visitor was likely to be someone looking for money, perched expectantly on the wide front steps, he lowered his head and continued reading. The bell rang again, imploring him to set down his worn copy of Guy Vanderhaeghe's *The Last Crossing* and glance out the front window. Meaghan Byatt's little economy car was parked neatly against the banked snow. He'd often considered the possibilities of reverse wiring the doorbell to give out shocks, like an electric fence. Worked to keep horses away.

Detective Byatt, a former partner for mere days. Kid in big girl clothes. She was a star over in robbery, and top brass had wanted to profile her, so they transferred her to the prestigious homicide unit. She was the youngest detective by far in homicide. Clever, dedicated, and attractive in an unconscious way. She looked impressive on a recruitment poster. He wondered if her virtuous looks were helping her solve crimes. Maybe that was unfair. After all, it wasn't her fault he'd packed it in.

Charlie heaved himself up from the high-backed mahogany chair and ambled to the door. She waited eagerly on the verandah, snowdrops highlighting long ginger hair that framed her confident face.

"Hey, Detective Smeg. Just checking in, wondering how you're doing." A pause suggested it was his move.

He didn't take it. People checking in, asking how he was doing, were beginning to piss him off. He'd retired, not lost a limb.

"I'm sorry. Did I wake you?" Her furrowed brow mirrored his own.

Smeg tried to remember when he'd last combed his hair. "No," he said. "Not a problem."

"I've been digging around in this case we were working on." Her hand moved toward the file folder tucked under her arm. "Got a few minutes to chat?"

It was unusual, this re-engagement. Smeg had watched, over the course of his forty years with the force, a disappearance of sorts when officers retired. He often thought someone should investigate. The same fate might have been his but for the fact that he'd been invisible for years. Obsolete, out of date. He was an old-style cop, dedicated to his craft, principled, hard-working. He watched younger, less experienced officers advance past him. That was fine, as he didn't want the desk job; the paperwork and bullshit grew exponentially the higher one rose in the organization. He could also live without the disdain that emanated from those who thought rank transcended skill and experience.

Byatt's hand dropped, leaving the file folder in its place.

Smeg breathed in the not-unpleasant fresh air and made no move to close the door. "Don't you have a new partner?"

"Oh god, where to start. Some sort of glitch with the paperwork is the short answer." Byatt's heavy parka, undone and wet with melted snow, seemed too much for the warm December day.

Paperwork? Since when did they put that much thought into it? In Smeg's experience, these matchups were made of convenience, like the way he and Byatt had been thrown together. His former partner was out on long-term disability, replaced by the next person in the door, as if a stellar career could be wiped out with one bullet to the leg.

He sighed. "Sure, what can I do for you?"

"Can I come in?"

Smeg stepped back, took and hung up her coat, then ushered her into the living room.

"I love this room." Her smile reinforced her words as her eyes took in each detail.

He knew she saw a living room filled with laughter. Its rose-patterned wallpaper grew out from under the chair rail and wainscoting Nancy had painted a soft Chantilly lace, an invitation to sit awhile. The ceiling and floor moldings had been replaced with less fussy versions of the originals that moved the eye toward the arched doorway. At least that was what Nancy told him. These days, his eye tended toward the floor-to-ceiling bookshelf with books stuffed in on top of each other.

"Do you play the piano?" Byatt asked, acknowledging the shiny black upright in the corner with a tilt of her head.

"No, that was my wife's."

She'd been gone five years. Cancer. He'd only had her with him for the same number. Byatt didn't know that, but he wasn't going to fill her in. Nancy had always pulled the drapes open in the early morning, fluffed the throw pillows, and polished the piano until it resembled the plate glass window. She was a concert pianist who gave the room heart and light. He couldn't bear to part with the piano. Nancy had taught Paul to play, but Charlie knew he didn't need to keep the piano for him. Paul's talent hadn't been sparked.

"Please," he said, and indicated she should sit on the loveseat. He took his place back on the still-warm chair.

"This case," Byatt said and leaned forward. "Human tissue found in a bathtub drain?"

Byatt's sandy sweater and dark jeans played to the room, and Smeg found himself relaxing. She, on the other hand, had bright pink spots on her cheeks and breathed a little too rapidly. They hadn't had much time together before he left. She was a good kid. Although at thirty-five, she wasn't really a kid. If he'd had the energy, he could have worked with her, but after he'd failed his former partner, leaving her alone in an alley while he chugged along trying to keep up, he couldn't bring himself to get involved again.

Smeg nodded. "I recall. Tell me where you're at in your investigation. Has the body been found?"

She leaned back and draped one arm over the back of the loveseat. "Two boys playing pond hockey found a decomposed body in a frozen-over swamp west of the city. Shot the puck into the reeds and hit him on the head. The lab tests have confirmed it's the same person. I have some thoughts I'd like to bounce off you."

He tilted his head, a little wary. If the department had valued his expertise, he might not have put in his papers. So, what did Byatt want with him now? He'd left her high and dry and little hurt, he knew. But he couldn't explain, not to her. Really, not to anyone, although the department therapist had tried to get him to talk when he'd gone for mandatory counselling after the incident. It was the end of the road for him for a number of reasons: out of sync, out of style, and out of shape. The opposite of Byatt, who oozed confidence and great physical conditioning, and who he realized was talking. Something about a contract killing. He pulled himself back to her case for the details: shot in a back alley, the body bleached in a bathtub before it was moved, no DNA evidence on the body. There were ties to organized crime. The accused lived alone in the apartment where the body was cleaned so he was the prime suspect. But with organized crime, there would of course have been others involved, especially to move the body.

"You've got a case with strong circumstantial evidence, given the human tissue match. Does the accused have known gang affiliates?" Smeg leaned forward.

"He's a member of the West Side Gang, and he's known to police."

"Have the victim's personal effects been located?" Smeg forgot he didn't give a damn about this case.

"A search of the dumpster behind his apartment revealed nothing, but a wallet, wrapped in a plastic grocery bag, was found in a dumpster one block over. We're checking for a match on the prints." She seemed to be getting on well on her own, figuring it out.

"What are you struggling with?"

"Someone else has confessed. I told Staff Sergeant Singer I thought the confession was false. The person, however, knows details that haven't been in the paper."

"Is there enough factual basis for the plea?"

"Singer and I talked about our mutual distrust of reliance on confessions. She agrees we need to find out the motive behind the confession."

"Coercion by gang members?"

"Singer isn't convinced. I just love her leadership, you know? We have an impressive success rate in homicide, and much of it is because of her. Anyway, I have an interview set up with the confessor for tomorrow."

Smeg's stomach was beginning to remind him of why he'd quit. Byatt had quickly learned how to get into Singer's good books by drawing her in, making her feel like a mentor. Smeg had been an actual mentor to his former partner, but the fresh-faced climber in front of him was a new breed of cop.

"Where's the gang unit in all this?"

"Protocol is that homicide retains lead on the investigation. Until we've determined for sure that it was a contract killing and that it was ordered by the West End Gang, it's ours."

"Sounds like that determination can be made. Don't you think Gangs would have some useful intel?"

"Singer's okay with our approach at this point. Sometimes the Gang Unit messes things up, you know?"

In Semg's experience, the cock-ups usually came when individuals got territorial.

"Well, if you don't need anything more from me, I'll get back to my day." He pushed himself forward in his chair. It was time to get back to the things that mattered, like removing stressors from his living room.

A shadow crossed Byatt's face. "If the confession doesn't work out, I'm going to need a partner to help pursue other leads."

"Maybe they'll have assigned someone to you by then. These arrangements don't usually take very long."

Byatt stared, seemingly unable to process what he'd said. "Singer's the one who wanted me to talk to you. I don't care if you help out or not." In the dim light, Smeg was unsure if he'd imagined the little pout of her lower lip.

"Sorry," Smeg said. "I'm done with all that." Although, he did wonder what Singer was thinking. She used to be one of the good ones.

A blur of black hair flew by the open living room doorway.

"You have a dog?"

"No, a stepson."

Byatt turned her attention back toward Smeg as she rose to her feet. "Anyway, I was supposed to leave the file with you. Do whatever you want with it." She glanced toward the fireplace and headed to the door. Smeg followed.

As she stepped into the hallway, she ran right into the speeding stepson coming back the other way with a bag of chips and a Coke in hand.

Charlie reached out a protective hand to keep her from falling backward. "Paul, watch where you're going." He rubbed the top of his nose where a headache was forming.

"Sorry," Paul mumbled and looked at the floor.

"No problem. I'm Meaghan." She extended her hand. "You're late for something?"

Paul took it. "Always in a hurry. I was thinking about my writing and not paying attention."

"Cool. What are you writing?"

As they exuded the virtues of modern poetry, Charlie briefly saw another world he didn't belong in, a world that was young, bright, and opened up like the blooms of a Christmas cactus. They moved on to a television show and its subtexts of race and gender, both enamoured of its in-depth writing of complex themes and accurate representation of the times. Even television had left Charlie behind.

At the door, Charlie thanked her for stopping by. "Stay in touch," he heard himself say.

Returning to his chair, he noticed a long, ginger hair curled up on the love seat, which he promptly disposed of. Stay in touch indeed.

Chapter Two

The usual mid-day noises reminded Charlie that it was time for lunch: children ejecting as from an oscillating tennis ball machine out the front door of the school across the street; traffic catapulting off the High Level bridge in a big hurry to get somewhere; and, the magpies gathering for their noon-time meal behind the diner, enjoying it at least as much as the patrons inside. He made his way to the kitchen, steadfast in his mission to secure a BLT. The phone in the nook tucked under the stairs jangled as he walked by, and he might have jumped but for the fact that he was no longer capable. He could imagine the searing pain in his left knee were he to land such an event. The bad days were starting to outnumber the good ones; this was a painkiller day.

He lifted the phone from its cradle before it could ring again. Without preamble, Quince from Human Resources said in her plummy voice that Charlie needed to sign papers to start his pension. He sighed. He was pretty sure he had already done that, but at any rate, they couldn't locate said papers.

"We can email them, and you can sign electronically," she said, helpfully.

Charlie was reminded of his grandmother and her many attempts to teach him to cook. His grilled cheese sandwiches worked better as barbecue briquets, and there was that disastrous cake he made for her birthday that looked like it had been baked in a Bundt pan. Now, Quince was telling him in the same soft, measured tones that he hadn't got his retirement papers right. He tried to imagine what signing electronically entailed. Was a special kind of pen required?

"Detective Smeg?" she prompted.

"I'll stop by," he said.

He unwound the phone cord that was inexplicably twisted around him as Paul bounced down the old staircase, the wood creaking like ice cracking. Charlie thought maybe he was coming through the roof. Bits of plaster dusted the photo wall Nancy had curated upon finding a large cardboard box of photos under the bed in the spare bedroom. She'd sorted them on the dining room table with a constant stream of questions about each one. He couldn't tell her much about his parents; his father had died when Charlie was three, and memories of his mom were wrapped up in the farm in Bonnyville and the hired hands he thought were family. She died when Charlie was ten, and only then did he realize he was alone—the farm workers were there to look after the sheep, not a child. Charlie's grandmother retrieved him, and that was the end of Bonnyville, his friends, his school, and the skatepark. He reached for his wedding photo and lovingly dusted Nancy's joyful face with his shirt tail before hanging it back in its place.

"You know, you can get phones now that aren't attached to the wall." Paul's phone was attached to his thumbs.

"What would I need a cell phone for?" Charlie had carried one when he worked; the department required it. They likely meant for it to be turned on and not left under the passenger seat of his truck.

"So people can find you? Communicate with you?"

"Who's going to need me that urgently that they can't wait until I get home?"

Paul shrugged. "Me, maybe?"

Charlie considered that for a moment. "I wouldn't know how to use it."

Not exactly true. He just couldn't be bothered. But now he wondered if maybe he should put in more of an effort. A portable phone was convenient, but also annoying. Before retiring, he was out on a call with one of those Millennials who didn't put his phone down during lunch. Charlie stared out the window through most of it. Blessing in disguise, really; what would they have talked about? Police work, maybe? Imparting knowledge following the call out? Not my problem, Charlie thought, just filling in for the day while his partner's in court. On the way out of the restaurant, the kid took a selfie. Charlie stared at him. Apparently, they'd just had lunch at the trendiest kabob place on the north side. For the next ten minutes, he heard about the need to support socially conscious restaurants with sustainable food sources such as fake vegan meat. He sincerely hoped that wasn't what he had just eaten.

"Mom wanted you to have one." Paul's voice had gone quiet. "I can show you, help you get set up."

True, she had. She had worried about him. She'd worried about Paul, too. He knew Paul wouldn't call him if he didn't have a cell phone. He needed immediate gratification and wouldn't leave a message on the land line. Or maybe it was because Charlie often forgot to check for messages. He needed to up his game in the parenting department.

Paul shrugged again. "I'm going to the mall to pick up wireless earbuds. I could help you choose a phone?"

At the very least, it wouldn't hurt to do something with the boy, and he did have to go that way to get to the detachment. "Okay, but something simple. I don't want any bells and whistles."

"They come with cameras, storage for music and movies, internet."

Paul's smile took away any further defence Charlie might have wanted to mount. "I'll get my coat."

He stepped carefully over the buckled concrete of the front sidewalk and cracked driveway.

"When are you going to get your learner's permit?" he asked Paul as he gave the dented hood of the old truck a rap on the way by.

Charlie found it on an acreage out by North Cooking Lake and put it back into active service. He'd been on his way to fish when the early morning sun bounced off the truck's cobalt blue roof that gleamed like porcelain. It wasn't until he pulled into the long drive and neared the truck, left to languish in the trees, that he realized very little of it shone like porcelain; most of it was more like the metal garbage can he'd run over in the alley last spring. But still, there was something about that truck. One of the farmhands had driven one much like it, he recalled. The older one who took him to school when his mom was at work. When the owner of this current model and the property wandered over, Charlie asked how much. "Are you asking me how much I'd pay to have it hauled away?" he'd asked, not ironically. Once they settled, no money exchanged hands except for the tow truck Charlie had to commission to get the thing back to Edmonton.

"I don't need to learn to drive. The light rail transit doesn't belch carbon into the atmosphere."

Charlie had a mind to make him walk.

Paul shuffled the papers off the passenger seat and climbed in. "At least you aren't letting it idle." He cupped his hands and blew into them to warm them up.

Unwinding through the maze of one-way streets required a drive-by of the remnants of last night's annual pig dinner on the front lawn of the neighbourhood's most active fraternity house. Beer bottles mostly, but also articles of clothing that might have been best left on their owners, given the frigid overnight temperatures.

The moment they crossed the threshold into the Apple Store at Southgate Mall, Paul morphed into a different person. One whose shoulders aligned with his straight back and stretched neck. One Charlie had to tilt his head upward in order to look in his eyes. At least until he raced off like a puppy in a pet store, sniffing here, sniffing there, embodied by overstimulation. Smeg stood rooted. A young woman, wearing her digital upbringing like a brightly lit screen, approached him with an easygoing smile that was more of a question mark. 'Are you lost?' she seemed to say. 'Wandered off from the group of retirees having coffee on the concourse?' He looked around for Paul and, making eye contact once again, waved him over. The young woman looked visibly relieved; some sort of secret code passed between her and Paul. The question mark turned to an exclamation mark of recognition like she'd found someone to whom she shared a planet.

"What can I do for you?" she asked Paul.

"We're looking for an iPhone," he said. "It doesn't need to be the latest generation."

She looked at Charlie. He didn't respond. She turned back to Paul.

"Can you show us some with basic features?" he said. "Nothing fancy?"

She bent down to the cabinet and pulled out a black phone. "This iPhone is more basic than the Plus but still supports LTE-Advanced networks and Apple's 3D Touch displays. The new ones are due out any day, so I could give it to you at a reduced price."

Paul's head went up and down. "Sweet." Then his head stopped. "Do you have any discontinued models? That would be cheaper?"

Charlie felt her assessment of his fixed income. It wasn't that he couldn't afford a more expensive phone. He just didn't see the point.

"That are still supported?" She pushed her toxic yellow-green hair back to reveal a train track of metal running up the side of her ear. "Yeah, we have a few? I'll check in the back."

Charlie's eyes moved from one flashing display to another as they waited for the spike-haired spawn of Dr. Seuss to find the phone. "Will a discontinued model work? Why aren't they making it anymore?"

Paul shrugged. "It's Apple."

"Does that answer my question?"

"They put out a new one every year so people will buy more phones."

"Why would a person buy more phones? Don't you only need one?"

"They upgrade to a better phone with better technology."

"Isn't that wasteful?" Like driving a car.

Paul shrugged again. "Gotta have it."

The sales assistant returned and handed a compact box to Charlie. He took it and turned it over a few times, looking for the way in.

She reached for a penknife. "I can open it if you like?" She was speaking more slowly and louder than she had earlier.

It honestly wasn't his fault his fat fingers couldn't release the box from its hermetically sealed packaging.

She seemed to be waiting for feedback. Charlie said, "That'd be great."

He watched with growing disdain as she peeled away layers upon layers of wrapping to reveal the phone's essence of glittery light. Once she'd retrieved her prize, she held it up with such pride as though she'd invented it herself. When she asked if he wanted her to get it set up, he turned to Paul, who nodded.

On the way out of the mall, he felt the phone vibrate in his hand. Looking down, he saw a text from Paul.

Enjoyed shopping with you today. Followed by, *just heading into the shoe store to check out the sweet boots on display!*

And so it begins, he thought.

The first person Charlie Smeg saw upon entering the detachment was Staff Sergeant Singer. The sliding glass doors were barely closed behind him when the sharp click of her boots marched toward him. He was still a little miffed at her for springing Byatt on him. Singer was responsible for staffing her unit, and her current lack of personnel was no concern of his. Just his luck, she'd be in the office right when he arrived. Although if he had given his memory even a cursory search, he might have found she was usually at her desk after lunch. She smiled; he held out.

"Detective Smeg." She extended her hand. "I was just about to call you."

The corners of his mouth turned up before he could stop them. "Good to see you." He grasped her hand firmly.

"Do you have a few minutes?" Singer clipped in perfect military likeness.

Her severely pulled back hair would have passed inspection any day of the week and her tailored button-down shirt was tucked tightly into her uniform trousers. Singer had done a stint in the Navy and had only partially transitioned to civilian life. Smeg marvelled at his inability to pinpoint her age and also at the fact that age was the least interesting thing about her multi-textures. Beneath the crust, Smeg knew a non-combatant existed; crunchy on the outside, soft on the inside like a loaf of his grandmother's French bread.

"I was on my way to HR, but I guess they can wait. God knows I've waited long enough for them."

He wasn't in a hurry for his pension cheques, but he did wonder at the ineptitude of a unit that could lose signed papers. And staff requisition forms.

Singer waggled her finger toward her office. Upon entering, Smeg tipped his head back and gave tribute to the wall of portraits that circled her starkly clean desk, impressed as always at their ability to silence any who dared to enter. Once they were seated, she got straight to the point. Smeg appreciated that about her.

"I should have told you I'd sent Byatt your way. That may have caught you off guard. She said it didn't go well. I'd hoped you could help her out."

"I'm retired. And not looking for a post-retirement contract. Any involvement would be a stopgap and likely not helpful once she's assigned a partner."

"According to HR, you're classified as on leave. I could return you to active duty any time."

"On leave? When I called about my pension, they said I hadn't signed the forms. Apparently, they also classified me incorrectly." It now crossed Smeg's mind that Singer might have had something to do with the misplaced papers.

Singer tented her fingers and leaned back. "Usmani seems to be doing well. She stopped by last week."

Coby Usmani was his former partner, a woman who'd honed her numerous skills as a law enforcement officer in the Taliban controlled region of Afghanistan before her arrival in Canada in the dead of winter ten years ago. He liked her right away and asked to have her as his partner. She was straight talking, dedicated, and didn't take shit from anyone, including him. She had a bit of a limp at times, left over from a childhood tussle with polio. It had never slowed her down. But the bullet in her leg had. He didn't know what the last two months had felt like for her, but to him it had been an eternity. The longer it went on, the less he wanted to do police work.

"Glad to hear. She's a good cop."

"So are you. And you know that incident wasn't your fault."

He lowered his eyes. He disagreed. "She was never reckless."

"Her report filled in what yours left out. She ran in ahead without waiting for backup."

He mentored her carefully and was deeply disappointed in himself when she'd taken that action. Clearly, he hadn't emphasized safety first. At least not enough.

Singer continued, "She misread the signal. Had she waited for it, you would have been by her side and would have had her covered."

Smeg had heard the shot. A brief few seconds of not knowing whose gun had discharged punctuated the smell of fear and exertion that bubbled up from his body as he moved toward the sound, no longer waiting for backup. He rounded the corner of the crumbling warehouse in time to see a man closing the passenger door of a moving vehicle. Usmani lay partially hidden behind a dumpster. Their years together exploded like a grenade in his head as he plugged toward her. Blood pooled from her leg. She'd looked up at him from behind dust-covered hair. Backup arrived just as he was calling for an ambulance. He didn't leave her side until she was out of danger.

"Still," Smeg said. "It's time."

"You have expertise I could use. No one has as many murder convictions under their belt."

"Only because I've been around for so long." Smeg hadn't been able to see under his belt for many years. Perhaps she had missed that part.

She shook her head. "Percentages. You're way up. The younger detectives are in too much of a hurry to wrap things up and get on to the next one."

"Like Byatt?"

"She's different. She reminds me of you. The fire in her eyes burns to solve crimes. But she needs mentoring."

Something began to stir in Smeg. But then he remembered his first impression of her. The suck up. "Not sure I saw that in her."

"Take another look." She pierced him with dark eyes that shone from beneath heavy eyebrows.

Smeg stared out the window, unable to form the word no. Maybe it was Alzheimer's. He rose to his feet.

"Think about it." Singer didn't smile; she might have used up her quota for the day.

Smeg was halfway home before he realized he'd forgotten to go to HR to sign his retirement papers.

Chapter Three

The basement stairs, unlike the spacious spiral heading to the second floor, were steep and narrow. Charlie had just managed to get himself down them and into a chair in front of the hockey game when his phone buzzed. He tossed the TV remote onto the coffee table and rummaged through the Big Mac wrappers, napkins, and paperback novels for his phone, mildly pissed at the disruption. And a bit disgusted at the rank smell of cold grease he had just released from the pile. He'd recorded the game from the night before but couldn't for the life of him recall why; it wasn't like he had a stream of social calls preventing him from watching the game live.

The call display said Edmonton Police Service. "What?" he growled into the phone.

"This is Officer Battle. Sorry to bother you, Detective Smeg. We got a body. Singer said you'd want to have a look before it's moved."

Apparently, his delay in saying no had by default become a yes. Smeg sighed, mostly for Battle's benefit. He had to keep up the pretence but, really, he couldn't turn down the chance to get back in. At sixty-five, maybe he should retire, but a small hole in him had begun to fill the past two days since his meeting with Singer. At any rate, it wouldn't hurt to do this one case with Byatt, like a free trial, before deciding on further investment. Singer was usually intuitive in her assessment of people.

"What you got?" Smeg had forgotten about the game which droned in the background.

"Woman, about fifty, Caucasian. Her SUV is sitting in the brush below the Quesnell Bridge. Drove right off the road, no skid marks." Smeg saw the inevitable shake of Battle's head as he launched into a lengthy description of the crash as if he were reporting live on location. The officer in charge—at least until the message was delivered.

Battle had signed up to serve and protect, but along the way, his judgment clouded. Walking the beat downtown, he became attached to some of the regulars, kids with nowhere to go. Battle had prodded and pestered Smeg to come with him after work to meet the three young guys who loved their music. Battle had called it rap, but the boys corrected; it's spoken word. The pieces in Cree were particularly melodic, even to Smeg. They had dreams of competing in festivals, but Smeg knew they'd never get there. But not for lack of talent. One night, the following week, Battle rounded a corner and encountered two men beating on the youngest musician. Somehow, the two men wound up in emergency, and though it couldn't be pinned on Battle, he now worked the front desk.

Smeg cut him off, "Could have suffered a medical incident prior to the accident." There was now some urgency that required an end to the phone call. He knew he should be at the scene already.

"An eyewitness says a car bumped her from behind. A car driven by her husband."

"Anything else?"

"Your partner says she hasn't heard from you."

Until this very moment, he hadn't had a partner. But maybe that wasn't the story being told in the precinct.

"I'll call her," Smeg said.

He hung up, then punched her number. Given different circumstances, he might have wondered how her contact made it into his new iPhone. She answered on the first ring.

"Detective Byatt? Detective Smeg. Looks like we're working together."

"Yes, I heard," she said, hesitantly. Then, with more assertiveness, "I'm pleased."

Smeg hoped she was. He would have liked to reunite over coffee or at least in conversation in the office. He'd need to make amends after the call out, restart on the right foot. Byatt would be familiar with hesitancy, having worked in robbery where a lot of male officers eschewed a female partner. Smeg needed to ensure she didn't feel that attitude had followed her over. A reminder that he'd already had a female partner wouldn't be remiss. But that was secondary to his belief in the importance of a real connection if they were to work together. He also might have liked more time to consider his decision to return to active duty.

"Got a body," Smeg said. "Meet me at the Quesnell Bridge. Or do you want me to pick you up?"

"No, I'm close by," she said. "I'll meet you there."

Smeg preferred to arrive together, a chance to review what was known before arriving at the scene, but he wouldn't push her. He recalled the cockiness of her earlier visit to his house and wondered if he hadn't been quick to judge. The confident façade was perhaps easily shaken.

"Did headquarters give you the details?" he asked.

"Oh, yes, I did hear a name." The phone gave a momentary crackle into which Smeg imagined her head nod. "That's a slippery section of freeway in a storm."

"Indeed. I'll meet you at the top of the bank."

Smeg pulled onto the shoulder of Whitemud Freeway behind a row of vehicles. Two marked police cars had been positioned as sentries as though the stream of footprints led to a secret cave. He stepped out of his truck and was pelted in the face by icy spray from the monster tires of a lifted pickup weaving in and out as it raced to the head of the line. He swore and wiped his face with his hanky. His decision to leave the warmth of his basement was in question as they worked their way slowly down the slick slope. Now he was the one who hesitated. Byatt could clearly negotiate the treacherous hill.

Based on Smeg's experience, there probably wasn't even a crime at the bottom; more likely an accident. He looked to the river beyond, at the late afternoon sun reflecting blue off the corrugated ice jams. Two coyotes watched back, wary of the activity so close to their corridor, wondering if there might be anything to scavenge. Reporters wouldn't be far behind.

Byatt quickly began taking pictures and measurements. Like the coyotes, her observation skills were tuned in as she foraged in the snow. Smeg remembered how thorough she was from his short stint with her earlier. He watched for a moment as she moved around the scene, collar up against the wind. He glanced down at her fashionable boots and wondered how she had made it down the hill.

"Came from the mall," she said in response to his glance. "Christmas shopping."

She handed him the camera, set her clipboard down on the roof of the SUV, and pulled her hair back into a ponytail. Wet snow smeared her glasses.

"What do we have?" Smeg asked.

Byatt shook her head. "Nothing out of the ordinary. I've done a baseline." She reached for the clipboard, flipped over the plastic cover, and read her notes to him.

Her baseline was cursory. "Treat it as a crime scene even if it doesn't appear to be. Better to err on the side of caution."

Byatt stared at him, one eyebrow higher than the other.

Smeg clarified. "Make a note about securing the scene from onlookers."

"No one's gonna come down that bank in a snowstorm."

"Except the husband," Smeg said.

"Right, right." Byatt nodded, apologetic.

"What else?" he asked.

"No signs of defence injuries in the hands or arms. Apparently, the husband's anxious to have the body moved. He doesn't like her lying out here on the frozen ground." She tucked the clipboard under her arm and pulled on her gloves.

Despite the cold, the dead woman's muscles hadn't begun to stiffen. The longer rigor mortis was delayed, the more time investigators had to do their work, but it was inevitable, like the coming darkness. The body would need to be moved before lighting had to be set up. Byatt's camera kit had a powerful external flash, but the coroner didn't have the advantage of an artificial light source at hand and moved quickly to capture the essentials. Rigor, they were fond of saying, not rigor mortis.

"Right," Smeg said. "Let's have a look at the vehicle."

"Based on the lack of skid marks, she didn't attempt to stop or slow down. She could have been unconscious before the vehicle left the road. The underbrush would have slowed the vehicle before the tree stopped it completely. Not likely the cause of death."

A guardrail would also have stopped her. Crashing into the Talus Dome, the city's latest expensive art installation, conveniently located at the top of the bank, would have served the same purpose. As a piece of art, it wasn't his favourite. He appreciated that the artist wanted to represent the river valley cliffs, but actual rocks and dirt would have been less costly than a thousand stainless steel balls. The savings might have paid for a guardrail.

"Brakes could have failed," Smeg said. "Although it appears she didn't protect herself from the impact."

He turned to a uniformed officer. "Who was first on the scene?"

"I was. Well, after the husband." He looked toward a man standing under the bridge.

Smeg pushed his wool cap higher on his forehead. "I understand he was following in his own vehicle."

"That's his black car up top."

Smeg followed his gaze to the Mitsubishi Outlander, then glanced back at the husband. Small, wiry, scowling. Smeg didn't have trouble putting the tough guy vehicle together with the image of its driver.

"What's his deal?"

The officer replied, "He said he was going to a medical appointment with her. Apparently, they both work downtown, so he met her after work. Says he was back quite a ways and didn't see anything until she left the road. Then she was over the edge, so he didn't see the impact. He called it in."

"But an eyewitness says he bumped her from behind. Ran her off the road."

"There're no marks on the bumper. Although the snow could have masked it."

Smeg also hadn't seen any marks, but the husband could have wiped them. "Think he touched anything?"

"He said he knew she was dead, so he waited for emergency crews."

Smeg looked over at the coyotes. They, at least, were waiting for an official announcement.

"Let's go have a chat with him," Byatt said to him.

Trudging through the deep snow, he thought about the ways in which a glance at a body would be enough to know with certainty that death had occurred. There were cases in which the body was mutilated beyond the point where life was still possible. And there were cases where death had occurred long enough ago that decay was obvious. Neither of those scenarios applied here.

"This is ridiculous," the man barked, before they could even say hello. "She's been lying there for an hour already. Get her moved."

The fire in his eyes could have melted snow.

"I understand your concern," Byatt said. "We just want to make sure all the bases are covered. We've seen what we need to and taken pictures so they'll move her now."

"I'd have thought everyone could get here quicker." He looked directly at Smeg, who had been the last to arrive. "This should be a priority."

"What's your wife's name?" Smeg asked, ignoring the scorn in the man's voice. He'd seen lots of different reactions to the loss of a loved one. And lots of assholes.

The flame dimmed, and the voice softened. "Deena Hammond."

"And yours?"

"Jay Rodriguez."

"Kids?"

He nodded.

"Tell me about your wife," Byatt said.

"She was sick and had been for half a year. The doctors couldn't figure it out. Idiots. All that high-priced education. She'd used up her sick days at work and was getting set to go on long-term disability. Except she didn't want to. She'd already been passed over for a promotion because she was too sick to go through the application and interview."

"Where did she work?"

"Alberta Environment. She was an upstart, a go-getter," he said.

Smeg was a cop. It was all he knew. He could read deception in speech patterns; knew what actions were coming next from micro-expressions, a slight movement of the eye; and he could quickly identify how various poisons cause death. But he didn't have a clue what it meant to be a government upstart. He waited but wasn't further enlightened.

Rodriguez also waited, possibly for a follow-up question. "Where are they taking her?"

Smeg looked over to where the body was being lifted to carry up the riverbank."The morgue. They'll need to do an autopsy."

Rodriguez would need to sign the consent form, but it might be best to wait until he calmed down. If there were enough evidence of a suspicious death, like a vehicle forced off the road, they wouldn't need his consent, but they'd need to present a case for that.

"What do we need an autopsy for? She was sick, she died. We know that."

Jay Rodriguez is a particular breed of asshole, Smeg thought. "We can determine cause of death. Maybe what her illness was."

"Why does it matter now? She's dead." Rodriquez's shoulders slumped.

"Maybe your kids would like to know," Byatt said softly.

Even before Charlie stepped into Café Blackbird, the scent of toasted bread and melted cheese seeped out. His stomach rumbled, and he looked about to see what was on offer, but couldn't read the chalkboard and its specials in scrawling pastel. He ordered a Dead Woodsman for Byatt, recalling her drinking something similar from their earlier time together, and an Ichorous Imperial Stout for himself because he could see it on tap. The words of Guy Vanderhaeghe came to mind. *Do not follow your present course. It is a dead end.* He was sipping and remembering that he hated stout when Meaghan Byatt arrived.

"I had to park down the block," she explained as she shook the snow off her head and sat down. "Traffic's crazy."

Charlie smiled. "Every snowstorm."

He watched with envy as she took a long drink of her beer, then set it down. Her eyes followed.

"So," he mumbled and waited for her to look up. When she did, he gave her a candid smile. "Back to working together. Hope you don't mind." It had occurred to him that since Singer had orchestrated the whole thing, Meaghan might have hesitations, too.

"I'm pleased. You're a legend."

If he'd been outside, he would have kicked at the snow. It was one thing for Singer with her ulterior motives to say such things, but he hadn't expected it from the attractive and intelligent young woman across from him. He might rightly have expected resentment for the way she'd been bounced around the past few months.

"In my own mind." He laughed, then took a mouthful of stout which he gagged on. "Molasses."

Taking direction from Guy Vanderhaeghe and deciding not to follow his present course, he waved the waitress over. "Got a Bud Light?"

Meaghan smiled at him. "I see your taste in beer hasn't improved."

"The beer list hasn't improved," he said, slightly irritated. "Catch me up on the past couple of months."

"Oh god, where to begin?"

He listened while she told him with great sincerity what had gone on in the office since he'd left. First, it was the facts, cases she'd been peripherally involved in, but only to research old files and fill in on random call-outs. With prompting, she moved on to her frustrations, how she felt she was being sidelined and wondered why.

"Some days I feel like I'm partnered with Battle."

He grimaced. "Sorry about that. My fault. I think Singer was waiting for me to get over the incident with Usmani and return to work."

She cleared her throat. "You and Usmani were close."

He waved the thought away.

There was a momentary twitching around her mouth as she reached for her beer. Then she looked at him with dark eyes, both brilliant and bold. "What do you think about today's accident?"

"Husband's a bit of an ass." Charlie gazed out the window at the snow that glittered under the streetlights as it fell softly to the ground. "We're going to have to wait for the autopsy results."

It's the most wonderful time of the year, poured like syrup from the speaker in the corner.

"Got your Christmas shopping done?" Meaghan asked. "Only one week to go, and the mall is insane."

The width of Charlie's face expanded like a balloon as the thick folds of his eyelids came together like bread rising. He didn't know why Christmas caused him such disquiet. Or maybe shopping malls were the problem. He lifted his beer to his lips and chugged most of it back before bringing the glass back to the table with rather more force than intended. Chatter filled the dimly lit room. He reached for a handful of nuts, popped them all in his mouth at once, and chewed slowly.

"Suppose I should pick up something for Paul," he said. "But I don't know what."

Charlie wasn't particularly good at paying attention to details. Paul came along at the right time in Charlie's life, just as he'd begun to feel the tugs of missed parenthood. They had bonded early over endless games of balloon tennis, and there was that time they'd built and launched a model rocket only to crash it into a tree and damage it beyond repair. He smiled to himself, recalling another afternoon when Nancy was out and he'd ignored the squeaks of Paul using his bed to practice his trampoline jumps. When the bed broke, Charlie quietly fixed it.

"How old is he?" Meaghan asked. "I couldn't tell in the dark hallway the other day."

"Early twenties. I married his mother, Nancy, when he was twelve. I lived with them for five years before she died, and that was five years ago."

"Good math," Meaghan said. "Add ten to twelve and you get early twenties. I'll take care of the numbers end of things."

Charlie's laugh started low in his belly and rolled upward before erupting. "Good idea."

"So, what about Deena Hammond?" Meaghan asked as they paid their tab.

"I'll go to the autopsy," Charlie said. "I don't expect much resistance to having it done, given the suspicion she may have been run off the road."

Chapter Four

Smeg limped as fast as his bum knee would allow into the narrow room of the morgue, aware of the precarious line his flawed frame walked in the company of bodies without souls. Perhaps that was too ominous. But he was getting old. The creeping hesitation he felt after a two-month unexplained absence was new. Kris Cross, the pathologist, was at the first table. The rest were empty.

"What are you staring at?" Smeg growled and went to hang his coat on a hook.

"Nice to see you too," Cross said.

"Sorry I'm late," Smeg said. "Assholes didn't give me the right start time."

"No worries. Although I'm surprised to see you at all. I'd heard you packed it in." The Meercat circles around his eyes were a deeper purple than Smeg recalled.

"Yeah," Smeg muttered. "Me too."

He had known Cross for thirty years. At first, he wondered why a guy named Kris Cross would become a pathologist. Had he taken his name as a literal challenge? A call to incise? He'd been tempted to ask but wanted to avoid the glare that would have resulted. He soon learned the puritanical doctor didn't have a sense of humour. What he had was a severe attitude emphasized by his crew cut, now grey, and heavy, black framed glasses matching in austerity. And a high level of skill. Smeg couldn't recall a mistake in all their years working together. If ever things went wrong, it was with how the body had arrived, not with what Cross had done to it.

The room, while long enough to accommodate seven chrome tables that gleamed in the bright light, wasn't big enough to absorb the rot that hovered in the air and permeated his nostrils. He'd attended many autopsies and knew the ventilation was up to code, but he'd never get used to the smell. Without a protective covering, Smeg's clothes would need to go straight into the washing machine when he got home. With bleach. The pathologist, decked out in long rubber gloves and an industrial apron, cut a straight line down the centre of the breastplate, made a Y-shaped cut from both shoulders joining over the sternum and down to the pubic bone. He then spread the ribs open and anchored them with a large clamp.

"No saw?" Smeg asked. Other autopsies he'd observed involved cutting the ribs down both sides with a grinder saw and lifting them out. Metal on bone; osteoarthritis on hyper speed.

"Her bones are soft and somewhat pliable," Cross responded.

A much quieter process, at any rate. Smeg could see everything now: heart, lungs, liver, stomach, spleen. Cross removed them one by one and carefully weighed each. Smeg stood still and tried to keep his mouth shut. As the afternoon wore on, the pain in his knee grew.

Cross noted, "She shows early signs of liver hepatomegaly, but only slightly enlarged. We'll need to wait for toxicology to see if there's any elevation of enzymes. Heart too shows some injury; its weight is high. I'll send a blood sample for testing. Could be genetic. Any idea if there's family history of heart disease?"

"I'll ask." Smeg scribbled in his notebook.

Cross poked around the abdomen, noted how the blood had pooled, and then cut open the stomach and examined the contents. A sour smell hit Smeg in the face. He covered his nose and mouth with a handkerchief rescued from his pants' pocket.

"Lot of liquid," Cross said. "We'll test that along with a urine sample. Can't rule out poison, so something may turn up in either of those places."

He moved his hands along the neck and sides of the face. "Head injury appears to be post-mortem."

"Consistent with the crash?" Smeg asked.

"Yes." Cross was making a triangular incision across the top of the skull. "But why didn't the airbag protect her?"

Smeg shrugged. "Secondary impact?"

Cross removed the brain. "No visible signs of brain trauma."

"Possible poisoning might be an issue here. Could be she was targeted?" Smeg needed to ask, although he knew it was his own job to figure it out.

"Maybe. We can keep her until toxicology and blood and tissue results come back. Two days tops. If nothing shows up, we'll have to release the body to the family. There's not a lot of indication of wrongdoing here."

Cross pushed his glasses up with the back of his hand.

"Oh, one more thing," he said. "There's a tattoo of a collie on the small of her back." He rolled her over, and Smeg took a few pictures.

He then took his leave. Replacing the organs and sewing her back up would take hours.

Charlie lifted the small pot of Hoya Hearts, a Valentine's gift from Nancy that he had managed to keep alive, and gave it an ample drink of water. The plant, with its clusters of white blooms, required little maintenance. He supposed the rest of his plants had names as well, but he didn't know what they were. Nonetheless, they needed moisture. He continued, without urgency, removing dead leaves and rotating plants in hopes their withered branches might reach for the fleeting winter sun. Today, that sun was intensely dazzling but would roll orange toward the horizon and slip away in a quick burst of red well before Charlie sat down to dinner. The plants would need to soak it up quickly.

He put the watering can away under the kitchen sink and paced the hallway waiting for the phone to ring. They needed the autopsy results. They couldn't investigate a murder if there wasn't one. His mind was already on the case. There were enough unanswered questions, beyond those that were health-related, to make him want to know more about the woman, with a jerk for a husband, who drove off the road in a snowstorm. Or was pushed off by another vehicle.

He sat down in front of his laptop and opened the uploaded accident scene photos. The woman's facial features were oddly peaceful in a frame of cuts and bruises. A few strands of light brown hair stuck to the sides of her face. She had a bump on her forehead, likely caused by secondary impact with the steering wheel. Around her neck, skin lesions were visible along with a dark patch that didn't look like a bruise. The interior of the vehicle held his attention. He hadn't had time for more than a cursory glance at the scene and now he studied the contents of her bag that were strewn across the floor of the front seat on mud-splattered floor mats: phone charger, planner, hair ties and elastics, tissues.

A close-up photo of a research report on personality disorders gave him pause. She worked in Environment, so it was unlikely that report was for work. Maybe the workplace was strange; possibly so were the personalities within it. Mostly what he saw was a sad end to a life. To die alone in a cold vehicle. He wondered if she knew it was coming. A middle-aged wife and mother who didn't make it home. It was hard to imagine someone would have intended to harm her. But he'd seen it before. When his phone finally buzzed, it wasn't the call he was hoping for.

Paul. "You called?"

"I don't think so."

"Pocket dialed?"

"Pocket dialed?"

"Never mind. Hey, ever break into a house?"

"What? Why?"

"Writing a story. Trying to get the details right."

"You need to get a job."

"I had an interview. For an editing position."

"How did it go?"

"Go?"

"Did they like you?"

"I don't know. I guess that's what the interview was about."

"Okay. Let me know if you hear anything."

"About what?"

"I need to go now, Paul. Another call coming in." Charlie shook his head. Kid didn't get his mother's brains. Maybe didn't get anyone's.

As he hit reply, he heard Paul moving around in his bedroom and realized his call had come from inside the house. It was like a recurring nightmare.

"Smeg."

"Officer Battle. The pathologist's report is in. Cause of death: arsenic poisoning." The triumph in Battle's voice was palpable.

"Okay, on my way."

Smeg crossed over the North Saskatchewan River, midway through the largest stretch of urban parkland in North America. Midway through the shortest day of the year, only seven and a half hours of daylight. And midway between mosquito seasons. As he exited onto River Valley Road, he hit Byatt's number. Paul had set up the Bluetooth in the vehicle, which reminded him that the kid did have skills. Maybe he needed to direct the boy toward them. With technology industries rapidly growing in Edmonton, it might be a good time for a young guy to get on board. And if he didn't get a decent job, he'd never move out of Charlie's house.

"Hey," Byatt said. "What's up?"

"On my way to the office," he said. "Looks like we need to investigate the Deena Hammond death."

"Where to begin?" she mused. "In Robbery, we'd examine the crime scene and talk to the victim. I'll start searching for details about Hammond online."

Not wrong thinking, Smeg thought.

Smeg found Meaghan Byatt at a desk in the corner, leaning into her computer, typing. The light was bright, the space cheery. Faint remnants of citrusy cleaner hung in the air. Byatt chewed on the corner of her bottom lip as she glanced over to her notebook, seemingly unaware of Smeg's presence.

"Report on the Hammond incident?" he asked and pulled up a chair to sit beside her.

"Yeah." She turned toward him, recognition wiping the concentration from her face. "The one filed by the uniformed officers is bare bones in keeping with a car accident. I'm finishing up the death report and classifying the death as undetermined pending autopsy."

He handed her the autopsy report. "The salient points include dark patches of skin and the beginnings of skin lesions that could be called pre-cancerous. Or signs of long-term arsenic exposure. Brain slightly enlarged; early signs of heart disease. Lab results show traces of arsenic in blood and urine."

"She could have been murdered?" Byatt asked after scanning the results.

"Not necessarily," Smeg said. "The most common cause of arsenic poisoning is contaminated drinking water. And that's a messy way to murder someone."

"Arsenic's hard to come by," Byatt added. "Unless you work in production of pesticides, medical labs, or maybe a veterinary lab."

"What's Rodriguez's line of work?"

"He didn't say," Byatt continued. "He was reluctant to have the autopsy done."

"He'll be our first stop this morning," Smeg said. "You driving?"

Byatt grabbed her keys off the desk and jiggled them.

Warming temperatures had turned the parking lot to a sheet of ice. In his younger days, Smeg would have enjoyed drifting across the lot. Now it just looked like a trip to emergency waiting to happen. Makes and models of cars had turned into an assembly line of snow-topped sameness. A bike rested against a wall, belonging to some hardy soul, given it was cleaned of snow but covered in mud from a recent ride. All these things Smeg noticed because he rarely walked to the back of the lot. If he couldn't find a parking spot near the door, he parked illegally.

"What is this?" He frowned as Byatt unlocked the doors of an '87 Saab sports coupe. "Where's your other car? The one with four doors."

"I'm having the winter tires put on today. This one's my summer car."

"Why the hell aren't your winter tires on already? We've been driving on snow and ice for a month. And am I right in assuming this one doesn't have winter tires?"

"All seasons on this baby." Byatt smiled and patted the roof of the car.

"I'm not getting into this." Smeg patted his belly. "I can't get into this." He didn't smile.

"Want to take your truck?"

"No." Smeg opened the passenger door. "It's over on the other side of the building." He slowly stuffed himself into the car, moved the seat back as far as it would go and flipped the visor up.

Byatt turned the engine over four times before it started while Smeg contemplated having to get back out again. And then having to walk from wherever this tin can decided to break down. As they pulled onto the street, a tension filled the small air pocket inside the car. He knew he needed to replace it, but he wasn't sure with what. When he was partnered with Usmani, they spent hours together in comfortable silence. But it had taken time to get there.

"So," he eventually managed. "How are things?"

"Good." Byatt nodded.

Smeg also nodded and thought maybe the two of them would be well placed as bobble heads on the dashboard.

"Did you find anything interesting about Hammond in your online search?" he asked.

"Some academic stuff. A couple of research papers on the social effects of climate change, and one on how increases in extreme weather impact mental health. Another one on the rise of TikTok and its impact on popular culture. Although that one appeared to be a different Deena Hammond."

"Hmm."

After a brief pause, Byatt said, "I'm looking forward to working this one with you, Smeg,"

"Hey, me too."

"And not just because it gets me out of the office." Byatt turned and gave him a smile he knew he didn't deserve.

The house was half a block from the light rail transit tracks and street parking was a bitch. Byatt pulled into a spot that wasn't a spot.

"See how easy it is to park this sweetheart?"

Smeg scowled, put one hand on the car door and the other on the frame, and heaved himself out. The car, which was almost touching the pavement, rose with him. Hammond's family lived in the McKernan area, close to the university, in an Edwardian home that should have had old-world charm. As he stood gazing at it, he decided it did have character, but that of a ghost story, as its exterior walls bulged outward, possibly constraining otherworldly things within. The paint was chipped, and the porch sagged. He stepped gingerly, not wanting to fall through the rotting floorboards. A rap on the door was answered by a young man, late teens or early twenties, in yoga pants, with legs like stilts and rubber band arms. Smeg pushed aside thoughts of malnourishment.

The kid was clean-cut and sporting a pencil between his teeth. He removed it. "Yes?"

"Good morning." Byatt was also respectable and was carrying a notebook. "Have we interrupted your studies?"

Smeg recalled it must be exam time. The kid could certainly be a student.

The young man stared at them.

"Police detectives," Smeg said. "Is your father in?"

The kid eyed them up and down. Smeg's thigh-length overcoat hung open. Byatt paid more attention to how she dressed and, on this occasion, looked quite professional in dress pants and heeled boots. Side by side, they could have been Jehovah's Witnesses. Smeg pulled his badge from an inside pocket and flashed it.

"Yeah, come in. I'll get him." The kid turned around and yelled, "Dad!"

Then he wandered into a den off the foyer that was overwhelmed with a blaring television. Smeg followed. The curtains were drawn, and a small lamp on a desk in the corner provided just enough illumination to highlight the grime on a tattered Persian rug. He resisted the urge to cough in response to the musty air. The kid plunked himself down on the sofa and reached for a textbook before noticing Smeg in the doorway. He glared.

Smeg moved on. He found Byatt inspecting a smattering of head shots of the skinny kid and a young woman that ran the length of the hallway. The sister, it appeared, who was likely in her early twenties. If the length of her neck was any indication, she was also tall. Rodriguez thumped down the stairs looking like he'd just woken up. Or hadn't bothered to comb his hair.

"What do you want?" he croaked, then cleared his throat.

"Excuse us." Smeg smiled apologetically. "Need to ask you a few questions. May we come in?"

"Looks like you already have."

Jay Rodriguez had the air of a man who'd been strikingly handsome in his youth. Now, tired and aging, with grey creeping along the edges of his shaggy black hair and deep dark circles under his eyes, he was beaten down.

"What questions? This is a bloody inconvenience right now."

"Sorry if we woke you up," Byatt said.

Rodriguez opened his mouth, then closed it; an air of resignation took hold of him, beginning with his shoulders and slumping downward.

"Are you alright?" Byatt asked.

"We're in the middle of planning a funeral," Rodriguez muttered.

"We understand and are sorry for your loss," Byatt said.

"Won't take long," Smeg said. "We have the autopsy results."

He watched for some sort of reaction, but none came.

Chapter Five

Smeg scanned Rodriguez's living room for a sturdy chair. He chose one of ample girth and hoped it wasn't of the same vintage as the front steps. He also hoped the large collection of flowers germinating from the dining room table, emitting a fragrance that was chokingly intense, didn't include chrysanthemums. Roses, lilies, he could see. The rest of the flowers in the show-stopping perfume smorgasbord, he didn't recognize. Byatt had wisely chosen the spot farthest from the source. Smeg couldn't control a loud and forceful sneeze. Apparently, there *were* chrysanthemums in there somewhere. Rodriguez glared.

"You off work for a while?" Smeg asked.

"Couple of weeks. We'll see how it goes." Rodriguez hovered in the doorway like he was late for his next meeting before opting for a spot on the couch.

"Your employer sounds supportive. Where do you work?"

"I work for the city in pest regulation. I manage a unit that does mainly mosquito control. It's our slow time."

Smeg scratched his head.

"So, the autopsy," Rodriguez said. "Cause of death was sickness?" he added with a large dose of sarcasm.

"Other family members showing signs of illness?" Smeg asked, ignoring the question.

"No. Why would they?"

He spoke like a man who was used to being interrogated and didn't like it. Maybe it came with being in middle management. Smeg tried to envision Rodriguez at a dinner party, chatting pleasantly, and failed. He had no more success imaging what it must have been like to be married to him. Hammond, having put up with him for years, he decided, was a saint. Again, he felt some empathy for the dead woman. Byatt had him well in hand as she manoeuvred through a series of sympathetic questions about the children to which he responded with increasing calm. Rodriguez picked up a throw cushion, fluffed it, and placed it carefully in the corner of the couch. Without looking up, he reached for a glass figurine of a collie from the coffee table.

"Do you have a dog?" Byatt asked.

"Used to. She was Deena's, but she died last year."

Smeg wondered if this was the point in time when Hammond had its likeness tattooed on her back. Collies were gentle, although also herding dogs. What did the tattoo say about her? Had Hammond been controlled by her husband? Her employer?

"She must have missed the dog," Smeg said, surprised he'd said it out loud.

Rodriguez looked confused, like he didn't understand an attachment to a dog. Or the connection between pets and positive interpersonal relationships. Maybe he was more of a cat person.

"You mentioned your wife had been passed over for a promotion at work recently. What happened there?" Byatt asked with the soft quality in her voice that Smeg had noticed earlier in the car.

"There was some bullshit the first time she applied for promotion. Someone else wanted the job and spread some nasty lies in hopes of securing the job for herself. Worked too, for a time. But Deena shone. She would have got the next one if she hadn't become sick."

"Can we look around the house?" Smeg asked, beginning the slow rise to his feet.

"Got a search warrant?" Rodriguez said, the quick anger returning.

"Calm down, we're just looking to learn a bit more about your wife."

"Feels more like I'm a suspect here. If she was sick, why the need for all this?"

"Just covering our bases."

"Fine," Rodriguez said. "But don't take all day." He stayed where he was on the flowered couch and stared out the window at the falling snow.

"I'll look upstairs," Byatt said as Smeg headed off to the kitchen.

The kitchen was messy in a homey way, with a pantry that displayed a convenience store selection of canned goods, including cases of minestrone soup stacked on the floor and more kitchen gadgets than Smeg had ever seen. He checked the fridge; again, the cans, this time of Molson Canadian. He discovered that the stove had recently been turned on when he put his hand on an element. As he ran his burnt fingers under the tap, he remembered to fill a vial with water to send for testing. Next, he checked the drawers and cupboards for instruments that could be used to inject arsenic, but found none.

He wandered into the half bath off the kitchen and opened the medicine cabinet. Advil, dental floss, a pill bottle promising a homeopathic treatment for anxiety, asthma, cough, blood cancer, and a number of other unrelated health conditions. He turned the bottle around to read the back label. Medicinal ingredients included arsenic trioxide. Smeg retrieved his cell phone from his pocket and took a picture. As he was finishing up on the main floor, Byatt came down the stairs, left through the front door, and returned with an evidence bag.

In response to his raised eyebrows, she said, "There's makeup in the upstairs bathroom that isn't of high quality and might be worth testing."

He thought about the need for a search warrant conversation, but quickly realized Byatt knew the line and when not to cross it. Besides, cheap makeup wouldn't be enough to make a person seriously ill, nor would it be an effective murder weapon. Smeg went into the living room where Rodriquez was still staring out the window.

"Mind if we take some makeup from upstairs for testing?"

"Go ahead," Rodriguez said.

"Lovely still life paintings in the den," Smeg said. "Someone in your family paint them?" He'd noticed the neatly rendered signatures that said Rodriquez.

"Me," Rodriguez mumbled, still focused on the window, which, as far as Smeg could see, was also still of any life or movement at all.

He waited a moment for a laugh. Hearing none, he had to conclude the man was serious. Smeg didn't know much about art, but he thought the paintings were done in acrylics. They were striking. The one that jumped out at him when he first walked into the room featured a larger-than-life wine bottle, grapes, and a cut pomegranate centred by a half-full stemmed glass of red wine. The colours were so rich he could almost taste them. Two other paintings, both of flowers, adorned the wall on either side.

Smeg suddenly felt bad about their intrusion into the family's life. "That is, um, sorry for all this. We'll be gone shortly." He fumbled with his cell phone.

Rodriguez's face went slack, and he turned to look at Smeg. "It's alright. I guess I'd like to know, too. Although it would have been helpful to know the problem when she was still alive."

"Yes," Smeg said.

"We'll be in touch," he said when Byatt finally came back downstairs.

"When can we have her? For the funeral?"

"Not sure," Smeg replied. "Given cause of death, the coroner may want to delay the release of the body. We'll let you know."

"What was the cause of death? You didn't say."

Smeg hesitated. "Arsenic poisoning."

Rodriguez looked like he'd been the one poisoned. "Bullshit."

"Where might she have encountered arsenic?" Byatt asked.

"No idea."

"We'll need a statement," Smeg added.

Rodriguez's eyes turned black.

Smeg watched through the car window as a tall, thin woman wrapped in a thick scarf and light jacket rounded the corner and headed toward them. As the face came into focus, he recognized her from the photos in the hallway. She stopped in front of Rodriguez's house and stared at Byatt, who was brushing snow off the driver's side windshield. Smeg cracked the window an inch or so.

"You visiting my dad?" she asked.

Byatt looked over at her. "Are you Katie?"

The young woman shook slightly and waited, either for Byatt to continue the conversation or get in her car. Smeg thought maybe she shouldn't linger too long, as her feet must be cold in her thin canvas sneakers; they'd freeze to the sidewalk. She hoisted a small pink gym bag higher on her shoulder.

"We're detectives. I'm Meaghan Byatt." She jerked her thumb toward the car. "That's Charlie Smeg."

"Why would detectives be here? We were expecting police to follow up on the cause of the accident, but detectives seem like overkill."

"What do you know about the accident?"

"Single vehicle. Snowstorm. Maybe her brakes failed."

"What about your mom's health?"

With a furrowed brow, Katie said, "What's that got to do with it?" Then she scowled. "Except those bitches she worked with are probably doing a happy dance right now. Someone else will get the promotion now that Mom's out of the way."

Smeg pulled out his notebook and jotted down a reminder to follow up on that thought with Hammond's work colleagues.

"Well," Byatt said. "Maybe our investigation will help answer some questions about your mom's death."

Katie stood for another minute, then turned and headed up the steps.

Byatt slid in behind the wheel and handed her phone to Smeg. "I took photos of Hammond's journal."

"That would explain why you were upstairs for so long. Did you read the whole damn thing?" Smeg's face, he knew, revealed he was anything but annoyed.

Byatt drove. Smeg read.

I can't shake this horrible sickness, can't bear the abdominal pain, the headaches and now my friggin' hair is falling out. I look like shit, feel like shit. I can't keep wearing scarves on my head at work. It's not a fashion statement when you do it every day. I guess if I go on medical leave it won't matter anymore.

That was her most recent entry. Clearly, the woman was upset, even angry, but Smeg didn't see any more than that. He didn't see suicidal. Reading back over her words, he thought she displayed an innocence, one that didn't resonate in a work climate that required mental toughness. A blowing of one's own horn.

Smeg scanned back to the first photo. "Listen to this: *Had I known he was damaged I might not have chosen to spend my life with him. Although who knows? Young love, love is blind, blah, blah. I saw how his parents treated him, but didn't connect it. Horrible people. Now I know what all that criticism does to a person. It causes insecurity, control issues. So why am I still here?*" Smeg interrupted, "Bit of a clinical take on things. Like Katie's response to her death. All of this suggests a family that doesn't talk about or deal with emotions."

Byatt nodded. "Her husband appears to have been the reason she started the journal, given that it was the first entry. Once she was done venting, she moved on to work grievances. Look for one about the kids," she prompted.

Smeg scanned through, giving highlights. "High school graduations were happy days. Everyone on best behaviour, it would appear. Doesn't like Katie's boyfriend very much. Seems she's following her mother down the path of choosing controlling jerks. Logan's flirted with drugs a bit, but not seriously enough to affect his life."

He closed the photo app and set Byatt's phone down. "Lunch?"

Byatt glanced at the time on the console. 11:10. "Will anything be open yet?"

"McDonald's."

Byatt made a face like she'd taken a big bite out of a lemon. "No chance. Sugarbowl's likely open. You can get something healthy there. You know? Salmon, quinoa, fruit salad."

Smeg's face was more like he'd swallowed the whole lemon. "Anything edible?"

Byatt laughed. "They make good burgers."

Charlie ordered the bratwurst with warm potato salad, and Meaghan opted for the vegan sausage tofu scramble.

Charlie was visibly horrified. "Do you have a medical condition?"

"I like tofu." Although her face said otherwise.

"Isn't it tasteless? Like Battle's jokes."

"You mean the ones that shouldn't be told in the office? Or anywhere." Meaghan's shoulders lowered as the corners of her mouth turned upward. He had noticed she needed time to shift gears from work mode.

"You know ..." Charlie hesitated, collecting his thoughts. "Well, maybe it's tough being a woman in a male-dominated profession." He watched her carefully, not wanting to lose the camaraderie that had started to slowly seep into their relationship.

"I can handle it. And hey, it's not as bad as it was over in robbery."

Charlie played with his fork, bending an errant tine back into place. He wasn't guiltless. His forty-year career had spanned waves of misogyny, xenophobia, and homophobia in the workplace, even arachnophobia that time the exterminator hadn't done their job properly. He tried to keep his mouth shut through all of it, but he knew that wasn't enough. The many times he'd let his colleagues' comments go unchallenged came back to him.

Meaghan's cell phone buzzed on the table. She glanced at it. "Mom," she said, and pressed her fingers against her temples. "This is just so ridiculous." She declined the call.

"Oh?"

"She thinks she's being helpful, but her never-ending suggestions drive me crazy. She's on about my boxing at present. Apparently, I should choose an activity that's more lady-like. She thinks my sister could offer some suggestions."

"Ouch. What does your sister think?"

"She's on my side, but she won't stand up to Mom. Not when she's the favoured child."

"Maybe your mom just wants to connect?" he ventured.

"Maybe."

Charlie felt a bit inadequate to continue giving advice, but brightened when the food arrived. They ate in amiable silence; Charlie with a satisfied look on his face, and Meaghan casting longing glances at his plate. The lunch crowd began to fill the empty seats: students in gloomy heavy-knit sweaters, jeans with holes in the knees and bare ankles; middle-aged women in dark-coloured exercise gear sipping lattes; and a smattering of folks from surrounding offices in black coats.

"Not much Christmasy about that Rodriguez house," Meaghan mused, and pushed away her plate with its half-eaten tofu. "Maybe they don't celebrate."

"Or Mom was too sick to organize it."

"Could be last-minute people. There's still four days."

"Lots of time." Charlie grinned.

"Three for me," Meaghan said. "I celebrate Christmas Eve with my parents. Did you pick up something for Paul?"

"Thinking video games."

"Do you guys want to come to my place for dinner Christmas Day? I can probably manage a turkey."

"Could you be a bit more confident about that?" Charlie joked to cover his surprise, and pleasure, at the invitation.

Meaghan laughed. "Sorry. And maybe that was a little too forward. We don't know each other all that well."

"It's okay. We'd love to come. I have every confidence in your cooking."

Charlie pulled into his neighbourhood, named after Laurent Garneau, a soldier during Louis Riel's Red River Rebellion before becoming a prominent leader in the Alberta Métis community. The neighbourhood was special to him, particularly because his grandmother was Métis, so he had read all the history books he could find on Edmonton's early years. He parked under the elderly and gnarled elm tree in front of his house. The neighbourhood, which included the century-old University of Alberta, was one of the oldest. The trees themselves told a story: it was a sad day when the Garneau Tree, a 143-year-old Manitoba maple on campus, had to be removed. Planted by Garneau himself, along with his wife Eleanor, the tree had survived many an area revitalization project.

In any event, it was a great place for walks, Garneau. Or so Charlie had heard.

As he passed the open bedroom door, he glimpsed the hunched figure of his stepson, as if waiting for inspiration to pour out through the top of his head to his waiting fingers, at his desk. Chewbacca watched him from a ceramic *Star Wars* mug filled with pens. A pile of shoes by the door appeared ready to be boxed for pick up by the Salvation Army. Charlie doubted they would ever make their way to the nearby closet, its door open to receive more than the army-style jacket hanging solo inside. Take-out coffee cups formed a neat line along the edge of the table by the unmade bed.

"Love what you've done with the place," Charlie said.

With his high hairline, Paul could pass for a laid-off ad executive. Today's T-shirt read, *I paused my game to be here*. His head bobbed up and down as he reached for a box of Timbits cereal and poured out a handful. Charlie eyed it suspiciously.

"Chocolate glazed," Paul said and tipped the box toward him.

Charlie thought about that for a minute and wondered if a breakfast food needed to taste like a doughnut. But then he realized the kid came by it honestly. The breakfast cereal doesn't fall far from the box.

"What have you been up to? I feel like I haven't seen you in a few days. Did you go out on the weekend?" Charlie vaguely remembered Paul's friend Femi had been home from college.

"Went out for a few drinks? You know, that new brew pub on 104th street?"

Charlie didn't know. But he did know it wasn't really a question.

Paul sniffed in the unconscious way of a kid with chronic allergies. And a kid who was preoccupied.

"How did your interview go?" Charlie asked. "For the editing job."

"I haven't heard anything. It doesn't pay much anyway. Contracts. Work from home. I thought it would give me more time to write. The hours would be better than the split shifts I'm currently doing at The Keg."

Charlie saw the whole editing scenario as untenable. Paul was social; he wouldn't survive long holed up in his bedroom. Charlie had often heard him role-playing *World of Warcraft* online, yelling animatedly at the screen. Battling monsters with swords and magic, in a massive, multiplayer game. It was the connection with others that Paul craved. Then Charlie realized Paul would spend all day at it, rather than editing or writing.

"They reported on the news last night that Home Depot is adding a thousand new tech positions," Charlie said. "Online shopping and workforce management need advanced software systems. You interested in that sort of thing?"

"Don't know if my digital media and IT diploma would be enough." The softness around Paul's jawline would benefit from facial hair.

"Could get you in the door."

"Maybe."

"I'll send you the link to the job ad."

Paul smiled. "Yeah, thanks."

On the way out the door, Charlie paused. "Hey, what are the new games this year?"

"*The Witcher.*" He looked wistful. "I'd love to get my hands on *Wild Hunt.*"

Charlie headed to the mall.

Chapter Six

Charlie wasn't interested in the long drive to South Edmonton Common, a veritable small town of big box stores, or fighting for a parking stall, but now that the last independent electronics store had been subsumed, he didn't have much choice. Edmonton could no longer claim to have the largest indoor mall in the world, to which he felt a sense of relief, but now seemed to be striving for that distinction in an outdoor mall. The front doors of the store slid open to allow him generous room to enter, and the security guard more than enough time to assess him. Charlie walked up and down the aisles of home audio and theatre, media streamers, computers and tablets, televisions, appliances big and small, until eventually he found an escalator that deposited him in front of the game consoles. He must be getting close.

"Can I help you find something, sir?" A friendly young man dressed in a store logo T-shirt and black polyester pants peered at him from behind a handheld price checker. Smeg tried not to fixate on his platinum nose ring. Instead, he pulled a crumpled slip of paper from his pocket and peered at it.

"I'm looking for either *The Witcher* or *Wild Hunt*."

He was met with a confused look. "I think you are looking for *The Witcher: Wild Hunt*. Just one game, not two. I'll show you."

Charlie was certain he'd found his saviour and happily followed him. On the way, they encountered two more employees in branded T-shirts who greeted them with enthusiasm. He met their smiles with his own and wondered if they thought he was visiting from head office. The thought amused him, and he nearly ran into the back of his leader, who had stopped abruptly. He reached for a game and then handed it to Charlie.

Charlie turned the colourful box over to check the price. "Are there others similar? I'd like to get two."

The young guy reached for *Fallout*. "This update's good."

"I'll take your word for it." Charlie nodded his thanks.

As he made his way to the checkout, his phone rang. He was inclined to ignore it, but when he saw the call display said Meaghan Byatt, he smiled and answered.

"Hey," she said. "I've been looking at Hammond's journal entries, and there are quite a few passages that can be read as suicidal."

"Such as?" He stopped walking.

"She definitely felt hopelessness, you know, about her future. She had undiagnosed health problems that wouldn't go away, and a husband that she wished would go away, never-ending roadblocks at work."

"What kind of roadblocks?" He stepped aside to let a cart filled with electronics and two kids, pushed by a young woman, get by him.

Byatt's phone spat static in his ear. "A number of times she felt she was in line for a promotion, was told she was being prepared for it, and then at the last minute it went to someone else."

"That shit happens all the time. Especially with government. Entitlement, not merit, leads to promotion."

"Maybe she took it personally."

"Likely, but still not an indication of suicide. And besides, a person wouldn't kill themselves with low-dose arsenic poisoning."

"Maybe she just drove straight off the freeway. We haven't tested the assumption that she was unconscious when the vehicle left the road," Byatt said.

"Okay, I'll check with the coroner to see if she was conscious prior to the accident."

"Price check on till five," the PA system said.

"Where are you?" Byatt asked.

"Buying video games for Paul. They're pricey. When I was his age, I could walk into a store like this with a hundred bucks and come out with a Sony Walkman."

"Yeah," Byatt said. "But nowadays it's difficult. There are CCTV cameras everywhere."

A noise like a pained dog barking in a tin can had Smeg quickly setting down his coffee before he spilled it. If he'd been prone to terrors, this might have caused an episode. Once he'd married the sound to his phone, he realized Paul had changed the ringtone. Again.

"Charlie Smeg here."

"Brokks Testing Service. We've got your lab results. The water sample you submitted tests well below Health Canada's guideline for arsenic."

"Okay, thanks." The home water wasn't a problem, but there was still the office.

Smeg opened his front door, original to the house and sporting a nine-light window still intact, and grabbed the mail. There were the usual development notices from the city and pleas from the community league to have his property designated as historical. He really should start that process; he tossed the mail on the front bench. Pulling on his lightweight parka, he headed out. The old truck coughed in the cold as he again turned onto 109 Street, then it sputtered as he made his way down the hill to the Walterdale bridge. Maybe he could get his truck designated, too.

His first case as a detective had been years earlier; the victim—young, pretty, going places—was raped behind a downtown nightclub before she was stabbed. It made Smeg question becoming a cop, thinking about a promising young life snuffed out senselessly, but he soon turned his questions to seeking justice. He'd been working part-time in a bicycle repair shop, one of those assembly-line storefront places, to put himself through university. A guy with a long grey ponytail, whom Smeg had assumed to be ancient, would come into the shop first for repairs, then parts, and eventually, he started helping with the bicycles. They shared a love of detective shows, and one day the man said, 'You should be a cop.' Smeg had laughed; he was studying history. But, of course, he mused as he pulled into the police parking lot, there weren't a lot of jobs tied to a history degree. And now he couldn't imagine what his life might have looked like if he'd pursued that instead. He knew he'd made the right choice with policing. He knew he'd made a difference.

Officer Battle was in his usual place inside the front door. He would have been the epitome of authority if his uniform wasn't a size too big.

While he sported close-cropped hair and a back as straight as a nightstick, his unpolished shoes clouded the image. His face, while seamed, retained the chiselled quality of a movie version of his role. On cue, a smile cracked his face.

"Hey," Battle said. "What are you doing here?"

Smeg glared at him. "I work here."

"I thought they'd ruled your case an accident."

"Higher-ups are always in a hurry to get things wrapped. Pad the year-end stats to wave in front of City Council."

"Not an accident?" Battle's tone was light.

Smeg knew the guy was happy in his job, staying on top of the office gossip. And now he was digging for tidbits he could dole out along with the sweets from a bowl on the counter containing lollipops, jujubes, and mini tootsie rolls.

"Not likely." Smeg liked Battle, but he wasn't going to give him this one. He'd have to wait for the report.

Smeg ambled back to his desk with its barebones allocation of out-of-date equipment, including an old rotary phone someone had left as a joke. The stapler, tape dispenser, and sticky notes were standard issue, although his had been issued in an earlier decade. Everyone else had new Polycom desktop phones with speakerphone background noise suppression and three-way conferencing headsets. They said his was coming, but he guessed they weren't going to bother. Assholes. He wouldn't likely know how to use it anyway.

He softened at the sight of Byatt waiting for him. She looked up at him and smiled.

"Where are we at?" Byatt asked, removing her feet from his desk.

It seemed like a good use of the desk to him.

"Water at the house tests fine. It's not the source of the arsenic." Smeg sat on the edge of a table, which complained audibly. "Let's head over to her office this morning." He stood up. "I'll drive," he said before she could offer.

When he was Byatt's age, he would have loved her minuscule sports car. But now the truck suited him just fine.

Deena Hammond had worked in the Wildlife Diseases division of Alberta Environment in the South Petroleum Plaza downtown, a building that had seen better days. Its ethnography would have put the most ardent observer to sleep—years upon years of government offices moving in and out. The vertical slats on the exterior walls were reminiscent of prison cell bars, smokers let out for a break. A pattern of slimming lines continued through the panelled lobby to a bank of mirrored elevators. He hit the button for the ninth floor and hoped the elevator was working better than the slimming lines were.

Byatt read from a poster in the elevator titled, *What's bugging wild critters*. "Whirling disease, West Nile Virus, Bovine tuberculosis, Deformed antlers, Black spots in fishes."

"Working here would bug me," Smeg observed as they stepped out into the hallway and made their way to the reception desk.

The first thing that hit him about the place was the smell. It was off; earthy, like rotting plants. He wondered if any of Hammond's symptoms could have been related, such as headaches and the discoloration of her skin. The room itself was befitting wildlife disease: emaciated like chronic wasting with no pictures on the discoloured walls and a sagging couch that looked like it had been visited by someone without bladder control.

"Can I help you?" the receptionist asked, turning from his computer to face them.

Smeg paused, taken by surprise. He had expected a woman, not the young man in front of him, and was reminded yet again of his outdated notions. But this guy took his outdated notions a step further. His neatly combed brown hair ended in a curl just below his collar and his clothes were not befitting the office in Smeg's mind. Tight jeans were shoved into red high tops that flashed like a streetlight, and his dress shirt didn't completely cover the Superman image on his T-shirt.

"We have an appointment with Hilaria Golding," Smeg said.

The receptionist glanced up at a phone list on the wall. "First week." He grinned. "I'm from the temp agency and haven't learned the numbers yet."

It would have been hard not to smile back. "Temp agency," Smeg said.

"Yeah," the young guy said. "I'm a graphic artist. Temping pays the bills while still giving me time to do my drawing."

Smeg was happy to listen to the guy chatter about art and his heavy metal band. Mostly to avoid being invited to sit down.

"Nice place," Byatt muttered as a plump, forty-something woman emerged from around the corner.

As she made her way down a long cubical passageway with self-important strides suggestive of a need to be elsewhere, she slowed to check her phone. The pallor of her skin told Smeg she didn't spend any more time outdoors than he did. She was dressed from head to toe in shades of taupe, her light brown hair framing a genial face that gave her a bit of a mushroom look. At the sight of Smeg and Byatt, a comely smile appeared out of nowhere.

"I'm Hilaria Golding," she said, and extended her hand to each of them. "And you are?"

"Detectives Meaghan Byatt and Charlie Smeg." He reached out a hand of his own.

"How can I help you, detectives?"

Her jaw moved ever-so-slightly as she worked what appeared to be a very small piece of gum. Or they'd interrupted her breakfast.

Byatt responded, with an equally kind demeanour, "We'd like to ask you a few questions about Deena Hammond."

"So unfortunate," Golding said and gave her head a minute shake. "Such a lovely woman. Please come back to my office."

As they passed the kitchen, she asked, using air quotes, "Would you like a 'coffee?'"

While not well-versed in the meaning of air quotes, he did get that the coffee was a bit of a risk. Yet, he accepted her offer of bitter-smelling brew so that he could fill a vial with tap water from the sink. Music that had been absent from the elevator played softly in the background, accompanied by a fridge motor that may have been on its last legs. The coffee was vile, still black after adding two large scoops of powdered creamer. He dumped most of it in the sink before continuing to Golding's office.

"Did you work with Hammond for long?" Byatt asked.

"We started out together five years ago, actually on the same day. We did similar work but had responsibility for different parts of the province."

"When did you become her supervisor?" Byatt asked.

"Three years ago. I got the director position when it became vacant and then the senior director a year later. Now I'm executive director." She laughed. "Making my father proud."

Smeg wondered how many levels of director it took to get to the top. He also wondered if there might be a punch line to follow that thought, but he couldn't work out what it might be.

"At that point, did Hammond apply for the director job?" Byatt asked.

"No, I decided not to fill it. Leadership was looking for cost savings, so I offered up that position. Deena applied for a few opportunities outside the branch but didn't get them. I think some folks may have been concerned about her health."

"Are there others in the office who are sick? With chronic illness?"

"Not that I'm aware of," Golding said. "Although there always seems to be one or two people on long-term leave. Last year, a man fell down his basement stairs while changing a light bulb and landed on the top of his head. He was away for six weeks."

Smeg listened in awe as she repeated multiple versions of the story, each with slightly different details, but all resulting in people being off work for some indeterminate length of time.

Smeg intervened. "What about illness?"

"That might be a question for HR," she said.

"Indeed." Smeg nodded and wondered why the list of injuries wasn't also a question for HR.

"Did Hammond talk to you about her desire to move into management?" Byatt asked.

"Oh sure, I encouraged her to do so."

"Was she frustrated at all?"

Golding looked momentarily confused. "I don't think so. I mean, she was useful here and I appreciated her talents as a researcher. She wrote great reports for me, and I often praised her for them. I don't think she was as ambitious as me—you know, she didn't like to take work home, and that's more the level of dedication leadership is looking for."

Smeg considered the utility of a useful employee, an occupational hazard that may have left Hammond vulnerable to exploitation. While being useful was her job, being used was not. The boss sitting in front of him might have confused talent with ambition, although he suspected she knew exactly what she was doing.

"Can we see her office?" Byatt asked.

"Sure," Golding said, and she led them down a hallway. "Are you looking for something in particular?"

"Not really," Byatt said. "Just covering our bases."

"Her death wasn't an accident?"

"We have to investigate fully," Smeg said. "Mind if we just poke around?"

"Go ahead," Golding said. "I'll be in my office if you need me."

After she disappeared into the bowels of the building, Byatt observed, "She's a bit of Christmas cheer in this gloomy place."

"She was a monochrome of beige."

"But pleasant enough." Byatt began poking around the papers on Hammond's desk. She sat down in the office chair and opened the desk drawers. "Not much here, dozens of pens, a box of granola bars, an old letter opener, paring knife, a lighter. Oh wait, here's a syringe."

"A syringe?"

"It looks like it hasn't been used in a while. The plastic is discoloured and there's no needle."

"There's enough here I'd like to look more closely at," Smeg said.

He pulled a pair of rubber gloves from his pocket and put them on. He reached for a bright pink water bottle and put it in an evidence bag to keep it clean. He added the syringe.

"We'll get these tested," Smeg said. "The water bottle for arsenic and the syringe to find out what she was using it for."

Smeg thought about what it would mean if the water bottle tested positive for arsenic. It would at least narrow the possibilities of how she was being poisoned. And if there was a problem in the office, they'd find more evidence. The syringe, he imagined, was likely not implicated. There were too many possibilities for its use, and they weren't all medical. She could have been using it to apply glue. Maybe the low-budget furniture needed periodic repairs. Maybe that was the smell that permeated the place.

"The office doesn't really have the making of a crime scene," Byatt observed.

"No," Smeg agreed. "Pretty normal office. Well, except for the receptionist."

Byatt laughed. "He was actually quite charming."

"In an elf-like way."

"Office towers would more likely be the scene of theft, not murder," Byatt said.

Either way, the security camera kept an eye on them on the way out.

"What did you make of Golding?" Smeg asked. "Why was she rambling on about accidents?"

"I can't quite put my finger on it, but there was something about her. She was friendly enough. We likely made her nervous. And there was the weird comment about her father being proud of her. Like her rising through the ranks was being done to impress him. Who says stuff like that?"

"Lots of strange people in the world. And lots of folks who spend their lives trying to impress Daddy."

He dropped Byatt off at her car in the police department parking lot.

"Four o'clock for dinner tomorrow?" she asked.

"Looking forward to it," he said, and meant it.

He was surprised to realize it was almost Christmas Eve. He had planned to go into the office to write up his notes, but instead considered what he would make Paul for dinner. Nancy would have done an Irish stew with soda bread. He could manage the stew; the bread would need to come from the bakery.

Chapter Seven

Charlie and Paul arrived at Meaghan's condo with two bottles of medium-body French Chardonnay twenty minutes late. If Charlie had been alone, he would have been on time. Paul had fussed over what to wear, exposing an entirely new side of himself. Insecurity was characteristic; concern over wardrobe was not. Meaghan answered the door in a sleeveless black dress, exposing arm muscles indicative of regular workouts. On some women, a dress that clung in such a way might lead to thoughts of what was underneath, but the addition of an apron adorned with holly and ivy, not to mention a few grease stains, gave the whole look a seasonal feel. She hugged them both briefly, wished them Merry Christmas, and invited them in. The place smelled like the comforting aroma of roasting turkey and its partner, mince pie.

"Mmm, smells awesome," Paul said. His ever-so-slight Irish accent still clung, even though he'd only been to Ireland once. "All I've had to eat today is a bag of Chips Ahoy."

There were other remnants of his mother: a quiet laugh ready to erupt at any time.

Meaghan chuckled and led them down the hall to the kitchen. "I've got healthy things on the menu. Hope you like roasted veggies."

Light streamed in through a kitchen window and illuminated the set table, inviting with its cheery red tablecloth and candles, mismatched both in shape and size. She lifted the lid from a pot that bubbled on the stove and stirred its contents, her face flushed from the heat, giving her rosy cheeks the look of a small child. Her glasses, now covered in steam, she pushed to the top of her head. Paul pulled up his jeans, which were down around his hips, and slid onto a high stool at the counter while Charlie opted to stand. He thought that with all the time Paul took in deciding what to wear, he might have produced a belt.

"He'll actually eat anything he doesn't have to cook himself," Charlie said. "His mother did the cooking in the family."

"My mother, too." Meaghan turned from the stove, her green eyes somehow bigger and brighter before she lowered her glasses back into place. "She was also a task master, activity planner, army drill sergeant, and controller of family resources. As a teenager, I hid from her, either to avoid chores or to avoid family outings. We bowled, hiked, walked, biked, went to movies, concerts, parks and playgrounds. Some of my friends were over-programmed by their parents; we were smothered. They had helicopter parents; we had cyclone parenting."

"But you did stuff? Like activities?" Paul looked at her with wide-eyed envy. "My mom was usually busy working, at least until we moved in with Charlie."

Charlie chuckled. "And I wasn't exactly an event planner."

"We did go on that trip, you know, to Banff?" Paul checked his phone, then tucked it back in his pocket.

Charlie recalled the adventure fondly. Had there only been the one? He felt a twinge of guilt, realizing Paul might have wanted more. There were likely other parts of the province left to explore, he thought wryly. The Badlands and Head Smashed In Buffalo Jump came immediately to mind, but those were more his choices with their ties to prehistory. Paul talked about Calgary's Studio Bell and its museum, which housed the Rolling Stones Mobile Studio. "Cool," he'd said. If given the opportunity, he might have more ideas. Meaghan pushed a tray piled high with nachos and guacamole in front of Paul. He dove in.

"I see you survived Christmas Eve?" Charlie said, giving Meaghan's hand, which rested on the counter, a pat.

"Yeah, Mom's calmed down a bit. Also, Dad puts a little extra rum in her eggnog."

Extra rum was nice, but so was extra eggnog. If it were him, a large one would be on offer.

"Would you like me to open the wine?" Charlie asked.

Meaghan handed him a corkscrew, one of those winged ones that was close to foolproof. The cork released with a burst.

"Sounds like your father has it figured out." Charlie poured wine into three glasses.

"What did your dad do?" Paul asked, reaching for his, its delicate bowl lost in his outsized hand.

"My dad's a retired cop," Meaghan said. "He spent all day barking orders, so I guess at home, he was happy to let Mom do it. He'd tag along on group escapades if he wasn't asleep in a chair."

"You decided to become a cop, too? Like him?" Paul leaned on the counter and propped his head on his hands.

"I used to follow him around the house. I think I liked the calm of him. Over time, I associated his demeanour with being a cop." Meaghan mashed potatoes in a large mixing bowl while Paul watched in fascination.

"Yeah, I know what you mean." Paul pulled his eyes from the potatoes to give Meaghan a conspiratorial look. "Charlie's pretty relaxed, too. I've often found him asleep in a chair."

Paul lifted his wine glass toward Charlie, who responded with a nod.

"What about you?" Meaghan asked. "Are you going to follow in his footsteps?"

"Huh?" Paul asked as if there was no way to make sense of the question.

"He's more into technology," Charlie supplied.

Paul, recovering his composure, added, "Cop work seems a little too strenuous; I mean, I know it isn't all sleeping on a chair."

"There are police jobs that require technical skills—information technologists, data analysts. Cops use a lot of those supports ..." Her voice trailed off, and Charlie wondered if she thought she'd overstepped her bounds.

"His mother said similar things," he added quietly.

Paul watched them carefully. He took a big gulp of his wine. Then he checked his phone. Paul had some affinity for solving mysteries. His technical skills, honed by hours of video games, could be a means to get there. And his diploma gave him a marginal amount of theoretical knowledge.

"Sit in," Meaghan said and set steaming platters on the table.

Paul's eyes popped like a Christmas cracker.

The mood of the previous evening clung to Charlie as he stirred boiling water into freeze-dried, instant coffee granules, the bittersweet aroma making him wonder why he hadn't made a pot with fresh beans. He tended not to reminisce about social events, but did note with curiosity a warmth with Meaghan's name attached to it. Charlie now lived parallel to the universe of women and so had ceased thinking of himself as in any way attractive. But what he currently experienced was something different. Paul had engaged in a buoyant jaunty fashion, responding, Charlie sensed, to an almost forgotten familial feeling. Maybe that was it for Charlie, too.

The black heads of chickadees bobbed between the seed in the feeder and the suet hanging in a mesh bag below. From Charlie's perch on a kitchen chair, the backyard had an air of English garden, or at least one covered in a blanket of white. Come spring, the yard would be accentuated with the smell of snow mould and rotting plants that hadn't been cleared away in the fall. He reached for his laptop out of habit, even though there'd be no urgent email on a holiday. He checked the news headlines: Boxing Day lineups in the mall leading primarily to the Apple store; a pileup on the freeway resulting in one dead; a spike in stabbing victims arriving at emergency wards overnight. Any connection between these stories was surely coincidental.

He found his phone on the counter and called the forensic engineer in charge of traffic collision reconstruction. "How's the analysis of the Hammond accident going? When can we expect the results?"

"It's Boxing Day, Detective. We're short-staffed."

"But still," Smeg pressed, mildly pissed. "The investigation doesn't go on holiday. What do you have so far?"

"There was ice on the freeway where her vehicle left the road. There was some sliding prior to impact, likely caused by the slippery conditions rather than by braking. Photographs taken at the scene have limited usefulness given how rapidly the snow was falling."

"3-D laser scan?"

"It's the computer model that takes time here. We need to evaluate all possible hypotheses and conclusions. Once we create an animation simulation, you can come in and see it."

"Okay," Smeg said. "Thanks for this." It wouldn't hurt to keep the guy in his good books.

"One more thing," Smeg said. "How did you get the department to agree to 3-D scanning? There's a lot of demand for those resources, and it doesn't seem like this one would be a priority."

"Well, there's a traffic safety issue given there was no guardrail that could have prevented her leaving the road. And the eyewitness account that suggested she was run off the road."

Smeg was hopeful there'd be new information from the 3D scan, as every tidbit could help point them in the right direction. So far, the indications that Rodriguez had helped the accident along were inconclusive. The aim of most reconstructions was road safety. Data from the accident would be added to a larger databank to see if the interaction of components at the site could highlight problems and countermeasures. It could also determine if the car had changed direction, caused by an impact from behind. He made himself a second cup of coffee, sat back down at the kitchen table, and called the coroner.

"Cross here."

"Hey," Smeg said. "Working the holiday?"

"Anything for you, Smeg."

Smeg chuckled. "Listen, that Hammond autopsy. Was she conscious when she left the road?"

"Let me pull up her file."

Smeg could hear the humming, whistling, and clicking of Cross's vintage computer with its monster hard drive. He supposed Cross only needed it to store files. Anything he wanted to look up was in books. Smeg recalled them spilling out of bookshelves and stuffing every crevice of the office.

"No, not conscious was the conclusion," Cross said.

"Dead?"

"That's more difficult to determine. Time of death is not exact, and narrowing it to before or after she left the road is virtually impossible."

"Could any of her symptoms have been caused by black mould exposure?"

"Why?" Cross sounded surprised.

"I think there's mould in the office where she worked."

The kind that thrived in spaces of human habitation, such as a post-war, brutalist-style, high-rise office tower with mis-planned aerodynamics that don't benefit from sunlight. It's called 'sick building syndrome.' It wasn't hard for Smeg to imagine based on his brief visit to Hammond's office.

"Generally, the symptoms are different. Did she have sinus issues or nosebleeds?"

"Those weren't mentioned by her husband." Smeg made a mental note. "What about skin infections?"

"I didn't find any spots consistent with infection. The discoloration of her skin is more likely arsenic poisoning."

"Hmm, okay, thanks. I'll let you get back to work." Smeg started to take the phone away from his ear, then remembered. "Hey, one more question: how would the husband have known she was dead when he arrived at her vehicle? He said he didn't touch the SUV because he knew she was dead."

"He couldn't have known by looking through the window. She was pronounced dead at the scene but only after examination by ambulance attendants."

That, Smeg knew. But he wanted to hear someone else say it. So why hadn't Rodriguez opened the vehicle door to check on his wife? It seemed cavalier at best not to do everything he could to save her. At worst, well, how *had* he known she was dead?

Smeg picked up the coffee cup from his desk and moseyed down to the cafeteria to fill it. The first day back after the holiday break might presumably be a letdown, but for Charlie, it meant an escape from obligatory eating and visiting with relatives. The cousins he only spoke with once a year came to mind. The office was hopping. Periodically, in union negotiations, someone put forward a motion to extend the Christmas holidays. It never passed. Under normal circumstances, the department was home to activity like ships passing in the night with little interaction beyond a signalled greeting, a wave, or a nod. This day, there was a buzz, a scene replayed every year, and Smeg rose to it accordingly.

He stepped into line behind Battle, who turned toward him and launched into an extended greeting as he filled his tray with yogurt, fruit salad, and granola.

"Getting a jump on your New Year's resolution?" Smeg asked, looking toward Battle's tray.

Smeg knew his own resolution should involve a reduction in caloric intake. He also knew that was unlikely.

Battle shook his head. "Just getting a jump on breakfast while I wait for my order of bacon and eggs."

Smeg also shook his head, ever so slightly. "I wish," he said, and reached in and filled his mug. And he did wish for breakfast all over again, even though he'd already had two Sausage McMuffins on the way to work. "How was the holiday?" he asked.

"I picked up one of those backyard ice rink kits. You know, the ones from Canadian Tire? For the grandkids." Battle pulled out his wallet and tapped his bank card. "My son didn't want it in his own yard. Guess he thinks my lawn's expendable." He laughed. "Anyway, I get to see more of them this way."

Smeg noted, in the rising hum, a glow as Battle shifted gears toward his grandchildren. In rare moments, Smeg experienced a fleeting melancholy connected to his own lack of progeny. He loved his stepson, but somehow couldn't visualize him with offspring.

"Ever think about retirement? You know, spend more time with them?" Smeg dropped a handful of coins into the coffee jar.

"Definitely thinking about it. As they say, if I had known grandchildren were this much fun, I would have had them first." Battle's eyes scanned him before he asked, "How was your holiday?"

Smeg knew better than to mention having dinner with Byatt.

"Nice," he managed.

"Paul home?"

Smeg nodded. "He still lives at home." Then, with a sigh, "He doesn't have enough of a job to move out."

"Oh," Battle said.

Smeg followed him to a table by the window and sat down.

"I'm trying to spark his interest in some of these tech jobs I'm seeing advertised. Seems to be a lot of them popping up."

"The department is looking for a data technician, some data entry, data manipulation, developing GIS solutions ... all reporting to Raj Agarwal in the Data Analytics unit. They're doing some cool stuff: enhanced efficiency of incident investigations, identifying trends, driving planning, and use of police resources."

Smeg nodded as if what Battle was saying made sense. He did know enough to understand Paul would know what all that stuff was. He hoped the job was one Paul wanted. It was hard to tell what his true passion was, and Smeg was aware of a nagging thought that he should let Paul figure things out for himself. Nancy might not have agreed that her boy was a data geek. She'd have fostered his love of people, pushing him into maybe teaching or nursing. Helping professions. But Smeg hadn't succeeded in encouraging much of anything. And, for sure, the kid needed to start somewhere.

"Hey, thanks for that. I'll mention it to Paul."

"It'll be in tomorrow's bulletin," Battle said enthusiastically.

Smeg's cell phone rang. He marvelled at Battle's insight into everything before it happened and nodded his thanks as he got up from the table to take the call.

"Brokks Testing Service. We've got your new lab results. The additional water sample you submitted is well below Health Canada's guideline for arsenic. The water bottle, though, had levels above what we consider safe."

"High enough to cause health problems?"

"With long-term exposure, yes."

The arsenic couldn't have been added directly to the bottle, as that would result in astronomically high levels. If tampering had occurred, it was more likely that tainted water was added to the bottle. But from what source?

Chapter Eight

Smeg gazed out the window at the old strip mall across the street with its advertised cheap liquor and convenient snacks, as he waited by Byatt's desk while she finished scanning through files on her computer. A collective gathered by a streetlamp to smoke cigarettes, the resultant cloud reaching to join its cumulus partners that dotted the blue sky. With one hand, he reached out to close the slats on the blind, shutting out the sunlight bouncing off her screen. She looked up and smiled in a way that made him glance away. He couldn't think of what to say.

"Hey," she said. "What's up? Did you enjoy the rest of the holidays? Well, I guess it was just Boxing Day since we seem to be back at it today."

Generally speaking, Smeg hated the dead space between Christmas and New Years when the world was suspended like the half-open door of a college professor fulfilling a contractual obligation to hold office hours. He wanted to kick it wide open and demand action. He was open for business; it was hardwired into him, the need to not only work but do so without delays. Byatt, on the other hand, seemed able to chill. Maybe he could learn.

"I worked. Or at least bothered people who made the mistake of answering their phones," he said. "Thanks for a great dinner the other night. Paul's still talking about those Oreo rum balls."

She clapped her hands lightly and laughed. "I was looking for an excuse to try that recipe. It also gave me an incentive to go to the boxing club."

The idea of Byatt boxing confused him at first, but maybe she was taking control of her life, her mother, her job—putting her fate in her own hands. Maybe her inner conflicts were manifest in outward strength. He saw her stepping into the ring with confidence and relaxing into it. As she was beginning to do with the job. She had the ability to be a great detective, she just didn't know it.

Paul could use such a hobby. Charlie himself could, too, although it would need to be less strenuous.

"Club was open on the holiday?"

"There aren't classes right now, but I did find a few willing sparring partners. I used to go with Jerry when we were still together. Now I have to take whoever shows up. There is some satisfaction, though in lacing up the gloves and pretending it's Jerry I'm punching." She rolled up her sleeves and mimed a light punch.

"Where is he these days?" Smeg asked.

He knew their relationship had been rocky. The explosive breakup gossip between Meaghan and Jerry had made it even to him.

"Financial crimes. I don't see him much."

"Not committing any federal offences then?"

She laughed and crossed her left foot with its chunky boot over her right knee. "The stuff they see over there is mind-boggling: money laundering, terrorist financing, corporate fraud. And most charges are dropped. That would drive me crazy. All that work for nothing."

"Keeps them employed, I guess," Smeg said dryly. He pulled up a chair and sat down. "I heard back on the latest water tests. The water at Hammond's office isn't the source of the arsenic. But her water bottle might be."

"The water bottle? But not the home water or the office water. So where was she getting the water from?" Byatt asked. Her left foot began to bounce. "A different source?"

"Can't rule it out," he said.

Where else could she have filled the bottle? The gym? Did she stop anywhere on her way to work? She wasn't healthy enough based on her autopsy to suggest a strenuous exercise regimen, but maybe she had just started one. Could she have been going for walks? Or meditation? Maybe she was going to a yoga studio. He pulled out his notebook and added to his list of items to check with Rodriguez, along with why he had been reluctant to have the autopsy done.

"What do we know about Hammond?" he asked. "Would someone want to harm her, and why? What else was going on in her life besides work?"

"The water bottle was found at her workplace," Byatt said. "It seems like that's the place to start."

"True. But we'll need a search warrant to go back there."

The last time he sought a warrant, he'd arrived with a smug attitude and a poorly developed argument. He tried to recall the name of the magistrate who turned him down. It was a woman. Something about her made his thoughts turn to poison.

"Have we come across other cases where arsenic appears?" he asked.

"I'm just starting to look through the case files," Byatt said. "I've asked analytics to help narrow the search."

Contrary to the musty locale of the analytics department's basement premises, there was a lot of action in the unit; its predictive modelling had helped the department reach its crime reduction targets in the past couple of years. They'd been able to map hotspots and put resources where really needed. They sped up the process of sifting through archives.

"Speaking of analytics, I'm trying to get Paul to apply for that data job," he said. "I think he'd be good at it."

Byatt returned her foot to the floor and leaned on her knees. "I love that idea. He's thoughtful and smart. I sense he pays attention to detail."

Smeg smiled at her. "True. I said I'd help him if I can."

"Good," she said. "Wish I had him now; he could help narrow my search. Is there anything in particular I should look for?"

"Source of arsenic. How is it being accessed? It's easy to come by if you work in a lab but not so much if you don't. Check robberies, cases of chemical theft."

"There are cases where chemicals were used, but nothing with arsenic specifically so far."

While she scrolled down through the files saved on her screen, Smeg recalled a case not that long ago where formaldehyde was found in the bloodstream and bleach was used to wash the body before dumping it in a shallow grave. He shook his head. After all these years, he'd become clever at seeing inside the minds of killers, but that case had pointed out there were still surprises. It was classified as a cold case: no evidence had been left behind on the body. It had been sanitized, ironically, to the point of purity. She was killed elsewhere and transported. There were never any real leads.

"Here's one that's interesting," Byatt continued. "A thirty-year-old woman who worked for Alberta Environment went missing two years ago. She'd been at her office in Edmonton on a Saturday afternoon, catching up on some paperwork. Two colleagues had spoken with her. She left the building and vanished, her car still in the parking lot. After an extensive search, her body was found four days later in a wooded area in the foothills. It was ruled a suicide."

"I remember that one. Getting yourself to the mountains without your car seemed like an extreme measure to commit suicide. There was a note, though."

"Still," Byatt mused. "Might be worth talking to the missing woman's colleagues who spoke to her that day."

"And the roommate." Smeg smiled encouragingly. "Keep at it."

He stood up and stretched. "I'll see about that search warrant."

Smeg turned onto Jasper Avenue toward the provincial courthouse. The headlights of his ancient truck pierced through the low-lying sepia fog that gave the city a dense, grainy look like an old photograph. He envisioned horses coming toward him, the clip-clop echoing on cobblestone at a time when arsenic was an ingredient often used in agriculture. Arsenic also had a murderous history; its lack of colour or taste when mixed into food or drink and availability in nature made it an ideal choice for foul play as early as the Middle Ages. He recalled, as he peered through the haze of the twenty-first century at the original Hudson

Bay building, that still today arsenic was used in pesticides, insecticides, wood preservatives, copper and lead alloys, glass, semiconductor devices, and veterinary medicines. There were more effective murder weapons available now; that in itself might make arsenic a killer's choice. Who would think to look for it?

Rodriguez worked in mosquito control, but in an office, not a lab, and he wasn't spraying chemicals, so that seemed like a bit of a stretch. And besides, most jurisdictions used pyrethrin to kill mosquitoes, and he had heard Edmonton had switched to *bacillius thurengensis* a few years back, a biological insecticide that was less invasive to other species. So, who else in Hammond's life might have access to arsenic? He stepped out of the parking lot and into the recently refurbished courthouse with its own chemistry, both literal and figurative. The distinctive scent of the foyer's lemon trees was overtaken by fresh paint in the long hallway that rolled into new oak as Smeg stepped up to the counter. He'd brought with him a carefully filled-in Information to Obtain form, which was tucked under his arm. He was directed to Faloney's office. That was the name he'd been unable to recall, the magistrate who'd turned him down the last time he'd applied for a warrant. He committed to doing better this time.

"Morning." Smeg smiled at her stony face. "Hoping to get a warrant." He handed her the form. "Probable grounds to believe a crime was committed at the Alberta Environment office downtown. A woman died of arsenic poisoning, likely put in her water bottle at her place of employment."

Light from the desk lamp reflected on Faloney's cool granite features, her small ears stretched by emerald earrings which hung like paper weights to her high shoulders. She scoured the document three times.

Smeg knew he hadn't missed a thing on the form, but he kept his face neutral. He forced himself not to shuffle his feet. She looked at him with mild disdain and reached for her water glass before instructing him to raise his right hand and swear to tell the truth. He relayed the facts of the case to date that outlined probable cause and reasonable grounds to search the office.

"Limited to Hammond's office." Faloney scrawled her signature across the bottom of the form and handed it back.

Smeg waited until he was back outside before breathing a sigh of relief. He drove back to the detachment to pick up Byatt. They would search Hammond's work environment, although he had to admit it seemed an unlikely place for a crime, at least one that involved death, even if unintentional. Government employees have been the butt of jokes since the dawn of government; wouldn't a maple syrup coordinator be a sweet job, after all. Although a person might die of boredom as a pencil-rounding machine tender, murder in the workplace was unlikely. If one were to acknowledge the fictional types of a *Parks and Recreation* department where nothing ever gets done, the eccentricities of *Brooklyn 99* might also come to mind. There were problems in his own department, but he likewise saw a lot of hardworking people. He pulled up to the front door of the detachment, and Byatt hopped in.

"How'd it go?" she asked.

"I got Faloney," he said. "She doesn't like me much. Last time I saw her was for an open-and-shut murder case. The guy had abused his wife for years, and there was evidence that the marks on her body were put there by him. The facts all lined up, only I failed to present properly and didn't get the warrant to search the home. No smoking gun, as it were. Charges were reduced to manslaughter."

Byatt looked down at her strong hands. She didn't look up, the dome of her head impenetrable. Smeg realized he was leading her in the wrong direction, and she might be thinking that working with him was career-limiting if he couldn't even secure a search warrant.

"I got the warrant," he said, quickly.

"Oh god," she said, with a slight drop in her jaw. "Of course. I was thinking about what we'd be looking for at her office, about government workers and what attracts them to the job. I would have thought they'd tend toward a balance between thinking and feeling, introvert and extrovert."

"I'm not sure an extremist would be misplaced." Smeg rubbed his chin. "Those people exist. And wouldn't cause suspicion exactly because people think their presence is unlikely."

"I think we want to talk with Hammond's former colleagues about their experiences.

Have others been passed over for promotions? Are they dissatisfied with the workplace? Their bosses? Jealous of colleagues? That sort of thing."

Smeg knew it was a line of questioning they needed to pursue. He thought about the woman who had died a lonely death in the mountains. It would be easy enough to unearth the facts; they were undoubtedly in a report they would need to read. He hoped there'd be something about the connection to Alberta Environment. Maybe she knew Hammond.

Charlie pulled into his driveway. As he got out, he came face-to-face with Paul. Well, face to top of head. Paul seemed to watch his feet meander in the general direction of the front sidewalk as he listened to tunes. Or maybe one of those podcasts. The tech job at the detachment was perfect for Paul, but he would need some convincing. He had the ability; it was the confidence he was lacking.

"Hi, Paul." Charlie caught a faint and pleasant whiff of mint citrus.

A new cologne and, not for the first time, he noted Paul's lack of a love interest. There hadn't been a high school sweetheart or even a prom date. At the time, with his mother recently gone, Charlie had been relieved Paul went to prom at all and really didn't think it beyond that. There were friends and continued to be. Charlie paid enough attention to see their influence; the families where a trophy for effort had led to the idea that expressing yourself was a basis for getting on in the world. The small, tight-knit group provided a cocoon from which he'd always expected Paul to emerge as a fully-formed version of himself, a man whose most fervent desire was to get a real job. Only recently had Charlie awoken to the gaps in his stepson's emotional security.

"Hey, Charlie." Paul yanked on his earbuds, which then came to rest on the front of his unbuttoned puffer jacket; the other end snaked out of a pocket.

"Leaving?"

"Yeah," Paul said. "Meeting a friend."

"Anyone I know?"

"Ah." Paul looked at the ground. "Femi's sister. Just having a coffee. At Starbucks, you know?"

It was only coffee, but still. Charlie reached for his wallet, pulled out a pair of twenty-dollar bills and stuffed them into Paul's pocket.

"Respect," Paul mumbled. "Thanks."

"Need anything else?"

"A job?"

"Yeah," Charlie said. "Was going to mention to you there's a tech job at work, something you could apply for."

"Bit of a stretch from video games to working at it for real, don't you think? I mean, my skills are low man, real low. I've seen guys who can do amazing things with technology, and I'm not one of them."

Charlie's own skills, as emotional mentor, were also low. But his grandmother had been an anchor for him when he was Paul's age, and he could draw on that. He'd just have to reach way back.

"It's entry-level, Paul. You'd be great at it." He gave Paul's arm an encouraging tap.

"How entry-level?" He scowled. "I don't want to do data entry all day."

Exasperated, Charlie said, "It's a starting point, Paul."

Paul shrugged. "Okay, I could give it a go, I guess?"

"I'll send you the ad."

"Great," Paul said, a little too loudly. "I'll take a look at it." He hesitated. "My gap year will soon be up anyway."

"Gap year?" Charlie knew what a gap year was, but he hadn't realized Paul did.

"Yeah, you know? Gave it a go as a writer?"

"Right. Not working out?"

Paul's head moved sideways, then up and down. "Different genre takes on the same story."

"What?" A cold wind ruffled Charlie's hair. It was time to head indoors. For more than one reason.

"This'll just be a new chapter. Tech instead of writing. Writing tech? We'll see, I guess."

Charlie thought about what it meant that Paul preferred to write his way through a gap year rather than experience it firsthand. Although from what he'd heard, maybe he should be grateful. Battle's son had sent an email from Nepal reassuring him that they hadn't actually been held hostage. And never once had the men who had taken over his train pointed their Kalashnikovs at anyone.

"Right."

"Maybe you could put in a good word for me?"

Not sure that will help, Charlie thought. "I'll do what I can."

Paul tapped the roof of the truck and walked away. The earbud had returned to his ear, and a rhythmic bounce was added to his walk. *So, not a podcast*, Charlie thought.

Chapter Nine

The intrigue of the case, bit by bit, pulled Smeg in. He'd always been the go-to guy for poisonings, and tell-tale signs were emerging: condition of the body, the water bottle, and a diary of dissatisfaction. He wasn't sure what he was expecting to find at the Alberta Environment office, but he did know he needed to look. The receptionist at the front desk, presumably another temp, had last night's party on her face and an essence of Zinfandel purchased at a gas station. Her hair was powdered, in a way that suggested she wasn't aware of its haphazard presence, with what was surely coffee creamer. Her fingers, hovering over her keyboard, trembled slightly. Her cleavage did the same. Whether from nerves or the remnants of alcohol in her bloodstream, Smeg had no idea. There she was, suspended, anticipating inspiration which, when it came, was from a small mirror in which Smeg and Byatt waited to be acknowledged. He regretted flashing his badge as she turned toward them, and her hands rose briefly into the air.

"I'm Detective Charlie Smeg, and this is Detective Meaghan Byatt. We're with the Edmonton Police, and we have a search warrant."

He waved the warrant at her. She didn't take it. He folded it and put it back in his pocket.

"Hilaria Golding is expecting us."

She reached for the phone. "There's someone here to see you," she whispered, then after a short pause, said in a more audible voice, "She'll be right out." The young woman turned back to her computer.

Byatt tugged on Smeg's sleeve and motioned for him to step away from the counter. At that point, he realized they were making her uncomfortable. The receptionist got up from her desk and took careful steps down the hall.

"Wonder what she was up to last night?" Byatt smiled. "She picked a bad day to come to work hungover. I'll bet she wishes she'd called in sick."

He smiled back. "I've had a few days like that over the years."

There were times, early in his career, where he participated in after-hours parties—drinking anything put in front of him, including rancid homemade wine and poor attempts at moonshine—followed by waking the next morning with regrets. And then it became a habit. A twinge of pain started at his temples, and he rubbed them.

"The bar's a place to unwind at the end of the day," Byatt said. "To make sense of things."

He also knew it filled a void, one that disappeared when Nancy came along.

"You seem to resist it." He had noticed her leaving work alone most days.

"It's complicated, you know. You want to be friendly but not blur the lines of professionalism. Maybe I overthink it."

Maybe he did, too. After all, he also left work alone. Because he preferred it that way.

Golding signalled her arrival at reception with a quiet cough. "Good morning, Detectives," she said, and extended her hand to each of them as they turned to face her.

The handshake was like granite. Her other hand drew attention with a large sweeping gesture. He was unsure which one to follow. There was a subtle change in her features from the last time they'd met, the charm a bit forced. The glasses thicker. In flats, she was shorter and dumpier. Smeg added five years to her age. She raised her chin. He stepped back and was rewarded with a smile and eyes that suddenly danced almost as if someone had hit the ON switch.

"You said you had a few more questions about Deena? Was it about her work? Relationships? I hope this won't take too long. I'm preparing for a meeting."

She reached over and carefully deadheaded the lilies on the front counter, giving the remaining blooms a gentle caress. Then she grimaced as she rubbed an obviously sore wrist.

"We have a search warrant for her office." He pulled the paper back out of his pocket and handed it to her.

She took it, stared at it, and handed it back. Her eyes hadn't moved as she looked at the document. Most people didn't know what to look for, so only pretended to read; the handing over was largely for show.

"I've seen these before," she said.

"Signed by a judge," Smeg said. "It allows us to search her office for evidence."

"Ah, evidence?" Golding stared, incredulous. "I've had to help out in such cases in the past. Usually, only when a crime has been committed."

"Oh?" Related? The place held intrigue.

"Just peripherally," she quickly added. "People come to me for information."

"What kind of information?" Byatt leaned in conspiratorially. "I love a mystery."

Golding considered her for a moment. In a lowered voice, she said, "You know that story a couple of years back? The predatory fraudster? I gave evidence in that case. I knew the guy who lost his life savings through an investment swindle."

Smeg thought she seemed very excited to have been involved in the case, one he recalled as having an unusually high media profile.

"Cool," Byatt said.

"Yeah. But I don't know what you're looking for here. This one's just tragic, poor woman."

"We're just covering our bases," Byatt said. "We don't know what happened to her at this point."

"She was sick. I'm not sure where you got the idea that something happened to her. Seems to me nothing happened. You know, it was just unfortunate, her illness." Golding seemed ready to dismiss them.

"The autopsy was inconclusive," Byatt said. "We have to check things out."

Golding's smile bounced back. "Shall I show you the way then?"

She hobbled off down the hallway mumbling something about a sore back.

"We know where it is," Smeg said, speaking to her back. "Oh, and we'll need to interview her colleagues."

Golding turned around, considering them like she was going to argue the point before that sugared smile affixed itself to her face once more. "Alright, I'll have Julia set up a schedule."

Julia, Smeg figured, must be the receptionist. *She'll be pleased.*

The office was untouched in the two days since their last visit. Smeg and Byatt donned gloves and began to open drawers, move furniture, books, potted plants, a lamp, and framed photos of her kids, then reached inside the pockets of clothing hanging in the cupboard. Contents of the drawer that had prompted the search warrant were placed in an evidence bag, including: pens, the box of granola bars, an old letter opener, a paring knife, and a lighter. For the next half hour, they read through the files and sticky notes on her desk. A laptop was also placed in the evidence bag.

"Here's something interesting," Byatt said, glancing up from a coiled journal she'd been reading. "It chronicles her interactions with a number of people, a record of dates and times she thought she'd been slighted or even bullied. Maybe she was keeping a record in case she wanted to file a complaint?"

"Maybe she filed one," Smeg said. "There's our in to talk with human resources. From there, we can ask about her employment record, including jobs she'd applied for."

"Okay." Byatt reached for her notebook. "Let's include the people Hammond talked about in her journal on our interview list." She paused. "Golding is one of the names."

"Hmm. And past supervisors?"

"Appears she thought she'd been persecuted for quite some time."

"Maybe she was just paranoid."

Smeg wrote the location of the recovery on the evidence bag and signed his name on the label across the seal. When they returned to the front desk, the receptionist had regained her seat and found her composure, her hair now neatly coiffed and arranged in a high ponytail. She had adjusted her bra and its contents to sit evenly so each breast could peer through the low cut of her blouse, and she now fussed over a large pile of file folders that required obvious precision in their arrangement.

"Julia?" Byatt asked and stepped up to the counter.

The receptionist looked up.

"I understand you are setting up interviews for us?" Byatt asked.

"Well, they're not ready yet," she replied. "I've only just heard from Hilaria."

"No problem." Byatt tore a page from her notebook and handed it to Julia. "Please make sure these individuals are on the list. We'll be back this afternoon for the interviews."

"Great," Julia said with a note of sarcasm. "The ones from other branches will take longer to arrange." The tone shifted to suggest she was used to defending a lacklustre performance.

"No problem. We can do those tomorrow." Byatt tapped the counter before turning away.

"Interesting place," Smeg said, as they stepped into the elevator. "How about that Golding?"

"What a joy she would be to work with. I'm not sure I'd trust her."

Golding was clearly not interested in any interruption to her carefully ordered day. Friendship with colleagues was not on the table, Smeg surmised, and success, defined by her, was found in pleasing bosses. He sensed that engaging in personal relationships would throw her off her game. Relationships were surface-level and served a specific purpose; that purpose being Golding. That, of course, didn't make her a killer.

Charlie would not have chosen a hipster bistro, but waiting for the interviews afforded enough time for a sit-down lunch, and it was close by. Honey Dijon chicken breast served over greens with a balsamic vinaigrette highlighted the star-studded daily specials. Carrot ginger chickpea bowl. Chipotle burrito bowl. Likely served with lime wedges he wouldn't touch for fear of spraying juice all over Meaghan. Not for the first time. Why do they have to say it's served in a bowl? He should ask Paul that. And there were those untamed beards again, but the place had an impressive beer list. Too bad they had to go back to work.

Meaghan joined him in line. "I had to park at the dental office on the next block. Hopefully, they'll cut me some slack if they know it's an unmarked police car. I backed in so the light bars on the grille and dash would be visible."

"You just don't want to piss off your dentist. He might give you an extra shot of Novocaine next time you're in the chair."

"She. And it could be worse. Like not enough Novocaine."

Meaghan smiled briefly and motioned to follow the host to their table. This one's beard was offset by an extraordinarily long and highly waxed handlebar moustache. At first glance, he appeared to be wearing long, patterned sleeves that turned out to be tattoos. Charlie tried to mask the pain in his knee as he struggled into the antique oak dining chair that didn't match the others. Meaghan gently slid the table toward her to create more room.

"How's the knee?" she asked.

"Feeling pretty good at the moment." He had been to see the physiotherapist the day before, and the knee was better. But a change in weather threatened to throw him right back to where he'd been. "Just hoping I don't need a knee replacement."

"Have you had cortisone?"

"I think that's the next step. Hopefully that'll do the trick."

Meaghan put her elbows on either side of the menu and lowered her head briefly. Charlie had noticed how faint lines formed across her forehead when she concentrated on small print. The lines quickly disappeared, and there was little doubt she appreciated the food choices more than he did.

She laughed quietly. "The menu here is predictable: organic and indie."

She reached for the water-filled wine bottle and poured it into their glasses. A shadow crossed the table as the server stepped up to take their food order. Backlit, he channelled an image of Jesus Christ, the superstar version. Meaghan smiled reverentially and offered her food order. Unsure of pronunciation, Charlie pointed at his selection on the menu.

"Hey," she said. "I heard Paul got an interview for the data technician job."

Paul hadn't said he'd applied. Charlie was disappointed; he'd wanted to help him with his resume. But it appeared Paul had figured it out.

"I hope he gets it," Charlie said. "Did you hear who's interviewing?"

"I can find out." Meaghan's eyes had taken on an intensity. "There's so much being done with technology. I was reading an article about how it's rapidly changing farming. A highly relevant topic in Alberta, what with climate change and the need to adapt."

"It's definitely a good time for anything data-related."

Their meals arrived. Despite the crafted flower garden sprouting from the middle of his plate, Charlie brightened at the sight of food. If he were a monarch of old, though, he'd probably sacrifice a food taster to ensure the strange-looking buds on his plate wouldn't be his end. By the time he got to the bottom of it, he was mopping up the last bits of chimichurri aioli with a nasturtium petal.

Smeg and Byatt arrived back at the Alberta Environment office shortly after 1 p.m. Julia greeted them in a way that suggested they had never met before. *Perhaps hoping for a fresh start?* he wondered as she reached for a breath mint. They had asked to interview all of Hammond's branch colleagues as a starting point in hopes of learning more about her and also to discern if others were dissatisfied with the workplace. Julia handed them a neatly compiled list of names and interview times.

"Follow me to the boardroom," she said politely, practicing her newfound professionalism.

First up was Delbert Abercrombie, one of the managers who worked closely with Hammond on a number of files. The notes provided by Golding indicated he had been with the department for thirty years. It had taken a great deal of sifting through reams of handwritten pages to find that detail. Smeg marvelled at how much Golding had been able to produce over the lunch hour. One of her superiors must have said it was important for her to respond so wholeheartedly. Or she wanted to shape the narrative.

"Good afternoon," Byatt said, and indicated Abercrombie should sit down opposite her.

He reached to shake their hands, his own childlike and out of proportion even for a man so small. He needed a haircut. Smeg was seated at the end of the table, close enough to create an atmosphere of casual conversation. He leaned back in his chair.

"Sorry I'm late. I go home at noon to walk our little dog and make lunch for my wife," he said.

He polished an apple on his pant leg. Smeg wondered if he'd had time for his own lunch.

"No problem," Byatt said. "We wanted to talk to you about Deena Hammond."

"It's so awful." He lifted the apple to his mouth and then lowered it without taking a bite. "She was young. And those kids without a mother."

"We're hoping to fill in some blanks," Byatt said. "Did you know her well?"

"Oh, yes, we worked together since she came to the department. Six or seven years? I don't know. I lose track of time." He stared at the table and had to be prompted to continue. "Nice lady. She was a hard worker. Friendly, but nose to the grindstone, you know?"

"Wanted to get ahead?" Smeg asked.

The apple was placed carefully on the table. "She applied for a few positions. I heard some stuff about how she'd been selected for jobs at a higher level, but then, you know how it goes. Higher-ups step in cause they want someone else in the position. That's how the world works.

Deena wasn't political enough or aggressive enough. She didn't play those games."

Smeg jotted in his notebook, *rationalizer?*

"This seems odd, these police questions about Deena." Abercrombie leaned in like he wanted to be the one asking the questions. "Is there a problem?"

"Hoping to understand a bit more about her," Byatt said.

"Her death wasn't from natural causes?" he asked. "I heard somebody here might have done something to her. That true?"

Smeg peered at his notes. "You've worked in the branch for many years. Do you enjoy working here? What is the atmosphere for employees?"

"I do enjoy the challenge. There's always new issues to delve into. I would have loved to move up the ladder as it were, but my wife is sick, and this position gives me the flexibility I need to take her to doctors' appointments and tend to her needs at home. It's a bit of a full-time job."

"Tell us about your wife," Byatt said.

"Oh. Well, she's always had migraines and had to stop working six years ago. She never worked full-time due to her health. At least not after we were married. Before, she had to work more with a young son to raise. And then after, well, we had our daughter, Amelia. We had to put her in daycare because my wife couldn't cope. Now, it's a bit of depression, you know, not being able to be productive and help out in any way. Then her ankle shattered into pieces from falling in the hallway. And now the pacemaker. She's pretty dependent."

Dependent seemed an understatement. With all those ailments, one foot in the grave might be closer to the truth. Did she really have all those ailments, or did she have Abercrombie's number? Was it she said jump, and he said, what would you like me to do next?

"How do you manage it all?" Byatt asked as she bit on the end of her gold-embossed pen, the words *Champs Boxing Club* visible along its side.

Abercrombie laughed. "It's okay. The kids are grown now. My daughter and her husband help out when they can. She worries about her dear old dad. But my stepson, he's a different story. He's washed his hands of it all. He thinks his mom is lazy, and he can't stand her outbursts. But it's all part of her condition. She can't help it."

"It must be stressful, though?" Byatt asked. "And what about your work? Is your supervisor understanding of the situation?"

Abercrombie glanced at his apple. "She's really supportive. My hours are totally without question. I come in on weekends, in the mornings when my wife is still in bed, and clear a lot of emails and stuff."

"You come in on weekends? When do you get to relax and putter at home? Maybe do something for yourself?" Byatt suggested.

Abercrombie shook his head. "My wife's a light sleeper. I wouldn't want to wake her."

After he left, Byatt turned to Smeg. "Yikes. How does he manage his life?"

"I was wondering the same thing," Smeg said. "He's so very positive and matter-of-fact, like he's twisted it all in order to justify the demands on his time. His story lines up with the notes from Golding. All the home life issues are there for sure."

"Do you think he could be taking out his frustrations at work? I mean, he would have access to a range of medications."

"Not arsenic, though, unless it's in her heart medication. Or maybe it was the cause of his wife's heart or other health problems. He would have cause for wanting her dead, I would think."

He wrote in his notebook, *follow up*. Is he stuck here in a job he resents? Not able to advance because of home commitments? Could he be happy here? Not everyone buys into the idea that advancement equates with success. Maybe he really does enjoy his job. It's certainly an escape from his wife. Of himself, Smeg was unsure of the answer. He loved the work, but would they have had him if he'd wanted to be sergeant? That was likely best left unanswered.

The afternoon wore on. And on. It began with a stream of interviewees who owned dogs and wanted nothing more than to talk about them: black lab with hip problems, a bernedoodle who could only eat boiled ground lamb, rescue dogs galore, and a long list of canine personality disorders. Much like their owners. Smeg had never understood the appeal of pets. Maybe because he'd been unable to find one that matched his own personality, although Paul had once suggested an iguana. Finally, a small tidbit that might be useful to them emerged from one of Hammond's colleagues, who said she'd applied for advancement herself several times but stopped when she realized they wouldn't let her go. "I have too much knowledge about how human health is affected by animal health. I don't know what they're going to do when I retire," she announced pompously.

The receptionist who had been around when Hammond was still there strolled in late and yawned throughout her short interview. She didn't need to tell them she only stuck around for the paycheque. Then there was a stream of recent graduates, happy to have a foot in the door, good at what they did, but not wanting to do much more. Friendships, they repeated, like a mantra, were more important than working twenty-four seven. Motivation to harm a colleague was lacking. The afternoon was like peeling back the layers of an onion that wasn't fit to eat but still released the juices that stung your eyes.

Golding poked her head in at five o'clock. "How's it going?"

"We've completed this group," Byatt said. "Should we get yours done as well?"

"No, my daughter has riding lessons at seven, and a briefing note is urgently needed by the Minister before I go."

At least it's not a dog, Smeg thought.

"And I'll have to walk the dog," Golding added.

Chapter Ten

Smeg wasn't sure what to make of Hammond's colleagues. His inclination was that they were a bunch of weirdos, but harmlessly so. Rodriguez was still the most likely suspect. As such, it felt like spending another day at the Alberta Environment office would pull them away from where they should be putting their efforts. He suggested Byatt do the rest of the interviews alone. But she had a different take on the place and felt he should be there to help assess. "They're a bit too nervous," she'd said, "there's something they're afraid to talk about." Smeg thought that was maybe a practiced skill in a large bureaucracy, but didn't say so. And now he found himself sitting in the same interview room as the day before facing Hilaria Golding who greeted them warmly.

"Tell us about Deena Hammond," Byatt said.

Golding's hand swept the room. "She started here when I did." She paused and then continued slowly, "She was teaching at the university and had studied animal diseases. She wrote a dissertation on antimicrobial resistance and infectious diseases that spread from animals to humans. Her area of expertise was useful."

"Is a doctorate necessary for the job?" Smeg asked.

"Oh, no. I've just started a Master's degree." Her fingers tapped the table. "I was hired for my supervisory experience and of course, attention to detail. I told them in my interview that I'm a bit of grammar freak, can't let something go forward unless Strunk and White would approve. I just can't stand it, and I'll send the work back until it's perfect. My superiors seem to appreciate it."

Attention to detail? Smeg wondered how tedious that interview must have been. He did appreciate in his own work the need to attend to the small stuff as ignoring details could lead to bigger problems. Failing to carry spare batteries for your portable radio and not recharging the taser were two examples. But Golding was droning on about amusing conversations with her father, who loved pointing out grammar errors.

"I've taken that love of words and brought it into my work."

Thank you for your *dead-ication*, he thought with barely concealed amusement.

"You're studying part-time then?" Byatt asked.

"Yes, it's looked on favourably to be working toward an advanced degree. I'm doing an online program at Athabasca University. Management," she added, then laughed. "I don't have a lot of time between work and family responsibilities. My husband's amazing, though. He does all the cooking. Loves it; there's always a cooking program on at our house. There's always a French sauce. Not like my home growing up when sauce came from a ketchup bottle. My father's illness caused my mother great stress, and she really didn't have time for fancy meals."

"Is your husband full-time at home?" Smeg asked, hoping to ward off a lengthy tangent.

"At home full time? No, Randy's a researcher at the university. He tends to get home ahead of me, so he picks up the kids from school and gets them started on their homework." Her voice dropped a notch. "The kids understand the Minister needs me at work. My job is important, and the work can't be handed off to someone else. The Minister wouldn't like it. Besides, it's Mommy's paycheck that puts them in riding and dance lessons, and buys their laptop computers and video games. They want a trip to Disneyland, but I can't take the time off. The lake cottage with Grandma and Grandpa will have to do again this summer."

It appeared a tangent couldn't be avoided, especially as Byatt circled back.

"Tell us about your father's illness."

"There's a history of mental illness in his family, and he didn't escape it, but he knew not to open that Pandora's box. 'Keep the lid on tight and move on' was his motto. He managed to hang onto most jobs, so things were good. I learned from him to set a path and not detour from it. And our work unit will move on from this current situation."

"You were Hammond's supervisor?" Smeg asked.

Golding clasped her chin and tapped her lips with one finger. "She had a lot of knowledge and was a good employee. She responded well to feedback. She wanted to improve herself. She did want to move into a leadership position and was taking courses and looking for opportunities to further those skills. I always encouraged her to do so."

"She had applied for positions," Byatt prompted.

"Yes, I'm not sure she was ready for them, but it's a good idea to apply and let people know you are interested."

Smeg wrote in his notebook, *Hammond—false sense of her own ability? Golding—pompous.*

Golding placed her hands on the arms of the chair in readiness to leave. Smeg, too, thought it was time to clear out. This wasn't the level of excitement he had hoped for in returning to work.

Byatt stared at her for a moment. "Tell me a bit about Abercrombie. What's his deal? Says he's here every day, even weekends."

Golding removed her hands from the chair and placed them on her lap. "I've been on him about that. His hours are a problem—no one knows if he's coming or going. He misses a lot of meetings. And I've had to talk to him about not recording his vacation days on his time sheet. He does a lot of creative timekeeping in order to deal with his home life."

"Abercrombie told us you were supportive of him. But it sounds like you have concerns," Smeg said.

"I don't envy him, but still, it's my job to make sure he isn't cheating the system."

"What about his work?" Byatt asked.

"He's thorough. I like that. I guess some of the analysts in the branch don't always appreciate him, especially the female ones. He tends to passive aggression. I don't ask him to supervise staff anymore because they keep quitting on us. They don't like his micromanaging. I've talked to him about that, too."

Golding certainly had commitment. And she was a hard worker who put in long hours. She was also clearly focused on doing the government's bidding. Was it a case of rats swimming to scramble up on the sinking ship? Maybe Guy Vanderhaeghe was instructive here. And Byatt thought there was something more going on. Were folks uncertain about their job security? Did Golding feel she had to go the extra mile to hang onto her job? To keep the government afloat? That would require a pretty big ego, but he suspected she had one.

"What did you make of her?" Smeg asked as he and Byatt took the elevator to the parkade. "She was distant, almost aloof before. Now she's babbling on about her husband's cooking. Mommy this, mommy that."

"Yeah," Byatt said. "I've been trying to reconcile that. When we talked to her earlier, she seemed to assess us as not having value in her day. Maybe her bosses told her this was important."

"Or maybe the sharing of personal details steered us away from discussing her work."

Despite her new focus, he shuddered to recall how many times she said the word 'Minister' throughout her interview. The highest level of politician in her world seemed to be the sole reason for her existence. She very much wanted to get ahead in the organization, but there was more. She seemed to need the validation of being important. It reminded Smeg of some of the detectives in his own office.

Paul loped, giraffe-like, his head and shoulders bobbing above the cubicle walls toward Charlie's desk in the bull pen. Charlie had been watching for Paul to come out of his interview, anxious and hopeful for his success. He knew Paul would be good at the data technician job; the question was whether Paul would project enough of the confidence Charlie had in him. He looked hireable enough: light blue dress shirt tucked neatly into dark blue pants, sports jacket flung across his shoulder. Charlie had suggested a haircut; it hadn't happened.

"So?" Charlie asked, unable to read the face in front of him.

Paul shrugged. "Don't know."

"Don't know good or don't know bad?"

Paul stretched his arms behind his back. "Okay, I guess? One of the interviewers couldn't say fluctuate and instead kept saying fucktuate. I couldn't keep a straight face." He couldn't keep one now either.

Charlie didn't want to know how that scene had played out. "Tell me about the job."

"Lots of data entry, which I can do; you know I've been on a computer since I was five. Also, retrieval of information, like when investigators want a search done, maybe of old documents to find patterns of a crime." Paul's cheeks flushed, and he raced on. "Like cold cases you can search and find patterns way easier now. The data analytics unit has contributed to the solving of five cold cases in the last year."

He was beginning to sound like a detective novel. That one where Harry Bosch unearths DNA evidence that points to something having gone terribly wrong at the regional crime lab. Maybe that wasn't a good one to dwell on.

"You'd enjoy it then?" Charlie said, although the answer was obvious.

Paul's head bobbed.

"Wanna get some lunch?"

"Definitely. McDonald's?"

Charlie nodded happily.

Paul pulled on his jacket. "Did you know seventy percent of crimes involve a vehicle? Data analysts can watch CCTV footage and find who was in the area when a crime was committed. The data technicians can help do that."

Charlie did know, but didn't say so. Paul appraised the bullpen office as if for the first time, although he'd been in it often. He chattered on as they left the building and walked down the block, and only stopped talking to place his order. Once seated, his Big Mac occupied his mouth.

Charlie seized three French fries and chewed them slowly, savoring the burst of salt. "How'd it go with Femi's sister the other day? Your coffee date?"

"Eloise?" Paul wiped his hands on a napkin. "Don't know if it was a date?"

Charlie still didn't get why most of his stepson's sentences ended with a rising inflection, but he was beginning to notice it in others of Paul's age, especially the young women in the office. He'd given up trying to talk to the one in the mailroom as she seemed never to be inviting a response. Maybe it was because he didn't know her name. Might be something to work on.

"What's she like?"

"Eloise?"

He couldn't think of who else it could be. Charlie knew his shoulders were up around his ears and made a conscious effort to breath.

"She was just home for the holidays, you know? She's taking a program at Red Deer College. Some drama thing she's into. She was big on that stuff in high school. I went to a couple of her plays with Femi. She's pretty good." Paul tilted his head toward the empty paper his burger had been wrapped in, traced a line through the grease, then licked the final remnants from his finger.

Charlie became acutely aware of what he'd just put in his body. Meaghan must be getting to him.

"We went to that new club before she left," Paul said. "You know? On the Rocks?"

"Mmm." As usual, he didn't know it, but that probably wasn't important.

"Had a few drinks, a few laughs?"

Charlie liked this emerging Paul, the one who seemed willing to talk with him. The one who was no longer a teenager. The one who didn't need to ensure the sides of his hoodie hid his face whenever they were out in public together. *Although McDonald's might not count as being out in public*, Charlie thought as they stepped out of the restaurant and said goodbye under the golden arches.

Paul headed toward his car; Charlie called after him, "Let me know if you hear anything about the job."

"I will," Paul promised.

"I hope you get it," Charlie said.

Having Paul in his workplace might pose some challenges, like perceptions of nepotism, but Charlie was developing an appreciation for the ways the two of them could grow together by solving crimes as a connection point. He was also too old to concern himself with other people's opinions. The job would give Paul self-assurance, a chance to be successful. And Charlie could help him with that.

When Smeg got back to the office, he found Byatt munching on a packaged sandwich and staring at her computer screen. He sat down in a chair and spun it around. The chair didn't appreciate it and nearly bucked him off. He regained his composure.

"Finding anything interesting?" He squinted at the map.

"I've found more details on that suicide death, the body found here in the Delberty Mountains foothills two years ago." She pointed to the location on the wall map in front of her desk. "I think I mentioned before that she worked for Alberta Environment. Same ministry as Hammond, but this woman was at Oxbridge Place on 106 street. She'd been there about six months after transferring from the same department Hammond was in, but a different branch."

"Anything to suggest more than a coincidence?" Smeg asked.

"Based on timing, she may have worked with Golding. Likely also Abercrombie, given he's been around forever."

"Still not much. What are the details on the suicide?"

Byatt glanced down at her notes. "She went missing after leaving her office on a Saturday afternoon. Her roommate reported it when she failed to return that night. Her abandoned car was found in the parking lot at her office. First thought was that she had been abducted. No witnesses were ever found. Two colleagues who had seen her in the office that afternoon were interviewed but shed little light on the situation. They had exchanged pleasantries but didn't notice anything out of the ordinary."

"How did it get to a conclusion of suicide?"

"The interview with the roommate. She felt the woman had been depressed, worked too hard, and had little social life. At thirty, she was in a bit of a rut. Roommate said she'd developed health problems that her doctor hadn't been able to diagnose. And there was a note but it wasn't definitive."

Smeg's eyebrows bounced up. "Comparable situation to Hammond. Any other similarities in medical condition?"

"Nothing in the file. Maybe we should ask her roommate."

Smeg nodded. "Yes, let's do that. Any idea how she got to the foothills?"

"Once the body was found by a hiker, they discovered she'd purchased a one-way Greyhound bus ticket. When she got there, she presumably just started walking."

"Autopsy?"

"Dehydration." Byatt frowned. "But the toxicology report showed a lot of stuff. All of it prescribed."

Now they had a second suspicious death tied to Alberta Environment. But there was still no obvious conclusion of murder. And no certainty of suicide in either case, just a growing number of coincidences. He knew a death was always a complicated thing. Byatt had been right to flag this one.

Smeg's phone rang. "Hey, Paul. What's up?"

"I got the job. Guess the interview did go alright." He sounded surprised.

"Congrats," Smeg managed to get in before Paul started talking again.

"They want me to start Monday morning, as soon as the paperwork is done."

Smeg could hear Paul's grin, and it made him smile.

"Raj Agarwal is cool, he knows all the programming languages, JavaScript, XML and others I've never heard of, and he's so good at using Big Data, you know? I'll be collecting data for the team, breaking it into chunks, cleaning the data, that kind of stuff."

"That's great, Paul. Sounds like you're pleased."

"Yeah. Hey, I gotta go, meeting up with Femi."

"Talk soon," Smeg said as he ended the call.

"That was quick," Smeg said to Byatt. "His interview was just this morning."

"They must have liked him."

"Yeah, and I didn't even get a chance to interfere." Smeg was prouder than he wanted to admit.

Byatt looked down and scratched the back of her head. "I might have."

Smeg appraised her. "That was nice," he said. "Thank you for doing that."

"He's a great kid. I have no problem at all giving him a recommendation. I think he'll be keen on the possibilities in data for police work."

"Who did you talk to?"

"Raj," Byatt said. "I went downstairs to talk to him about my data request. I could have sent an email, but I thought I'd use it as an excuse to talk about Paul."

"Well played," Smeg said.

"Where are we at for this afternoon?" Byatt asked. "We still have some questions for Rodriguez. Should we go talk with him?"

"When is the funeral? Do we know?"

"Paper says it's tomorrow. We could likely stop by and talk to him today. I'll give him a call."

And they'd need to set something up with that roommate. As he waited for Byatt to get off the phone, he wondered: what had driven the suicide victim to switch jobs; what were the specifics of her health issues; and what had caused her to end up in the foothills without her car?

Chapter Eleven

Smeg and Byatt met Rodriguez at his office. They stepped off the elevator and were brought to a halt by a big red hand. The kind that is embedded, palm open and forward, in a stop sign.

Inspect your property now. Before winter. Water-holding items can contain mosquito eggs. Unclog gutters, repair leaky outdoor faucets, drill holes in the bottom of wheelbarrows to allow water to drain, and ensure trash can lids are tight-fitting.

Smeg stared at the poster. He'd kind of forgotten his house had gutters. And the wheelbarrow already had holes, compliments of rust that resulted from *not* drilling holes in the bottom of it. He called Rodriguez, who met them in the lobby and invited them to sit down. Smeg would have preferred an office with a closed door, but since it was a Saturday and no one appeared to be around, he complied. Rodriguez told them he had come in to get caught up on paperwork and keep his mind off the funeral.

"Thanks for agreeing to meet with us," Byatt said and lowered herself into a padded armchair before setting her notebook down on the table in front of her. "We won't take too much of your time."

"It's okay," Rodriguez said, from a matching chair opposite. "But I still don't know what you're looking for."

Rodriguez presented a cleaned-up version of himself, a fresh hair-cut still razor sharp around bulbous ears, one of which he tugged on. His sweater, while not entirely festive, was noticeably colourful for early January in Edmonton, where a propensity to wear black reigned. Mardi Gras came to mind more readily than a death in the family. Even as a young man, Smeg hadn't the nerve to dress in bright tones. And now, of course, those colours would make him look like a circus tent. He did wonder, though, what Rodriguez's style said about him.

Smeg had taken the couch. "How long have you worked here?"

"Twenty years. I didn't plan to become an expert in mosquitoes, but here I am." A brief crinkle appeared around his eyes.

"Your yard must be mosquito-free," Smeg said. "Do you do the things on the poster?" He pointed to its location by the elevator.

"Some of them." Rodriguez chuckled and then ran his hand through his hair.

Evidently, Rodriguez, unbeknownst to local vermin, had a lighthearted side. Smeg felt a slight affinity for the man who appeared to find the mosquito police a bit much. He allowed himself a brief smile. An earlier thought, that grief is sometimes manifest in asshole behaviour, resurfaced. He focused on opening his mind beyond viewing Rodriguez as a manifestation of the anti-hero in an Ant-Man comic, as Byatt moved the conversation in a more meaningful direction.

"We're hoping to learn a little more about your wife," Byatt said. "We did find traces of arsenic in the water bottle on Deena's desk. Neither samples from home or office have the levels of arsenic that were in the bottle."

"You took a sample from my house?" He looked past Smeg to the wall behind before locking his eyes on him.

"The day we were over, I filled a vial." Smeg met Rodriguez's stare. "Could she have been filling the bottle anywhere else? Did she stop on the way into work? Go anywhere at lunch?"

"Where would she have filled a water bottle?" A crease formed between Rodriguez's eyes and lined up with one on his nose. "Where might that have been?"

"She was likely too sick for a gym, but maybe a yoga studio?" Byatt's well-defined arm muscles were visible through her form-fitting sweater.

Smeg watched Rodriguez, who no longer appeared amused. In fact, based on the way his eyebrows came together like the V in Vlad the Impaler, he was gearing up to roast someone. Smeg involuntarily leaned back, out of the way of his dagger eyes. He also watched Byatt maneuver the conversation with skill and sensibility away from parasites and toward other potential sources of disease, the kind that grew in insidious ways from a small amount of exposure to poison. He saw the detective who had been promoted to homicide for good reason. Not just, as stated, to profile a woman, but to bear witness to a department's efforts at breaking the gender barrier. Her face was a closed book, but Smeg could read the thought process as she gently, without breaking a sweat, interrogated Rodriguez. He realized that, similar to his relations with Detective Usmani, he could work with this partner.

Rodriguez shook his head slowly. "No, nowhere I can think of."

"Any medications that might have had arsenic in them?" Byatt asked.

"I'll look, but I can't imagine a prescribed medication that would have dangerous levels. She did take a few homeopathic medicines. She was getting desperate toward the end."

Byatt nodded, then looked over at Smeg. How desperate was a question that still hadn't been answered. Despairing enough to try unproven remedies? Despondent enough to take her own life? Panicked enough to drive off the road?

"What about family medical history? Any heart disease?" Smeg asked.

"Her mother had a heart attack doing the laundry in the basement of their condo in Canmore. Died still clutching a pair of folded red socks. They never knew how long she'd been down there. The pile of laundry, both clean and dirty, was enormous. Deena's father was upstairs surfing the net, also a never-ending endeavour. Otherwise, he might have noticed she was missing and gone to check on her." Rodriguez continued to drone on.

Would the outcome have been the same if the socks had been blue? Smeg wondered. Was Rodriguez trying to say his mother-in-law worked herself to death? Or that her husband was an asshole? Do daughters marry men who are similar to their fathers? Certainly, there was a propensity in Rodriguez to ramble when trying to avoid the truth, so perhaps Hammond's father also shared that. He glanced down to see what colour Rodriguez's socks were. A neutral brown.

Smeg gave Byatt a pleading look to which she responded by interrupting Rodriguez's monologue. "Any other family history? Heart or other medical conditions?"

Rodriguez shook his head. "Well, unless you count mental health. Her brother has been diagnosed with a smorgasbord of issues: schizophrenic personality disorder, anxiety, depression, and PTSD. They say he fried his brain on a bad batch of cocaine as a teenager. But who knows; it could have been a brain injury. He ran with a rough crowd, I'm told. I heard some tremendous stories. He was arrested once for siphoning gas from a police car. I mean, how high do you need to be to do that? The car was parked at the police station at the time. Anyway, he's never really recovered. Lives his life in slow motion."

Smeg shook his head; there were a lot of odd people in Hammond's life. And still the rambling. Why was Rodriguez telling them all this? "Would that explain the book on personality disorders found in the front seat of your wife's car?"

"I suppose." Rodriguez showed no emotion, nor comprehension.

"It was bookmarked to alexithymia, a disorder characterized by the inability to identify and describe emotions," Byatt said.

Rodriguez glared at Smeg. "Never heard that one before."

Neither had Smeg, but he'd read about it in Hammond's book. Alexithymia led to a personality characterized by the inability to identify and describe emotions, leading to un-empathetic and ineffective emotional responses. The core characteristics were marked dysfunction in emotional awareness, social attachment, and interpersonal relating. So far, this personality trait showed itself in most everyone they'd interviewed.

Byatt wrote in her notebook. Perhaps she was thinking the same thing. But more specifically, did Rodriguez think his wife was applying the diagnosis to him? Was that why the flash of anger? Smeg also read that sufferers may seem contradictory because they are capable of rages due to an inability to modulate emotions cognitively. Rodriguez was textbook on that front.

"Difficulty identifying feelings. Views things as black and white, can't see the big picture. Does that fit with what you know of your brother-in-law?"

"I think you're stretching there. Or maybe I've not heard the term because no one's able to pronounce it."

Byatt clasped her hands and watched him.

"Okay," Smeg said. "I think that's all we need."

They stood up. "Oh, one more thing," Smeg said. "How did you know your wife was dead when you arrived at the accident scene? The officer first on site said you hadn't opened the car door because you knew she was dead."

"The life was gone from her eyes," Rodriguez said in a flat monotone voice.

As the elevator door closed, Byatt shook her head. "I don't think he's our guy. There was honesty in all that rambling."

"But what was the point of it? Was he trying to throw us off? What are we missing here?" Smeg said.

He reviewed what he knew about Rodriguez. The man carried some anger, but it seemed to run deep, like it had built over a lifetime. Maybe he'd felt wronged along the way. The resentments didn't seem to extend to his wife. At least not on the surface.

"Let's stop by the funeral tomorrow. Maybe that will give us something more to go on," Byatt said.

Stepping out into the wind, bits of paper and plastic bags nipping at his ankles, Smeg appraised the day. Bright, bold graffiti with the words, *love is all we need*, on the rail bridge at the corner was visible through the leafless branches of a spindly elm tree and suggested good vibes. He wasn't convinced.

Thin, lacy-white clouds covered the grey sky like a casket veil and created a halo around the sun. Hammond's neighbourhood church had been chosen for the funeral. The family hadn't been members, and Smeg was surprised they'd opted for a religious ceremony. *Old habits die hard*, he supposed. Byatt had to park on the street two blocks over, an indication the church was already packed or that people in the community had more vehicles than garage space. They'd taken her car because it was more presentable than his truck, but they needn't have worried. Maybe the nicer vehicles were parked in the back driveways.

The church was out of place in its urban surroundings, quaint and small as though its parishioners should have washed the soil off their hands before putting on their Sunday best to walk up the hill and greet friends and neighbours in a ritual as old as time. Smeg could almost imagine the cobblestone walkway, the sheep foraging on the snowy hillside. The interior, once white before age turned the walls to the yellow of rancid candles, invoked memories of loss in Smeg that he'd thought vanished. His own experience of church was confined to funerals. He resisted the urge to turn around and leave. Open wood beams, plainly adorned solid pews, and worn carpet suggested this church was well used. He and Byatt slipped into the back row of the church just as the minister asked the congregation to rise. It did so as if attached by one long string.

"I am the resurrection and the life. The one who believes in me will live, even though they die; and whoever lives by believing in me will never die. Thank you all for coming as we celebrate the life of Deena Hammond. You may be seated."

Byatt bowed her head. Smeg viewed the room, surreptitiously, head lowered, eyes raised, squinting to take it all in. The church was full. Up front, seated beside Rodriguez and his two children, was an older man, in his eighties. Likely Deena's father, as beside him, a fiftyish man, emaciated with stringy, lifeless hair, fit the description of her brother. A few rows back, he recognized many of the people they had interviewed from her office.

Smeg rose and sat as instructed, but didn't partake in the singing and scripture readings. It felt a bit hypocritical when he hadn't attended a church service in forty years. Not to mention singing in general was beyond him and wouldn't be appreciated by anyone within hearing distance. As the crowd stood for a guitar solo of *Wind Beneath My Wings* that marked the end of the funeral, he and Byatt exited and found a spot under a tree where they could observe people without being in the way. Smeg watched Hammond's colleagues make their solemn way down the steps. At the bottom, Golding caught sight of them. She headed toward them.

"Didn't expect to see you two here." She extended her hand to each of them.

"Paying our respects," Byatt said.

"It was a lovely service," Golding said. "Deena would have loved it. And the kids, they managed well. I recall my grandfather's funeral. It was tough for my father to lose a parent."

"How old were you when he died?" Byatt asked.

"Oh, it was just a few years ago. He'd been ill." Her voice trailed off, but then she brightened. "He had a good life."

Smeg waited.

Golding continued, "He too always wanted me to be successful. Since I was little. But Dad believed I was gifted, and he wanted the best for me. I burned through junior and senior high school. We lived up north, where there weren't many opportunities, so my parents sent me to Edmonton for my last year of high school. It was perfect because I was able to slip right into university early."

It all sounded horrifying to Smeg. Wasn't high school about partying? "Didn't you miss your friends?"

Golding laughed. "I suppose I did make some sacrifices, but I met my dear husband, Randy, when I moved to Edmonton. He's my best friend. And I have my sister."

Abercrombie made his way hobbit-like through the crowd, along with a short, young woman he introduced as his daughter, Amelia. A colleague named Lauren Russo, whose wild black hair hung over the top of large, tortoiseshell glasses, joined them. Her walk was reminiscent of a springer spaniel.

"Glad you could make it," Abercrombie said to them, as if he were the host.

"She seemed to have a lot of family and friends," Byatt said. "Do you know many of the guests?"

"Jay's colleagues I've seen at office parties. And, of course, the kids and some of their friends pop in to the office sometimes," Abercrombie said.

Smeg turned toward him. "Is your wife here?"

"No, she wanted to come, but she's having one of her headaches and couldn't get out of bed."

"We don't think she's real," Russo said and gave Abercrombie a friendly jab. "In all the years I've known you, have I ever met her?"

Abercrombie frowned. "She's not much for office get-togethers."

After the three of them had wandered off, Smeg and Byatt watched the crowd disperse before heading to the car. Smeg stopped, one foot inside the passenger side.

"Something's weird about Abercrombie."

Byatt turned toward him from the other side of the car. "Yes. I know Russo was joking, but was she trying to tell us something about Abercrombie's wife?"

"I'll set up a follow-up interview with him." Smeg continued his quest to get into the vehicle.

The funeral had been a strange experience, as if it had been staged as a performance with untrained actors, everyone going through motions as in a hypnotic trance. There were few tears from the many heads dutifully bowed. The crowd had dispersed quickly once set free after short attempts at conversation without knowing what to say. Smeg was reminded to add the words 'no funeral' to his will. Rodriguez had kept his anger in check throughout, and he did seem to have a large circle of support in his life. But as a general observation, the entire crowd was lacking emotional attachment.

Chapter Twelve

Smeg wasn't an early morning person and not in the best position to judge what the office looked like at that time of day, but today it was surreal. Sun streamed in to turn desktops to shiny glass and walls into an opaque spectrum from mauve and pink to gold, giving a regal air to the normally pedestrian space. Smeg had hoped to beat the crowd and get caught up on paperwork, but chatter slowly filled the air and pulled his attention from his computer. The day was going to be eventful if the harried tone was any indication. He listened as two officers from Unsolved Crimes dissected pieces they'd unearthed and wove them back together in a collage of new scenarios, a new understanding of old crime scenes. Bodies that hadn't been found, missing motives, sketchy details. Smeg looked up from his desk as Byatt strode confidently across the room, gym bag flung over one shoulder. He assumed she was coming up from the locker rooms, her hair still damp from the shower.

"Did you sleep here last night?" he asked, only partly joking.

Byatt set her gym bag on the floor and sat on the edge of Smeg's desk. She gave his arm a light nudge, the corners of her eyes crinkling slightly.

"There are a lot of places I wouldn't sleep at night—this is one of them. Have you been in the locker rooms?"

Smeg could honestly say he hadn't. He shook his head.

"I'm not sure the cleaning staff have either," she said, and then her eyebrows furrowed. "I came from the boxing club. I prefer to go after work when I have more time but I promised Mom I'd go to my cousin's baby shower with her tonight." She twisted her fingers, a habit that seemed to accompany any mention of her mother.

"Good for you," he said, wanting to shift the conversation. "The boxing, I mean. I wish I'd started something like that years ago. I think it's a workout I could have gotten into."

"It isn't too late."

"Oh, I think it is." Smeg looked down at his belly which blocked out his belt from just about every angle.

"No, seriously. There are classes for beginners."

"One size fits all," he mused.

Paul arrived at Smeg's desk with a big grin, his cheeks flushed. He held a small stack of paper in his hand. Smeg thought, from where he sat, that Paul looked taller. The haircut he'd finally gotten made him look, if not exactly professional, a bit older. Like a guy who belonged in an office rather than a guy with a video game controller sprouting out of his arm. Something stirred in Smeg like he had somehow created this image in front of him.

"Hey," Byatt said. "How's the first day going?"

"I've got some preliminary data my supervisor pulled together. I have it on my laptop, but he said you wanted a printout?"

He lurched toward the desk and clumsily dropped the report. *Okay*, Smeg thought, *the boy hasn't been completed erased from the man.*

"Yeah," Byatt said and spread the pages out on a table.

Paul peered beyond her bent head and met Smeg's eyes. "This cool?"

Smeg paused, unsure of the question, before he realized Paul wanted his approval, to know if his new job was infringing. He examined the face in front of him, no longer a boy, but still eager to please. Smeg was proud of him, but clearly hadn't expressed it enough.

"Of course," he said. "Glad you're here." He hoped Paul would develop a thicker skin. He'd need it in this place.

"I see there have been a few reported cases of arsenic poisoning in recent years." Byatt highlighted each. "I'll check into them."

"Lot of data here," Smeg said. "Big data seems like something I'm about to miss the boat on, you know. Like, apparently, there's this thing called social media that passed me by. But data seems like something I should know about."

"I know you're joking? Maybe?" Paul said. "But let's open the department's analytics page on your desktop. Do you have it bookmarked?"

"I don't know." Smeg moved aside and Paul pulled up a chair.

"So, no." Paul quickly located the page.

"Look at this," he said. "There were more homicides reported by the coroner's office last year than were reported by police."

"Yes, that's interesting," Byatt said. "Our homicide numbers are extremely low in Edmonton. It's not like we have anything to hide. It could have just been missed."

"People make mistakes in reporting," Paul said. "It's one of the limitations of data. And one of things our team is looking at, making these types of comparisons and identifying where data needs to be cleaned up. Clean up's my job."

Smeg recognized the boy's tendency to get excited about new things. He hoped the newfound enthusiasm would stick around. The opportunity for growth had now presented itself and Smeg could foster it. He knew Raj Aggarwal, as Paul's new boss, would do the same.

"The kind of stuff we did by hand over the years," Smeg said. "Filling in the gaps in data. When we had time."

"Yeah, boomer." Paul smirked. "You were too busy running the economy into the ground."

"Hey, we were hard-working and committed."

"Then ruined the planet for your children and grandchildren."

Smeg had never considered grandchildren. Could the boy actually pull that one off?

Byatt watched Paul with interest, then turned to Smeg. "Your generation fought for environmental rights but then grew into a time of excess."

"True," said Smeg, tired of that old argument. "What your team does now is much more effective."

Paul laughed. "'Cause we're Gen Z."

"Look at this." Byatt pointed to a map of cold cases.

"Some show the victims had a history of sex work," Paul said. "We can look at the neighbourhoods where the homicide occurred and overlay with other types of data such as thefts, noise complaints, abandoned cars and drop-in centres in order to get at a pattern of perps targeting sex workers. Police can then be proactive in addressing the issues and preventing future crimes."

"You learned all that already?" Smeg asked.

"Raj explained the printout to me. Plus, I had to read the onboarding documents first thing this morning."

Paul had clearly been in early as well. Smeg thought he was still in bed when he'd left the house.

He pushed the chair back and jumped to his feet. "See you later," he said and loped back across the room.

From behind a file cabinet, someone called, "Welcome aboard, Galloway."

"Thanks," Paul said and disappeared into the stairwell.

Byatt smiled at Smeg. "See," she said. "I knew he'd be a good fit here."

"He does seem to have found his calling. So, where are we at for today?"

"I'll call the roommate of the two-year-old suicide case. If she's available, we can stop by and see her." Byatt headed to her desk.

The image of that suicide, made so by a note she'd left behind, a distraught bus ride followed by hours of walking before collapsing from exhaustion, came back to him. What must have been going through her head? The part that nagged at his consciousness was that she'd taken that action immediately following an afternoon at her office. Had something she'd seen there, an email maybe, triggered a response? And he continued to wonder about her connection to Golding and Abercrombie. On the other hand, someone planning to take their own life might just want to remove stuff from the computer they didn't want seen, like personal stuff.

Smeg checked his own email.

Dear Friend,

I am in hospital in Dubai. I am giving my money away as the doctor has told me I don't have long to live. Please contact my lawyer with your *personal information. Tell him I have willed $5M to you for your good work.*

Smeg replied.

Dear Friend,
I'm so sorry to hear of your troubles. What are you in hospital for? I had to pass some stones a few years ago and thought I was going to die too. Have you ever had gallbladder stones?

For some reason that was unclear to him, Smeg felt compelled to respond to scammers. Maybe it would keep them from targeting someone else. Or maybe he just liked toying with them.

The next email was from Abercrombie.

I've been thinking about our interview regarding my colleague Deena Hammond and I think there's more you should know. Deena had been sick for a very long time. I can fully appreciate the frustrations with such a situation as my wife has had similar struggles to find answers to chronic health problems. So I think a lot about these things. For Deena, her troubles began after she started working with us. She shared with me the many different diagnoses and treatments doctors had prescribed over the years. I think she thought I might be able to help her sort it out.

It's true Deena wanted to get ahead. I feel that Hilaria Golding was blocking her advancement. Deena was very smart. When she first arrived, she and Hilaria were at the same level and both were applying for the same positions. Hilaria got the first one but the choice between the two wasn't clear. Hilaria knew Deena was a threat and I know for sure that on one occasion, Hilaria convinced leadership to block Deena from taking another job by saying that she was short-staffed and couldn't afford to lose her right then. The job would have put Deena on equal footing with her and would have meant they could compete again for advancement. Hilaria's personable characteristics block a driving ambition. She needs to prove she is superior and craves external validation. I think it grows out of pressure from her father who drove her to success. I have heard he had a psychotic episode when Hilaria was eight and she kind of went off the rails. Anyway, I'm happy to talk more if you'd like.

Smeg thought perhaps he should put Abercrombie in touch with his new friend in Dubai. They might find much in common. He'd just finished reading the email a second time when Byatt returned to his desk.

"What do you make of this?" he said.

Byatt placed her hands on the desk and leaned in to read the email from Abercrombie. "Bizarre," she said. "Why would he send this?"

"That's what I'm trying to figure out. Russo alluded to his interfering nature and Golding did say his work was thorough and he has a tendency to micromanage. Maybe he's getting overly involved here?"

"Or trying to cast suspicion somewhere other than on himself?"

Smeg hit reply.

Thanks. Can we set another appointment time?

Byatt said. "Zadi Smirnov, the roommate of the suicide victim, can meet with us this morning."

A maze of one-way streets north of Whyte Avenue culminated in a water main break at the only street that allowed movement in the direction Smeg needed to go. Water gushed onto the already slippery pavement, darkening the snow-packed curbs as it found pathways in multiple directions. Cars created wakes as they passed through the growing lake. Smeg had been lost in thought, vaguely aware of the comfortable silence in the vehicle. He inched forward without putting his foot on the gas pedal, his already struggling truck not needing the added impact on its rusty chassis and barely breathing internal parts.

"What a mess," Smeg said. "This is going to be a nightmare once it freezes. Wanna give EPCOR a call?"

"That looks like them arriving." Byatt pointed at an Edmonton Power Corporation utility truck turning slowly onto the street. She brought her arm to rest on the seat behind Smeg.

Smeg's truck emerged from the water and slid to the right. He gripped the steering wheel as if it were a golf club and pulled the truck deftly back on course with much more success than his last golf excursion. At the department's last annual benefit tournament, his line drive had been straight. Unfortunately, the back of the sergeant's head got in the way.

"You're adept at conquering our driving challenges." Turning, her eyes met Smeg's.

He laughed. "There are year-round opportunities to develop one's skills. Potholes in the spring, construction in the summer, traffic accidents with the first snow in fall."

Byatt observed, "Or any combination in any season."

Smirnov's apartment building, like every other walk-up on the block, lacked defining features. Well, it could be defined; it was boxy, grey, and came with parking challenges. It was the kind of place one might imagine doing twenty years to life without parole. Smeg stopped in the middle of the road.

"What do all these signs mean?" Byatt seemed to be counting them. Or in awe.

"At least half of them are for the bike lane." Smeg had heard complaints when the signs first went in. They were undoubtedly excessive.

"Where's the bike lane?"

"Under the snow."

"Parking permitted after midnight."

"Until when?"

"That sign says parking of vehicles is authorized after nine a.m." Byatt continued to stare at the sign. "Does that mean parking after nine a.m. is okay or that only authorized vehicles can park here?"

Smeg pulled the truck to the curb in front of the building. "This one I recognize."

He pointed at the loading zone sign and tossed his police parking pass on the dash.

Given the state of his vehicle, parking patrol would undoubtedly think he'd stolen the pass. Byatt waited while he made his way around the back of the truck, one hand on the box for support and one eye on the slippery patches of ground. He motioned for her to go ahead up the sidewalk single file, past a young guy, smoking and checking his phone. The man was small and underdressed for the weather. He didn't acknowledge their presence or step aside to let them by. Between the doors, Byatt rang Smirnov's number and was buzzed in. Musty carpet mixed with the stench of industrial cleaner met them within. As far as smells go in this job, Smeg thought, this one was on the pleasant end.

A fleshy, thirty-something redhead opened the door, introduced herself and invited them in. Empty wine bottles stood waiting by a shoe rack piled with well-worn flats and scuffed-toed ankle boots. Smeg wondered if she'd had a party, or if the wine consumption was all hers. Stepping into the brightly-lit living room, it became clear from the half inch of roots showing that Smirnov was naturally a brunet, although her heavily shaped eyebrows didn't give it away. Her makeup was thickly applied.

"Your former roommate," Byatt looked down at her notebook, "Alisha Acharya. Had you known her for a long time?"

"We were roommates for three years. She answered an ad."

Smeg pondered what it meant to answer an ad for such a living arrangement. Was there an application process? Had the competition been stiff? Was it like speed dating?

"Did you get along well?"

Smirnov grimaced and looked down. "We were quite close. We had a lot in common."

"What do you mean?" Byatt asked.

"We'd both met a lot of assholes."

Had that been a criterion for a suitable roommate?

She continued, "Alisha was in a relationship before moving in here. Her unemployed boyfriend lived with her rent-free and was screwing other women. She was messed up, you know, like a woman in love who denies what's right in front of her."

Smeg wrote quickly in his notebook, then said. "Alisha's boyfriend. That was a long time ago. Was she over him?"

"Definitely. He pursued her for a while but eventually she told him to go fuck himself."

"More recently?"

"We went clubbing a lot, met a lot of guys. But she never really found the one, you know." The room was hot and sweat was beginning to seep through the makeup on Smirnov's forehead. "I mean, who does? Men are generally assholes, unfaithful liars."

Smeg hoped that wasn't true.

Byatt responded with what he wanted to say, "Assholes exist, but some women are attracted to them exclusively. Does that describe Alisha?"

"Maybe." She kept her eyes on Smeg, her cleavage pointed in his direction.

"Tell us about the day Alisha went missing."

"She was down. Maybe partly because she was hungover. We both were. She'd been rejected by a guy she liked, so we'd gone out the night before to help her forget him. She was beginning to think she'd spend her life alone and she'd wanted to have children. Anyway, getting married wouldn't have helped her with that. Her health had gone downhill to the point where she couldn't likely get pregnant anyway. She tried when she was still with the asshole, I mean, without him knowing. Lucky for her, she was unsuccessful. But still, I always hoped she'd get what she wanted."

"Did you know her when she was in her former job with Environment?"

"Yeah, she was still there for about a year after she moved in here. That's when her health problems started. She really liked the work over there and thought she had a future but it didn't work out. When her health issues really became a problem, she transferred looking for something less demanding."

"Did you know her former colleagues?"

Smirnov shook her head. "She mostly referred to her boss as 'the bitch'. I'm not sure I ever heard her real name."

"Did her health improve after that?"

"Getting rid of stress seemed to help."

"Did she say anything when she left for the office that day? Anything unusual?"

Smirnov slowly shook her head. "Not that stood out for me. I don't think she answered when I said, 'See you later,' but I might be reading too much in. Anyway, why would a person go into the office first if they were planning on killing themselves?" She looked down. "To clean up loose ends, I suppose, erase personal emails."

"Do you think anything happened at the office? Did she text or call you that day?"

"Not a word."

On the way out, Smeg handed Smirnov his card and told her to call if she thought of anything. The way she'd pushed her breasts at him had him hoping she wouldn't use the number for anything else. Reversing their way down the sidewalk away from the building, he noted the smoker was now a young woman also underdressed for the weather. This one didn't pay any attention to them either. Byatt pulled the passenger door open, hopped in and waited again for Smeg to inch his way around the vehicle.

"Does her story line up with what was in the original police report?" Smeg asked as he pulled the truck away from the curb.

"Yeah," Byatt said. "Not much then; not much now. I do feel we have a clearer picture of Acharya. Suicide is plausible. Interesting tidbits about poor health. Definitely Acharya's health issues line up with Hammond's."

"Any indication of why she went into the office that morning?"

"It appeared from a search of her browser that she was looking for how to file a complaint. Human Resources tends to bury that information in hopes of reducing the number of people who find it. Everyone's got a complaint, you know?"

"You figure?"

Byatt shrugged. "I certainly did."

Smeg wanted to believe all had been smooth sailing for Byatt, but he knew from earlier conversations that the path hadn't been easy. He accepted the trust she'd placed by inching into the conversation with him. The moment, albeit brief, felt significant. He'd heard enough stories about sexual harassment complaints, office Christmas parties being a particular point of departure from common decency, that he knew it happened. He also knew the grievances were why the department no longer hosted parties. Not that they entertained any of the complaints anyway. But this story hit closer to home, and it pissed him off. He hesitated, not wanting to say the wrong thing.

"I searched the province's website for information, thinking it might be as difficult to find as our own. I never filed, by the way. It wasn't worth ruining my career over."

"Harassment?" Smeg asked, quietly.

Byatt nodded.

"If you ever want to take it forward, I'll support you in any way I can."

Chapter Thirteen

For Smeg, sirens blaring meant a variety of things. If he'd called for backup and couldn't move in until he had support, he could hear a siren kilometres away. Other police sirens were so commonplace in the day-to-day operations of a large city police force that they barely registered. But there was something about a big red firetruck, and as one appeared in his rear view mirror, the familiar two-note siren amplifying, lights flashing, he pulled over to the side of the road to let it go by. In his mind, he saw one of those Fire Rescue Service trucks in front of Grandma's house. Two seasoned firefighters, surely as old as her, came to the door and asked if everything was okay. A neighbour had called on account of smoke pouring from the kitchen window; it was just young Charlie, learning how to cook. His grandma likely needed rescuing, having eaten his creations in the past, but she was unfazed, and the two left, helmets tucked under their arms. Easing back into traffic, he reached to turn up the volume on the radio and heard the newscaster say, "Alberta Environment."

"Police are investigating the suspicious death of a woman who reportedly died from arsenic poisoning on December eighteenth of last year. An unnamed source who worked with the woman said she'd been a long-time employee of Alberta Environment. The department said it could not make a statement at this time. Police would only say there is an active file on the case and it is too early to speculate on what happened."

"Police were contacted? I'm surprised Communications didn't seek out assistance from us," Byatt said.

"I heard there are problems down there. New staff who are giving standard responses to media inquiries and don't think they need to go any deeper."

Smeg was fine with that. He usually got himself into trouble when he provided responses for Comms. His tendency to be helpful usually meant he gave too much information, leading to more questions. The art of need to know hadn't been taught when he'd attended police academy. He thought a question asked should be answered. His blood pressure notched up.

"Media isn't helpful at this point," he said. "We'll be pressured to call it a homicide and charge someone or label it a death from natural causes and let it go. We would have done a briefing for them if there had been a story to tell. Who would have leaked the information and why report it?"

Byatt shook her head. "Probably Abercrombie. And as for why it was reported, consider the radio station you're tuned in to. CHAD needs to fill airtime. With their all-talk format, they run out of quality things to say fairly quickly, I've been told. I'm surprised you have it on."

"I was tuned in to the game last night. Never thought to change the station."

"That explains it. You're not really their target talk show audience. They're more focused on alpha males."

Smeg pondered that one. He definitely wasn't the type, and it pleased him to hear her say so. They drove the rest of the way in silence. If it was Abercrombie who spoke to the media, what did he hope to gain? Was he exposing a toxic work culture, or was this part of a campaign to cast suspicion elsewhere? Even if he hadn't openly accused someone to the media, being a whistleblower was a common technique used to divert attention. Media focus was all the government needed right now, on top of a global collapse in oil prices and an economy in the tank.

They waited at the red light across from the detachment. A man, clearly living rough, with shards of an old parka clinging to his body and flapping in the breeze, made his way to vehicle windows whose inhabitants likely wished the light would change.

Byatt turned towards Smeg. "Yesterday I was out for a walk and noticed that man beside me as I waited for the light to change. I hoped he wouldn't ask me for money. I hate giving to panhandlers."

Smeg parked in front of the building. There were loads of panhandlers in the area but this one was particularly aggressive.

She continued, "He didn't ask for anything and then he started to walk across the street. I was so focused on him and considering what had gone wrong in his life that led him here, I hadn't noticed the light had changed. He said to me, over his shoulder, 'It's safe for you to cross now, dear,' in the sweetest voice I've ever heard. Then I wondered what had gone right in his life, you know, someone had loved him once, maybe still."

They ambled up the sidewalk. Smeg said, "Combination of things. Lost a job. Mental health issues."

A wife who drove him crazy. Maybe Abercrombie's wife has a sister.

As he held the front door to the building open for her, he asked, "What did you make of Smirnov?"

"Rough around the edges but not harmful. The former roommate's illness connects the two cases, though. I'll check for an autopsy report on Acharya. We should also ask a few questions of HR at Golding's office."

"I'll see if Abercrombie has responded to my email," Smeg said and headed toward his desk. "I've a growing list of questions for him, too."

Smeg logged in and opened his email.

Dear Friend,

I know I can trust you because you respond to me and share your own health concern of gallbladder. My own health worsens by the day and I fear I do not have much longer on this earth. I am more committed to send you my wealth for your health and continued living. You live in place with good health care and I know you will fare better than me. I need your sincere assistance to secure funds which I have invested in a private company. Please contact my representative to ensure the funds safe transfer to your account.

Smeg replied.

I am sorry to hear of your worsening health. What is your doctor saying? Maybe your problem is also gallbladder. Are you still in hospital? Maybe they can remove whatever is causing you discomfort. Many things can be removed these days. If not, please have your lawyer contact me and I'll be happy to spend your money.

Then the email from Abercrombie he was looking for.

I do have some time this afternoon once I return from taking care of my wife's lunch. She is using medical marijuana now which she finds helpful and likes for me to cook into her food. Today she requests mac and cheese! I should be done with my home duties by 2 p.m. so could meet you then. Let's meet at Sunterra in Commerce Place where I'll be having my own lunch. Will that work for you?

Works for me. Question is, does all this running around work for you? Smeg thought. He replied in the affirmative.

The day had turned to wet flurries, the heavy kind that clings before it melts and leaves a chill. Smeg and Byatt brushed wet slushy bits from their clothes and laughed at the winter ritual as they rode the escalator to the second floor to meet Abercrombie. Smeg had been caught without a hat. It had seemed mild enough a short time ago before the sky opened and dumped a snow pile, as from a chute, on their heads. Stepping into the open seating area, with aromas of onion, garlic, and a hint of bacon grease in the air, they found Abercrombie happily slurping what looked like potato soup. They hung their coats on chairs opposite him.

"How's your lunch?" Byatt asked. She sat and pulled her chair in.

Smeg did the same and wished he'd grabbed a coffee on the way by the counter. And a bowl of that potato soup.

"Great. I usually get something here after taking care of my wife. I, of course, don't do marijuana mac and cheese." Abercrombie laughed and tipped his bowl to allow the last bit of soup onto his spoon. "I'm happy to make it for her, though. The alternative, which is her smoking it in the house, is not to my liking. How people get used to the weird smell, I'll never know. Makes me think the family of skunks that lived under the front step was back."

I, of course, also wouldn't do marijuana mac and cheese, Smeg thought. *What a good way to ruin mac and cheese.* Wouldn't it be more expedient to give her pot for breakfast and enjoy the benefits of her being stoned earlier and possibly for longer? Of course, it's possible he does, and the lunch dose is merely a top-up.

"How is your wife's health?" Byatt asked. "You mentioned chronic migraines when we first met, and a bit of depression. I hear there are many treatment options available."

"Been there, done that." He gave a wry smile. "Over-the-counter pain killers don't do a thing for her. She's had MRIs, CT scans, and injections of all sorts. She was on an opioid-based painkiller. That's when the mental health issues really flared up. She got desperate when the doctor tried to wean her off them, and her behaviour was unmanageable; anger, lying, anything to get her hands on the drugs. I had quite a time of it, cleaning up the messes she made. Apologizing to people she'd hurt, undoing the untruths. But she's better now, after the stay in hospital."

"Oh?" Byatt asked. "For migraine treatment?"

"No, she was in a psych ward for a couple of months."

Smeg was surprised they let her out.

Byatt asked, "How are you holding up?"

"I'm fine. I feel bad for her. I love her dearly, you know? She wants to be productive and help out around the house, but she just can't. The work does all fall to me but it's okay. I'd do anything for her. I'm healthy, and once we get her health back we can start doing things again. I love to travel, which isn't an option right now."

There was more than a small chance of his hopes being delusional.

"What about your wife. Does she enjoy travel? I mean, when she's healthy." Byatt seemed more concerned than she likely was. She was the good cop.

"Oh yes. I bought a timeshare in Paraguay many years ago, which we traveled to often before her migraines got really bad. She'd always wanted a place somewhere warm. I wasn't so sure, but like I said, she's my one true love. Anything for my princess. I think the air there would help her but now she has IBS, so she won't get on a plane. And the ankle still hasn't healed completely. She does feel bad, though, that I can't do what I like to do." He wiped his mouth with a napkin. "I do still have my choir group."

"Is she supportive of your involvement with singing? It's extra time away from her when she might need something done."

"She likes the extra income, so it's all good."

Smeg took over from Byatt. "Money must be tight with only one income."

"I'd like to sell the timeshare, but nobody wants one of those right now. Especially in Paraguay."

Given the travel risk involved petty crime, violent crime, smuggling, money laundering, and corrupt police, Smeg certainly wasn't looking to buy.

Abercrombie pulled a large chocolate brownie out of a bag and took a bite. "The other advantage of eating my lunch downtown. My wife doesn't know I'm sneaking extra treats."

You deserve them, buddy, Smeg thought. *And what else are you hiding from your wife?* Smeg had met a lot of people who buried their woes in food or alcohol; the question was whether Abercrombie had been pushed over the line. Was his unfortunate life too much for him? Did the woman he loves cause him more grief than he could bear? Or was Abercrombie fabricating some or all of her illnesses? Stress can do that to a person.

"Life tends to throw us curve balls, hmm?" Smeg said. "For better or for worse. Looks like you got the worse."

Abercrombie set his brownie down and looked off to the side. "I'm happy to have her, you know. I didn't date much as a young man. We were older when we met. I was thrilled when she said yes."

"Long time ago, no?"

"We're not getting any younger for sure. If I lost her, I'd not likely find anyone else."

Smeg had struggled at first, relearning to live without Nancy. But over time, he came to develop an appreciation for being alone. For one thing, you can eat all the brownies you like. He leaned back in his chair and folded his arms across his platform stomach.

"What about work?" Byatt asked. "You mentioned earlier you would have liked to seek out opportunities for advancement, but needed a less demanding job in order to take care of your wife."

"I enjoy the work I do, even with the frustrations." The brownie seemed to have been forgotten. "But sometimes I blame her. Why does love have to be so painful? When she gets really bad, I want to shake her, tell her to snap out of it."

They sat quietly, letting that one sit.

"All those drugs..." Abercrombie's voice trailed off.

"Do you think you're more deserving of advancement than others around you?" Byatt asked with practiced calm.

Abercrombie didn't hesitate. "Certainly Hilaria. She has that air about her, that ability to speak well, to present herself as competent."

"But she isn't?"

"She does some things to perfection but most of her work sits in a pile in the corner of her office and never gets done."

"Doesn't anyone notice?"

"Yes, but she blames it on her staff. And she's so pleasant, everyone believes her. She has flawless linguistic ability, but doesn't have empathy. Or is just so driven to succeed that she doesn't care who she steps on."

"Does she step on you?"

"Well, yes. If you get taken advantage of and are made to look bad in the eyes of your superiors you don't get selected for jobs."

"But you wouldn't have sought them out anyway."

"Years ago, I might have. Before my wife got sick."

"How about Deena?"

"She took advantage of me, too. I tried to help her out when she was new on the job. You know, tell her how to do things. She seemed more resentful than appreciative."

No doubt, Smeg thought. "You said in your email you thought Hilaria had blocked Deena's advancement."

"The women in the office seem to have a lot of ambition," Abercrombie observed. "There may be some drug use there, too."

"What do you mean?" Smeg asked.

Abercrombie ignored the question. "Below a surface of pleasantness, there was a bit of a cat fight going on. But I guess we can expect more of that what with the way the workplace is changing."

A report on toxic work culture had crossed Smeg's desk recently, which was apparently on the rise since the massive layoffs that accompanied budget cuts across all departments. There were people clinging to their jobs, taking desperate measures and hoping someone else would be let go instead of them, like self-promotion in the extreme that went along with outright lying to make others look bad.

"You mean the recent layoffs?" he asked.

"I voted for this government because we needed a fiscal reckoning in this province. But the layoffs have caused some anxiety in the office."

The ruling government treated all public employees with disdain; job security was out the window. *How far would people go*? Smeg wondered. Although the issue involving Deena Hammond began long before the current government. So, what was the motive here?

"Hey, did you hear that news report about Deena's death?" Smeg asked.

"Yes," Abercrombie said. "I listen to CHAD, the news/talk show station. I especially like the sports commentary. Now that I've given up my Oilers tickets, tuning into games and the morning-after game analysis is a solid replacement. Anyway, they reported the story of her death."

Smeg did understand the pleasure of a game. And given Abercrombie was just about as far from the manosphere, as Byatt had called it, as he himself was, his tuning into CHAD was likely just sports-based.

"Any idea how they got hold of the story?" Smeg asked. "Or why they wanted it? I also listen to that station sometimes and it doesn't seem like their thing."

"They're always looking for stories. They have a hotline for news tips."

"Oh?"

"Anyone could have called that in."

Wet snow had turned to ice pellets that bounced off the skylights and Smeg leaned in to speak over the din. "Why would anyone want to?"

"Just an interesting story, perhaps." Abercrombie was silent for a moment, although the dragging out of words suggested there were more to come. "Maybe the story needed to come out, if someone is poisoning people in the workplace. Bit of a health and safety issue, wouldn't you say?"

"Did you tip them off?"

Abercrombie shuddered involuntarily as if the thought were distasteful. "I would imagine the source is not to be revealed."

"Your wife?"

"No way. I strictly monitor her phone usage. She didn't make that call." Taking a stronger, more confident tone, he said, "I do have a meeting to get to, so will need to take my leave. Call me if there's anything more I can do for you."

Byatt turned to Smeg as they continued to sit side by side. "He seemed in a hurry to end the conversation for a man who was so anxious to have it."

"There's more to Abercrombie's story," Smeg said.

Beyond the obvious lack of a filter, the guy was strange, too even keel. Either nothing fazed him, or he was masking his emotions in the hopes of holding onto them, to keep the dam from bursting. They needed to meet his wife, but at the moment, there wasn't enough to warrant a visit to his house.

Chapter Fourteen

Charlie observed how Paul, with no motive beyond the thrill of the chase, coursed over every detail of the case. He turned up at work early most days, although Charlie didn't know exactly what time because he wasn't there yet himself. Arriving before office hours allowed him to focus on Charlie's case exclusively before Raj Agarwal showed up and gave him his assignments for the day. He knew Paul had viewed the photos on the computer and read any interview notes he could get his hands on because he asked Charlie a ton of questions, like why was it taking so long to get to anything concrete. There were lots of possibilities, but none of them seemed overly plausible. And with the clock ticking, this one wasn't looking good as Paul had rightly observed. Most cases break quickly. At least the ones that are solved.

Growing up, Paul had largely been left to his own devices, which could be why he'd turned to his computer and a world online. For many years, it was just he and his mom, who did her best, but was often at work or doing errands before throwing a load of clothes in the washing machine while heating a can of tomato soup for dinner. Charlie suspected she had fallen in love with him because he attempted to cook for her as she relaxed with a glass of Pinot and told him about her day. It certainly wasn't his gastronomical creations that were the attraction. She, on the other hand, was a talented cook when allowed that focus and he couldn't deny he loved her spinach and sausage lasagne and chicken pot pie, but that wasn't the reason he had fallen in love either. She had been thoughtful and caring in a way that warmed him like a chilli pepper.

Charlie was hesitant at first to take on an adolescent. He hadn't known how to be a father. Paul made it easy. Sure, there had been rebellious insolence toward new rules, but Charlie usually backed off. He hadn't wanted to overstep his bounds. Except with the language. Everything was either "sick" or "dope" to a twelve-year-old, and some days he wondered if Paul had a vocabulary at all. And he didn't understand why Nancy allowed the boy to choose his own clothes when he looked so much better in other outfits. "It's about self-expression," Nancy had explained, "about not crushing his spirit." That was a new concept to Charlie, but over time, he found that he liked it.

They played ball together and did the stuff kids do, like Lego and science kits. Although when Charlie introduced WWII airplane models, Paul called him old and he realized he'd need to get with the times. Once Paul's mom became ill, Charlie's attention was pulled away and the boy was on his own again, now with video games they bought to distract him. He'd developed a talent, Charlie realized, that now emerged as useful. It had grown out of the clutter heap in his bedroom. The old Xbox buried in the closet under a small television set and disks out of their cases. A person brave enough to dig through the dirty laundry on the bedroom floor would have found handheld devices and Wii game consoles. A shiny new PC they'd given him for his sixteenth birthday held a place of prominence on his desk, albeit surrounded by old comic books and chocolate bar wrappers. All of it overseen by Link and Zelda, who peered out from a poster above the unmade bed.

At any rate, Paul's digital skills had now found a home. He dialled his stepson's office number. Paul answered on the first ring.

"Want to come along this morning for the 3D scan presentation?"

"Absolutely," he said before barely having time to register the question. "What happens at those things anyway?"

"They'll give us a presentation of their reconstruction of the accident. I think you'll find it interesting, a virtual model."

"Like a video game." Paul had a smile in his voice.

Charlie smiled too.

"I'll check in with Raj to make sure it's okay."

Charlie knew it would be because he'd already asked.

Meaghan, squeezed between him and Paul in the cab of his truck, felt like a natural fit to Charlie, almost familial. She'd conceded to ride in his vehicle due to the recent dump of snow and the fact that the roads hadn't been cleared yet. Her car would have been stuck in a drift before leaving the parking lot. Unfortunately, the heater in his truck had picked this particular week to stop working.

"Smells like my grandpa's truck," Meaghan scrunched up her nose. "How did you achieve that?"

Charlie shrugged. "Back in the day, I thought that smell was from old potato sacks and rubber. But maybe all trucks reach old age."

"Maybe it's the owner?" Paul grinned. "You're not exactly a spring chicken."

Meaghan shivered and pulled her scarf up around her ears. "I hope the scan yields results. This case is raising eyebrows, folks asking why charges haven't been laid if arsenic poisoning is suspected; different folks, mostly my mother, asking why we don't back off on what is clearly a family tragedy."

Charlie patted her hand. "Are we consulting your mother now?"

"Oh god. Certainly my father never did, but that didn't stop her from giving an opinion on his cases. With me, it's worse. I didn't heed her advice to take up something more 'feminine' as a career so she loves to needle away at the choice I made. Teaching and nursing are apparently acceptable for women."

"Also acceptable for men," Paul said. "Most of my high school teachers were male and a good friend of mine's a nurse."

"Make sure you mention that to her sometime," Meaghan said. "And toss in that women can make good cops. I'd say she was a product of the past, as none of my friends' parents shared that sort of traditional ideation."

"Does she worry about you?" Charlie asked. "Often parents don't want their kids going into professions they feel aren't safe."

"I suppose. I do think she has too much time on her hands, which doesn't help her nervous nature any."

Charlie was relieved that Paul's interest kept him safely behind a desk. He thought about the bumps and bruises Paul had acquired over the years. Multiple falls down the stairs, bumping into a tree while reading a book, and crashing his bike into the front step. It would be an understatement to say Paul wasn't athletic. As he pulled into a parking spot,

Paul started to hop out before the truck was fully stopped. Even a desk job apparently wouldn't guarantee his safety.

Meaghan reached over and grabbed Paul's arm. "Easy Starsky, wait 'til we're stopped."

"Sorry, getting ahead of myself. This is going to be so dope."

The hope was to learn if driving conditions and the location of the accident contributed to Hammond's death. If indication of a crime emerged, the scan would be used to provide evidence in court. Tire marks indicated she left the road without being forced off by another vehicle, discounting the eyewitness account of Rodriguez's vehicle nudging her from behind, and no road debris had been found that might have caused her to swerve and lose control. Because her vehicle ended up down an embankment, it had been relatively easy for the data team to collect what they needed without traffic disruption, a factor that heeded other investigations where data needed to be collected quickly to minimize the disruption of traffic flow.

The presentation room was beyond bare bones; it was downright ugly, set in a 1960s building when flat slabs of moulded concrete were a thing and windows weren't. Since then, the interior walls had become covered in grime that bore a resemblance to black mould. Smeg coughed. Budget money was clearly allocated to equipment, not to removing asbestos or upgrading the elevators. Twelve hard, straight-back chairs faced two large-scale, wall-mounted computer screens at the front of the room. Larger displays could span the combined width, and the screens tilted for additional dimension.

Paul pulled his chair up, front and center, to a long table with laptop capability. Charlie imagined Paul almost salivated, presumably at the sight of electronics he'd only dreamt of. They watched the 3D animation of the SUV with Hammond's license plate as it slid and left the road. It followed a straight line down the embankment, slowed in the thick, wet snow, bounced off a large chunk of ice, and came to rest against a tree. The figure of Hammond was slumped over from the outset of the video and only moved to jolt back as the vehicle hit the tree. The machine learning engineer in charge of the analysis, Nala Bankole, explained that the team looked for animal tracks given the proximity to the river valley and concluded Hammond hadn't swerved to avoid animals. Although the park trails were popular walking spots, there had been no one in the area at the time.

"Moving on, we can conclude that road conditions were a factor in the accident, both in terms of ice and visibility. We know from the examination of the report that vehicle design or malfunction was not a factor. Her husband has reported she was slumped over before leaving the freeway."

"Just to clarify, there's no possibility a vehicle forced her off the road?" Smeg asked.

"The trajectory of the vehicle shows a gradual veering off, not consistent with a bump from behind."

A couple of tidbits had come in on the tips line—folks on the freeway who had seen a vehicle matching the description of Hammond's weaving—but there'd only been the one witness who had seen the vehicle leave the road. And Rodriguez claimed not to have noticed this detail. Slippery conditions could have caused the vehicle to slide.

"Can we get a copy of the scan?" Paul asked.

The officer, straight-backed, words clipped, said, "Your analytics team will have it by tomorrow."

Paul bobbed and weaved all the way back to the truck. “How does that all come together?”

“They use laser light at the scene to measure distances. Then, back in the office, they mesh them together to create a model of the scene,” Byatt explained.

Question is, what did they learn about this one? As it turned out, the scan primarily served the traffic safety unit. Clearly unsafe road conditions and a lack of safety measures contributed to the vehicle ending up at the bottom of the embankment, but there was nothing in the presentation that indicated a crime occurred.

Smeg’s call display indicated the staff sergeant wanted something, and he knew it wasn’t to inquire after his health. Today, right now in fact, what she wanted was an update on the Hammond case in light of the media attention it was now generating. “I don’t want money, I don’t want medals, I want your report on my desk, now,” represented her most favourite diatribe. Calls had been coming in from all sorts of news outlets since CHAD had reported the death. There was a limit to how long the police department could continue to say, “No comment.” Staff Sergeant Singer had called a press conference for three p.m. Smeg made his way to her office, where he met Byatt waiting for him by the door.

“Take a seat.” Singer closed the office door behind them and walked briskly to sit down behind her desk.

It had now been two weeks since Hammond’s death, and they had only paltry evidence to present. Smeg cringed—the meeting was not going to go well.

"Bring me up to speed," Singer said.

"We have yet to conclude that Hammond's death was accidental," Smeg said, knowing preamble was deemed unnecessary by Singer. "Autopsy confirmed arsenic poisoning as cause of death. Hammond consumed that substance in very small amounts over a long period of time. Traces of arsenic were found in her water bottle, at a level considered dangerous. Water samples from home and office have come back negative for arsenic. We have as yet been unable to locate the source of the arsenic. But we are operating on the assumption that water was added to her bottle by someone other than her."

"There were multiple lesions on the skin," Byatt said. "The brain was slightly enlarged, and there were early signs of heart disease. She had been unwell for about four months prior to her death."

Smeg picked up the thread. "Our strongest theory is that someone in the office setting was supplying her with tainted water. The office environment is unhealthy, characterized by worries associated with job security and competition over limited opportunities for advancement."

"Neither of which are reasons to kill someone." Singer removed her glasses and sat back in her chair.

Smeg had to agree. Unless they were looking for a psychopath. Under normal circumstances, people don't off their colleagues to get ahead. He was aware of the methods by which some folks climb the corporate ladder, and while at times it could involve stepping on people, that action wasn't literal and didn't require the bodies to be dead.

"There is one possible suspect," he said. "Abercrombie feels underappreciated and overlooked at work and has been pushed to the brink by a demanding wife who is both physically and mentally unwell."

"We're considering the possibility that the arsenic was only intended to make Hammond sick, not kill her," Byatt said.

"Why arsenic?"

"Availability. Someone had access." Smeg could envision Abercrombie mixing up concoctions in his basement. He certainly had the hairstyle of a mad scientist.

"Who?"

Smeg shook his head. "Don't know yet."

"What about her husband? Is he a suspect?"

"We haven't ruled him out," Byatt said. "Hammond was unhappy in the marriage, although there are no indications that she was planning to leave him. He works for the city in pest control. He could have had access to arsenic, but it wasn't readily available."

"Other suspects?"

Byatt continued, "We are exploring the connection to an earlier death of a woman with similar undiagnosed health issues. The death was ruled a suicide, but the evidence of that is inconclusive. The woman had worked with Golding and Abercrombie. We've interviewed her former roommate, who is currently not a suspect in either that or this recent death."

Singer locked eyes on both of them. "We need to apply pressure on this one. Best if we can rule it non-criminal, but, as always, let's explore all angles. Give me a list of the additional resources you need."

"Someone to sort through the tips line would be helpful," Smeg said. "I understand there's been a lot of calls since the CHAD story."

"I'll put Battle on it," Singer said. "He's been sniffing around this one for a while, looking for places to jump in and help."

Once dismissed, Smeg and Byatt wandered outside. Fresh air was always needed after a round with Singer.

"I always feel like I should salute her," Byatt said, to which Smeg agreed.

Smeg knew Battle had convinced Agarwal to lend Paul to him for help with analysis of the tips line. Under normal circumstances, this might have been seen as overstepping. But however the arrangement had come about, Paul would delve into the task with vigour. And Battle would not. He stopped by Battle's desk to tell him he would also send the security camera tapes from the Environment office. With that additional chunk of data to sift through, Paul would be needed.

Battle chuckled. "Paul's enthusiasm is turning out to be a bit overwhelming for poor quiet reserved Agarwal. Best he send him to me for a while. I'll mould and shape his young mind."

Smeg wondered if that would turn Paul into the office gossip.

"I've listened to the phone recordings and noted some calls that should be followed up first: people who had direct knowledge of Hammond either personally or professionally, and references to arsenic and its possible source," Battle said. "I'll email those notes to you. Galloway will upload the voice recordings and use a speech analytics program to convert speech to text, and then search for words or phrases relevant to the case."

Smeg still had to pause at the use of his stepson's last name. "There's only one security camera that's helpful," he said.

It showed a view of the main hallway running through Hammond's branch. Smeg knew it might provide very little as it didn't point directly into her office. From the main hallway, the camera captured people exiting and entering. Of particular interest would be when Hammond left at the end of the day. That would give a starting point to then view who may have entered her office once she was gone. The process could be painstaking and slow.

"Happy to help," Battle said.

And Smeg was happy not to have to do all that tedious work himself.

Chapter Fifteen

Smeg rang Rodriguez's doorbell, which was answered by his daughter, Katie. She wore an oversized, cream-coloured sweater that was slightly darker than her sun-starved face. Now that they could see her long neck, it appeared a football could have rested comfortably between her chin and collarbone. She gave him a look that was quizzical, almost affronted. They had given her a look, too, after her chilly response the last time they'd visited. Katie's reference to her mother's boss was a little too quick, like she wanted to blame someone. He'd run Katie's name through the police database and come up with a couple of misdemeanors, one for drug possession and the other trespassing that included public intoxication. Byatt found the details of that event on Facebook, too.

"Detective Charlie Smeg." He smiled.

She didn't smile.

"How are you this evening?"

"I'll get my dad."

Smeg stepped onto the hallway mat as she disappeared toward the kitchen. A video game, with incongruous sounds of beeping and voice tracks over classical music, blasted from the den off the hallway. He understood the concept that video game music was intended to blend into the background and enhance the experience by supporting rising action and directing the player to move on. But the whole mess was distracting to Smeg. About all the engagement he could manage was to note the boy didn't have homework on his mind.

Rodriguez appeared, wiping his hands on a grimy apron. Through the stains, Smeg could read the word: Grillfather. A tantalizing aroma followed. Smeg identified sautéed mushrooms, onions, and garlic. His stomach reverberated despite having already eaten.

"What can I do for you?" Rodriguez asked.

"Sorry to interrupt at dinner time." Smeg had thought it would be okay to stop by at eight p.m. but clearly dinner was still on the menu.

"I do have to keep an eye on the soufflé."

Smeg wondered if he was expecting company. Or was someone already there?

"Any news?" Rodriguez asked.

If his voice tone was any indication, Rodriguez had calmed down. Smeg couldn't speak for his mental state. He again thought it could be stress that had caused his snippiness.

"Not much to report at this stage," Smeg said. "Still early days. I did want to share the results of the 3D laser scan with you."

"They did a laser scan?"

"Because of the location," Smeg said. "There's potential for accidents at the site, given the lack of guard rail and speed of traffic on the freeway." He didn't mention the eyewitness account or that there was a high probability of wrongdoing. He didn't want to test the man's level of calm. Rodriguez invited him in. Smeg chose the same chair as before, the one he was sure wouldn't buckle under his weight.

"As you know, the autopsy was unable to determine the exact time of death and we do not know if your wife was dead when the car left the road or if she was unconscious. You have previously reported she appeared to be slumped when her SUV veered to the right and left the pavement."

"That's correct." He poked his head back into the kitchen and peered in the direction of the stove. Returning, he said, "I've got eight minutes."

"What?"

"Until the soufflé is done and has to be served immediately."

Smeg picked up his pace. "The scan showed poor visibility at the time of the accident and few witnesses came forward, even though there were lots of cars on the road. A few folks reported seeing her car slide prior to the accident but could not see into her vehicle due to blowing snow. You are the only witness to see her leaving the road. You saw her slumped over despite poor visibility. How close were you to her on the freeway?"

"Safe distance, but I could see her." Light from a multi-panel window left vertical lines of shadow on Rodriguez's face.

"What made you think she was slumped over?"

"It looked like her head was forward. I couldn't see her hat."

"You don't think your view might have been distorted by the snow? Or by a need to concentrate on driving, given the icy road?" Smeg thought it odd that the amount of detail Rodriguez saw was increasing with each telling.

"I was watching. She wasn't a confident driver, and I was concerned about her ability to manage the conditions."

"Is it possible that what you saw was her reaching for something? Are you certain she was slumped over?"

"I can't say for sure." His tone was beginning to rise. "But she did have fainting spells."

"Why didn't you drive her to the appointment in your vehicle?"

"She insisted on taking hers as it can't be left in the office parkade overnight." Rodriguez sat forward on his chair. "Anyway, you haven't told me about the scan."

Smeg outlined the report to him and noted there were no external environmental factors that contributed to the accident. He watched carefully for reactions. Rodriguez grabbed a stack of mags and crammed them into the magazine rack.

"If you think someone did this to her, I'd like to help," Rodriguez said. "I would look at her work environment. That's where her problems grew from. She didn't have health issues until she started working there."

Smeg wondered why Rodriguez was shifting the conversation away from the scan report. Was it because the scan supported the idea that death was not caused by the accident? And why was he suddenly offering to be helpful? Did he recognize the investigation was leading closer to the conclusion that someone had harmed her?

"No problems in your marriage?"

Rodriguez's nostrils flared fleetingly and thin lines flashed between his eyebrows. "None. I mean, all couples have their ups and downs but we had no more than most." He paused before saying, "I felt bad when she got sick. I knew she was frustrated."

"Beyond work, is there anyone she was in contact with that might have wanted to harm her?"

He seemed to seriously consider the question, judging by how scrunched up his face became. More so than he had the last time he was asked the same question. The clock on the mantel ticked. He might now sense he was a person of interest and was searching for a different plausible person. However, Smeg had noted in his many years dealing with suspects that those who sincerely want to help are not the guilty ones. He thought he might want to soften his own approach.

"She spent a lot of time chatting with our neighbour across the alley, who is always out in his garage with the big door open. Watching for her or any other woman who happened to walk by. He is creepy. Deena never saw it, though."

"Why would he want to hurt her?"

"I dunno. But I heard he did time for armed robbery and assault."

"What does he do in his garage? Does he have projects he is working on? Fixing cars?"

"Tinkering with things. He's always fixing something. The garage is filled with car batteries, semiconductors, and metal pipes. He's also into woodworking and making things out of metals."

If Rodriguez was hoping to provide a new suspect, he'd missed the mark on this one. A womanizer in the back alley had no apparent reason to slowly kill his neighbour. Smeg did wonder, though, about the arsenic risk present in all those projects in his garage. Could there be something Rodriguez had helped himself to? While the man did seem to have a genuine interest in moving the case forward and didn't appear to be hiding anything, he was a little too helpful. Smeg suspected he wouldn't get any further with him and opted to let him get back to his dinner. The oven timer went off as he stood to leave.

Charlie had been remiss in not visiting Paul's workspace to see his new digs. When he did, he was met with a bubble of enthusiasm. He had seen Paul effervesce before and hoped it wouldn't end in collapse. The first day he met Paul, he'd watched with admiration as an electric train engine was disassembled. *The kid's got the makings of a mechanical engineer,* he'd thought, until he realized Paul didn't have a clue how to put it back together. Then there was the time he changed his bike lock combination but didn't write down the new one. Charlie had to cut the lock off the school's bike rack. Paul wanted to do things and jumped in with both feet, but then couldn't get himself unstuck from the sludge he found himself in. This was an area of uncertainty for Charlie as a parent who didn't know when to let his son struggle and when to fix it for him. He realized the dilemma would be exacerbated now that Paul had entered his workplace. Of course, it was an opportunity to set him off on the right track.

"Looks like you're up and running here."

"I've started doing research on arsenic poisoning," Paul said, his voice rising along with the colour in his cheeks.

Paul had an armful of fresh supplies from the stationery cabinet, which he dumped on his desk: notebooks, five different colours of pens, two boxes of markers, sticky notes, and poster board. Charlie wondered if the kid was going to create a wall chart of his findings. Or if he was getting ready for the first day of school.

"I didn't know your unit did that type of work." Research seemed harmless.

"We don't." Paul laughed. "I came in early to access databases before my boss shows up."

Like I'd do, Charlie thought. Only Paul was sneaking around doing something totally legitimate. Charlie often snooped into other people's cases if he thought it would help his own, a practice that wasn't appreciated by his peers, even though they all did it. There wasn't the inter-jurisdictional sharing he'd like to see. He bemoaned the days when everything was in the hard files that he could access after hours. Open data only went so far. The previous year, he'd worked on a murder case that led to a pair of sex offenders who had abducted young girls from city parks across multiple jurisdictions. Because it crossed geographic boundaries, the case was assigned to the Intelligence and Investigations Bureau. When a boy turned up dead in a local park where the two had been spotted, Charlie wanted to talk to the Bureau. Compare notes, share data, that sort of thing. He was referred to the reciprocity agreements, a process for accessing information that would ensure, in a paint-drying way, that all leads would have gone cold. It occurred to him Paul might have the skills to hack the Feds' database, opening up a whole world of useful and currently inaccessible files. He erased the thought.

"I found a whole pile of research papers," Paul said. "Did you know arsenic was used as both a medicine and a poison in the time of Alexander the Great? If there's a killer here, they didn't come up with anything new. Could almost call them copycat, right?" He grinned.

Charlie chuckled. "Back then, though, you could generally get away with slipping poison into a glass of wine. If this case is murder, it took a lot more creative planning."

"I read a medical case where herbal and traditional medicines were the cause," Paul said. "It was a man who lived in Toronto but had spent years as a food factory worker in China, where they used many of the same ingredients. They were able to treat him after tracing his history. It seems knowing the victim's backstory is key. But you're the history buff. What do you think?"

The kid might have something there. Charlie had read a historical crime novel recently, *The Poison Thread*, set in Victorian times. A dark psychological thriller about a wealthy society woman who embroidered and claimed her stitching had the power to kill. Why would a wealthy woman who appeared to have everything set about to kill people? Was it a case of power, the powerful over the powerless? The powerless seeking power? Or did she have mystical powers?

"We're working on constructing the victim's historical profile in order to determine the source of the arsenic," Charlie said. "Much like your food factory worker. We haven't found an innocuous source for the arsenic, so we have to assume a crime has occurred."

"You need to dig further."

"Yes." Charlie thought about the chance he'd been given to shape Paul's observant and intuitive characteristics toward cop-thinking. "What are your thoughts?"

"The water bottle seems to be the best clue so far," Paul said. "I assume someone put tainted water in it, likely at work. Why would someone do that? Someone who likely has a good job and a good life. What would be the motivation?"

"Power, maybe. And a need for more of it. And someone with a psychological profile who would take it to the extreme."

"Hi, Smeg," Agarwal called out as he passed toward his office. "Slumming this morning?"

"You guys have great digs down here. Well, except for the absence of natural light. And the general greyness of everything. What did you do to deserve all this?"

Agarwal laughed. "Likely the same thing you did. I've seen your workspace. Have you heard about the Japanese decluttering trend? Throw out everything that doesn't give you joy?"

"Including my desk?"

Paul sat down and turned on his computer. Charlie headed back upstairs. He shoved his hands in his pockets as he waited for the elevator. Happily, his left hand landed on a Werther's Original, which he unwrapped and popped in his mouth. He was thinking there was no more perfect confection than a hard caramel with just the right amount of sweetness when he met both Byatt and Battle arguing by his desk.

"I still can't figure what you need boxing for." Battle scratched his head, looking genuinely confused. "It just seems like a sport for hulks from the 1960s."

"Hard-working men of steel?" Byatt said. "Those guys are relics. Today's fighters have modern methods, equipment, muscles built on supplements, weight and fitness training. It's more of a finesse sport. The heavyweights have shifted to weightlifting."

"But what made you choose boxing from all the sports out there?" Battle said.

"It's a good workout."

"And helps her deal with guys like you," Smeg added.

Battle shrugged and raised his hands in defeat.

"Where are we at with the tips?" Smeg asked.

"We've got two categories," Battle said. "Phone call-ins resulting from the press conference and tips from the caught-on-camera images we released. Where do you want us to start?"

Smeg, fresh off his thoughts about mentoring Paul, recalled that in relation to Byatt at least, it was actually his job to mentor. She seemed to be waiting for him to respond. Was it deferential, or was that only in his mind? He maneuvered his rotundity in an arc around the pole of Battle toward his desk chair and sat down. It was always a relief to get off his feet, but the time elapsed also allowed him to consider the question.

"Press conferences often incite sensationalist responses," he said. "Readers and listeners want a piece of the action, a chance to contribute something useful, to be able to talk about their place in the story. In my experience, you have to do a lot of sifting to find a gem from the resulting tips line."

He envisioned a call-in tips line as a throwback to an earlier era of crime-solving. He imagined a payphone booth. He saw himself as a product of that time.

"Yeah," Battle said. "And there's a lot of them on this one. Arsenic poisoning has sparked imaginations. Possibly because it's a highly irregular murder weapon in modern times."

Smeg turned to Byatt. "Have you done any of that type of analysis? On tips lines?"

"Not so much analysis, but I did a short stint answering phones on the open tips. We got all sorts of calls from all sorts of people, but once they heard a voice on the other end of the line, they often got cold feet. I spent most of my time coaxing the tips out of them. Patience is a virtue in that job. I'm really more suited to pounding the pavement for clues, but there was one caller who seemed like she wanted to talk, and for some reason, something in her voice, I kept her on the line for half an hour as she worked her way up to what she had to say. Her tip led detectives to a missing girl." She paused. "The caught-on-camera images might be the place to start, as most will likely be work colleagues and quickly identified. Were there many images released to the public?"

"Just one so far," Battle said. "We sent out a media alert asking for information. There's been a few responses. I can probably handle that myself."

"Sounds like the bulk of work up front will be from the tips line," Smeg said.

"I'll get Galloway going on that," Battle said. "He'll need guidance on what to look for, search words, that sort of thing. Then I'll help him analyze the relevant bits."

"Great. We'll leave you to it. Anything else we need from the phones?" Smeg asked Byatt.

Byatt said, "No, but speaking of phones, I'd love to get a hold of Abercrombie's cell phone. Forensics tells us so much about a suspect based on their cell phone: call list, text messages, photos, videos."

Smeg thought there was more he could learn about the uses of cell phones. He also knew they didn't have enough evidence yet to seize the phone.

"Let's go knock on Abercrombie's door," he said. "See if his wife is real or imagined."

Battle peered at him from his height of well over six feet, fluorescent light reflecting off what he called a 'high forehead,' although most would say he was balding. He rarely knew when it was time to leave, being a hanger-on at office parties and lingering at desks or in conference rooms beyond when he was needed. Smeg was set to dismiss him when Battle spoke.

"Real or imagined?"

"We don't really think he made her up, but he does display some elements of factitious disorder imposed by another, or FDIA," Byatt said.

Battle did not seem to comprehend. "Surely that isn't a real condition?"

"You might know it as Munchausen syndrome by proxy," she continued. "Abercrombie attends to a non-stop litany of ailments and grievances with an unflinchingly calm demeanour. He reaps the rewards of his daughter's praise for being an absolute saint. It seems she often meets him for coffee or walks in the river valley in a quest to support what surely must be his suffering."

"But that isn't enough to suggest he is doing harm to her."

Smeg picked up the thread. "His colleagues report he makes phone calls to her doctors rather than her making those calls. He presses medical professionals to see what they haven't seen and repeatedly asks for further intervention, no matter how risky. When doctors don't acquiesce, he adds new symptoms. Or switches doctors. It's all very strange."

"Wow," Battle said. "You two have all the fun."

"And speaking of fun, we're off to it." Smeg rose from his chair. "And you should too," he said to Battle.

Reluctantly, Battle turned to leave, but his shoulders lifted as the fire alarm sounded. Extended time standing in the parking lot provided unlimited social opportunity.

Chapter Sixteen

Smeg and Byatt arrived at Abercrombie's house to the appearance of no one home—curtains drawn, no lights shining through. Sharp, insistent yelps in response to the doorbell indicated the dog, at least, was within. The hope by arriving just ahead of the lunch hour was to find Abercrombie's wife out of bed and not yet down for her afternoon nap. Perhaps they had timed it wrong. They waited. Many years of law enforcement had developed in Smeg a heightened sense, and he felt they were being watched. Whether it was a movement, a sound, or he really did have eyes in the back of his head, he didn't know. He glanced at Byatt, who nodded, and he knew she too was aware of the presence.

Like every other house on the block, this one was a grey stuccoed wartime bungalow. Every neighbourhood in Edmonton built in that era looked the same. There must have been a sale. A curtain shifted slightly in what was likely a front-facing bedroom. The dog continued barking. They continued to wait. The curtain settled back into place. He rang the doorbell again. After an insufferable length of time, in which Smeg amused himself by knocking every minute or so, the door was unlocked and opened to the extent the security chain allowed. Through the small gap, he wasn't sure if he was seeing the dog or Abercrombie's wife. As his eyes became used to the dim light, he realized two faces were looking out, one above the other. The dog had a shaggy white face surrounded by a mop of ears. A classic Bichon Frisé. Directly above, the wide, wrinkled face of a woman with shaggy salt and pepper hair sat on top of a short, stocky body.

"Mrs. Abercrombie?" Byatt asked.

"Who are you?" The woman studied them with eyes that tried to squeeze through the small opening. The dog tilted its head to one side.

"I'm Detective Meaghan Byatt, and this is Detective Charlie Smeg. We'd like to ask you a few questions." Byatt removed her badge from an inside pocket and held it up.

The woman shook her head. "You should come back when my husband is home." Her slightly raised eyebrows jumped out of a taut brow. She took a small step back and began to shut the door.

Byatt smiled warmly. "We've already spoken with your husband. He's been very helpful. We'd love to have your help as well."

Smeg knew it was best to let his partner ask the questions. He could see he hadn't eased the woman's mind with his incessant hammering on the door. Hopefully, Byatt could repair the damage.

"What's this about?"

"Deena Hammond's death. You likely know she suffered from chronic illness. Your husband suggested you've had similar experiences with your own health issues."

He'd also suggested his wife loved to talk about her health. Without filter, he'd added. Byatt well knew to play on her desires. Smeg just hoped he wouldn't have to listen to too many details. He'd already heard them from Abercrombie, who hadn't held anything back.

"Can we come in?"

"Are you sure my husband said it's okay?"

"Don't worry," Smeg said, not wanting to lie outright. Although, he had done worse when necessary to get a witness to talk.

With careful precision, or maybe it was arthritic fingers, she slid the chain and opened the door. The dog did not seem to see their presence as a problem. It jumped, rolled, and let its tongue hang out, putting on a show for a new audience. Smeg reached down to rub its head and was rewarded by what promised to be a friend for life.

"Do you mind if we sit down, Mrs. Abercrombie?" Byatt asked.

"You can call me Dora."

She looked completely out of her element as she glanced around as if looking for guidance. Odd, considering they were in her living room. He wondered what it meant to be so fearful of the world. Did she ever go outside? Did she experience happiness? She waved at the couch, then took a seat on the edge of a high-backed chair. The dog sat between Byatt and him on the couch.

"I hope we didn't wake you?" Byatt said. "The house looked dark."

Smeg had no such hope. His actions had been focused on waking her up. Or at least getting her to answer the door. He tried to assess the room in the gloom. It was tidy enough and smelled of paint and oven cleaner.

"I don't sleep much," she said. "It's part of my condition."

"Oh?" Byatt leaned forward with her elbows resting on her knees. She gave Dora an encouraging smile.

"Anxiety. I toss and turn most of the night and then fall asleep in the wee hours. Delbert generally sleeps on the couch so he won't wake me." She wrapped her arms around herself to hide her trembling hands.

"Have you suffered from anxiety for long?" Byatt asked.

"I've had migraines forever, it seems. Delbert thinks they started when I worked in a flower shop years ago. He said it was the chemicals they sprayed on them and pressured me to quit and stay home. And of course my allergies—aster, baby's breath, dahlia, daisies. That could have been a problem, too." She smiled. "He always took care of me, said I didn't need to work. His job paid enough to cover the bills. I don't know about that. Sometimes I wish we had more money, you know, to buy nice things. I wanted my own car but he's happy to drive me everywhere, so I guess I don't really need one."

"How do you feel about being home all the time?"

"It's okay. I used to want to go out more, but now I don't really like to leave the house. At least not on my own."

Smeg considered the multitude of symptoms Abercrombie had laid out and wondered if a faked illness allowed her to leave the workforce and be waited on day and night. Although, that didn't seem like much of an existence. He also knew the symptoms could have been ascribed by her husband and may well have become real, the attention-seeking behaviour of an overburdened partner. Byatt maneuvered the conversation around to Abercrombie.

"Your husband says you have a lot of doctors' appointments. Are you pleased with your medical care?"

"Delbert says the doctors are very good. I don't know what I'd do without him." She bit her lip. "But don't you want to talk about Deena?"

"Yes, of course," Smeg said. "Did you know her well?"

"Not really. Delbert talked about her all the time. At first, he was impressed with her. She was very personable. But then it changed. She had a doctorate, something Delbert always felt was a bit uppity. He started with the government at a time when all these fancy credentials weren't needed. He learned and worked hard. It shouldn't require anything more than that," she said, her eyes glued to Byatt.

"I know what you mean." Byatt leaned back and crossed her legs. "We see that in our line of work, too. There are people on the pavement every day who understand more about policing than the high-priced superiors with their book learning. Delbert must be frustrated. He is likely very good at his job, what with all the experience he has."

"Delbert felt Deena didn't deserve the assignments she got. Things that he had coveted and he'd been there longer."

"Does he want to advance? Maybe into more of a management role?"

"He's such a hard worker," Dora said. "He hasn't applied for any other job recently. But I think he'd like to."

Smeg was losing patience. It had been twenty minutes since they arrived at the house. "Is he limited by having to spend so much time caring for you and taking you to appointments? He must be exhausted."

Dora's lower lip began to tremble. "He never says that he minds. It's just what people do in a marriage. It's not my fault I'm sick. My daughter says I'm a burden. But she doesn't understand." She picked up the dog, who had presumably sensed her discomfort and left the couch for a spot by her feet. "Anyway, once Deena got sick, Delbert had no reason to resent her. He became sympathetic, even suggesting she and I might want to talk, share experiences."

"And did you?"

"A couple of times. You know, she felt that somehow the office environment was making her sick. Is that possible?"

"I suppose in certain circumstances," Smeg said. "Did you ever ask Delbert what he thought about that?"

"He got a little angry, then told me not to be silly."

Smeg perceived that their time was up unless they wanted to launch into a therapy session. He wondered if Byatt was thinking about their earlier conversation. Maybe Dora was a burden, but one that Delbert had created. One that justified his lack of success. And one that led his daughter to admire his efforts. At any rate, Byatt must have agreed there was no point in engaging further, as she made moves to leave.

On the way back, he asked her what she thought.

"I'd love to get a look around the place. It's creepy. Does she float around in the dark all day?"

"Likely," he said. "And is their unhealthy lifestyle pathological or just weird?"

Byatt was silent for a moment. "You know, she didn't seem all that sick. I mean, other than the limp. She was pale, but that could be a result of virtually no exposure to fresh air and sunshine."

Smeg nodded. "Her voice was shaky. She seemed nervous."

It was Byatt's turn to nod. "So is it her or is it Abercrombie we should be focused on? I suspect it's him. Their relationship seems abusive. I wonder if we could talk to the kids."

Smeg knew they had no basis for those inquiries. He also knew they could figure out how to arrange it, if needed. Like in the context of a wellness check.

January fulfilled its promise as temperatures plummeted and the wind picked up, driving a frozen spike through the heart of outdoor activity. For Smeg, that meant his driveway didn't get shovelled. The old truck turned over with a groan and begged for extra time to warm up, making him late for work. Battle was pacing by the time he arrived. He offered apologies for his tardiness and took a seat. Byatt was already there. He started to take his coat off, but thought better of it as the vents in the conference room spewed cold air from above. Reconfigured spaces in the aged precinct building meant the heating and air conditioning no longer aligned.

Battle, quick to forgive, lowered his hitched-up shoulders and turned to face them with characteristic lightness in his eyes. His adolescent-like need to be part of the crowd meant not staying on the outs with anyone for long. Leaning his hands on the back of a chair, he cleared his throat and launched into a speech about security cameras and their effectiveness. He sounded like he'd swallowed a website. We live in a unique time, he pointed out. Cameras are everywhere, and his arm reached in a professorial sweep. Byatt's eyebrows rose along with the arc. Smeg hoped they weren't in for a full-on lecture. He'd never been keen on school and didn't see that changing now.

"Contrary to popular belief, security cameras aren't effective at either reducing crime or solving it," Battle said. "There are many reasons for that. Images may be grainy, lighting poor and, as in the case at hand, people tend not to look directly into the camera."

"Suspects should be more helpful," Smeg said.

Battle ignored him and continued, "Cameras are also not completely ineffective. They can be helpful in enclosed spaces with minimal foot traffic, such as the office where Hammond worked."

Not unlike the trajectory of Battle's career, Smeg observed, which had been neither effective nor ineffective but most helpful in enclosed spaces like the front desk which was generally his home.

"The cameras were installed in response to an incident where a disgruntled member of the public entered and located the unit that deals with complaints," Byatt said. "Apparently, he didn't like the response they'd given him and came to share a piece of his mind."

"You know, in a few years those cameras will be so small you won't even notice them." Battle's enthusiasm contained a trace of foresight.

"And they'll also have facial recognition technology, so we won't need guys like you to track down identities." Smeg gave him a pointed look. "What have you found out?"

"As the footage records the natural habitat of the work unit, we had to watch an extended period of time in order to ascertain the normal activity from the unusual or abnormal occurrences."

He went on to note they had identified Hammond's colleagues who could be seen walking the main hallway at all hours of the workday. Next, they moved on to a woman who delivered the mail, a man who picked up the bottles for recycling, the cleaning staff, and a person who watered the plants. The cleaning and plant staff entered Hammond's office regularly. There was nothing unusual but Smeg knew the video footage was only one piece of information.

Byatt jotted down a few notes. "The cleaning and plant staff, were they carrying anything?"

"The cleaning staff have a cart that was parked at the doorway to her office before entering. Plant maintenance had a basket that was taken into the office." Battle thumbed through his notes. "Each person who entered did so with confidence and seemed unaware or unfazed by the camera or other people."

"Easy enough to take tainted water in, especially in a watering can," Byatt said.

"True enough," Smeg added. "Some pesticides still contain arsenic, although it would be odd to be using them indoors."

"Both Abercrombie and Golding entered her office a number of times after she had left for the day. They always had a folder or an envelope they were dropping off; they come back out without it. Work must transfer from one person to another that way."

"What about Hammond?" Byatt asked. "Anything unusual in her behaviour?"

"At first, her coming and going was predictable. She'd arrive at 8:30 a. m. and walk briskly down the hall, calling a greeting to anyone she passed, whether in the field of vision or not. She wore lovely jackets: hunter green trimmed tweed, heavy wool in a white check, tailored pinstripe, with scarves that highlighted their colours."

Smeg thought Battle's catalogue of images might have surpassed the actual footage.

"Who are you?" Byatt asked.

"Tony the tailor?" Smeg grinned at her. "And I guess we know all of that happened during the day since there's an automatic shift to black and white at night." Smeg figured he should acknowledge Battle's efforts.

"Yes," Battle continued undeterred by the interruption. "Most infrared security cameras shift when the lighting drops. There are cameras with colour night vision but those would be out of the price range of most government offices." He flipped through his notes. "As the days and weeks go on, she becomes sloppier with her dress, perhaps because she loses weight and those tailored suits and dresses start to hang off her like her sole purpose is to ward off crows. Her hair begins to look like they've nested."

"Outstanding in her field?" Smeg asked.

"What? No. I'm talking about how she looked."

Smeg moved on. "Anything more about Golding and Abercrombie?"

"Abercrombie is at the office very early every day and on weekends. He arrives with a takeout bag and a disposable coffee cup each morning, seven days a week. You might think he lived there."

"Or is avoiding where he does live," Smeg said. "What about Golding?"

"She was generally in the office for about an hour after Hammond left each day."

"The folders? Could something have been carried into Hammond's office under a folder?"

"Certainly possible. Once the lighting dims, the images get fuzzy, so it's hard to tell what's going on." Battle checked his notes again. "Oh, and Rodriguez enters her office three times on weekends. He goes in with a briefcase and comes out with the same case."

"Thanks," Smeg said. "Good work."

"Back to Rodriguez?" Byatt said after Battle had left the room.

Smeg nodded. "What do we know about him?"

"The basic stuff, where he works, a largely unused Facebook account." Byatt booted up the conference room computer and did a Google search. "Oh, here's something. A woman claiming to have had an affair with him venting on Facebook about him dumping her."

"When did that happen?"

"A couple of years ago, although her complaints continued for a while after. Also on Facebook are a number of images posted by Hammond or the kids in which Rodriguez is tagged. Mostly happy family stuff. Which of course doesn't tell us anything since social media is a master class in creating the images you want the world to see." Byatt scrolled down. "Looks like some photos from his childhood. Maybe posted by a sister?"

"Anything there?"

"Likely some underage drinking, but no. Not really. I'll refine my Google search to earlier years."

Smeg removed his jacket. The air blasting at him was now hot.

"A charge, later dropped, for fighting. College stuff."

"Okay." Smeg made a move to get out of his chair. "It's likely worth another chat with him. I can handle that if you want to drop in on Hammond's colleagues. Maybe they'll open up more if it's just you, the friendly face."

He rose to his feet and went in search of a space in the building that was appropriately heated. Smeg didn't know much about social media, and even if it was an unreliable source, an affair was something that needed to be checked out. It could provide motive.

Chapter Seventeen

Smeg rang the rusty doorbell and waited. Rodriguez seemed preoccupied, even confused, when he opened the door, as if he didn't know whether to invite Smeg in. Not necessarily because he didn't want to; more like he wasn't sure what his role was, leader or follower. It seemed Smeg was interrupting something. Together, they executed a little dance on the front mat that allowed Smeg to close the door behind him. Really, what struck him most was the smell of marijuana wafting from the back of the house. He wondered if it was for medicinal use. And which family member was smoking it.

"Any news?" Rodriguez's eyes were red-rimmed.

"No breaks yet." Smeg stepped a little farther onto the mat. It occurred to him that Rodriquez was stalling in hopes of allowing the smoke to clear.

"Anything to indicate the arsenic was given to her?"

'No,' was likely what Rodriguez wanted to hear. Smeg suspected he wasn't seeking answers, just an end to the questions. He was tempted to hone in on Rodriguez's paranoia but knew it wouldn't lead anywhere productive. It was always better to be patient and build a case slowly. He'd need the small details if charges were to be laid.

"Not yet, but we can't rule it out." Smeg waited; possibly Rodriguez's reaction time had been delayed, and he would no doubt get around to inviting him in. To no avail. "I have a few more questions for you. The video footage from your wife's office shows you entering after hours on a number of occasions. What were you doing there?"

Rodriguez ran a hand slowly through his hair. "Sometimes when Deena wasn't well, she asked me to pick things up from her office so she could work from home."

"How did you get in? Security is tight in that building."

"Not that tight. I used Deena's pass card." He suppressed a giggle. At this point, Smeg no longer wondered who was smoking pot. He let him ramble. "No one stopped me. Guess I didn't look sketchy." He emphasized the point by looking directly into Smeg's eyes. "I picked up folders off her desk. Sometimes her laptop, if she had forgotten to bring it home."

"Did you see anyone in the office?"

"Abercrombie." A brief smile appeared. "Of course."

"Did you talk to him?"

"Yes. He's a chatty guy. At first, I think he wondered why I was there, but he likes to be helpful. He'd usually stop what he was doing and explain in detail what needed to be done with the work I was taking home."

"Was that helpful to Deena?"

"I doubt it would have been, and I never passed his long-winded comments on to her. She knew what needed to be done."

"Did you often have to help her with her work? As her health deteriorated."

"No. Her mind remained sharp, if that's what you're getting at."

Smeg had no doubt that was true. The autopsy had not found evidence of brain damage, and the quality of her work hadn't suffered. Rodriguez, at this point, was less sharp.

"How was family life during her illness? Were things a bit tense? How did the kids respond to their mother's inability to do things?"

"They're grown and pretty independent. They knew she was sick but didn't pay much attention."

A bit callous, Smeg thought. The interview wasn't going anywhere productive. He swung it to his purpose for being there.

"What about you? Did you have friends you could turn to?"

"I didn't need that."

Smeg waited a moment to let Rodriguez's comment hang in the air. He wanted to see a reaction, given a lone wolf can succumb to the stressors of life. There wasn't one.

"What about social media?"

Rodriguez rolled his eyes. "I dabble in it. The kids thought I should be communicating with extended family and set up a Facebook account for me a few years back. It's mostly a waste of time. Those cousins they wanted me to connect with post mostly memes."

"I noticed on Facebook you had an affair."

"How is that relevant?" He glared. "It was with a woman I knew years ago who had a thing for me. She resurfaced and started pestering me."

"Where did you know her from?"

"A business venture."

Smeg waited for details but none came. "Your venture? What kind of business?"

"I was involved in a lumber mill in British Columbia in my late twenties before moving to Edmonton. She was my business partner, and we dated. The business failed. We weren't especially environmentally conscious back then, and the protestors sank us. We couldn't fully operate with their interference and ultimately couldn't make money."

"And the woman?"

"The relationship, both professional and romantic, ended when I moved to Edmonton. She lives here now. I saw her downtown one day a couple of years ago and she approached me. At first, I was nice about it, but it became annoying when she wouldn't leave me alone."

His high seemed to have worn off. He was no longer enjoying himself.

"By 'nice about it,' do you mean you rekindled the old flame?"

"Maybe at first she might have thought so." He placed his hands on his hips. Sweat circles appeared under his armpits, followed by a sharp odour.

Smeg stepped back. "Did you have an affair at that point?"

Rodriguez looked out the window. "Briefly, I suppose, but then I told her to back off, that I was married. She was under some delusion that I was in love with her and wanted to leave my wife. She's a nut job."

"Did she accept your decision?"

"We argued a number of times. Like I said, she's a nut job."

"Would you say you have a temper? Have you ever got into a fight?"

"I'm starting to lose my temper now. Do I need a lawyer?"

"Just trying to put together a complete picture of Deena's life." Smeg gave what he hoped was a reassuring smile. He knew people were less forthcoming if they thought they were a suspect. "Did Deena use marijuana at all? For medical purposes?"

"No. If you're wondering if that's what brought it into the house, that was my son's doing."

Perhaps it was a family activity. His son seemed willing to share. Smeg stepped outside and took a deep breath. Rodriguez clearly hadn't liked the mention of his affair based on the way he rushed Smeg out the door.

As Smeg sat in rush hour traffic early the next morning, his phone rang. Byatt begged off for the day, sounding hoarse. He had never known her to take a sick day. He was also surprised; she wasn't the type to stay home if it could be avoided. He considered the day without her and hoped it would just be the one.

"Sorry," she said. "I can't shake this abdominal pain."

"No problem. Take it easy. We'll touch base tomorrow."

"I'll do some computer work from home. See what else I can find about our main suspects."

"Maybe check into Rodriguez again. If you're feeling up to it, that is. He said he was involved in a failed logging company. Would be about twenty-five years ago. The woman he had the affair with was one of his business partners, or maybe the sole partner."

"Sure. Do you know anything else about it?"

"He blames environmental activists for the failure of the company."

"Of course he does. They're an easy target for business folks who don't want to follow the rules."

"Yes," Smeg said. "But those activists were likely on to something."

"True. And not necessarily listened to twenty-five years ago. I'll check into what the issues were at the time. Beyond clear-cutting."

"How did it go at Hammond's office yesterday?" Smeg asked.

"We had a friendly chat about the cleaning staff, who all agree are lovely. The regular woman is Filipina. They're on a quest to help her improve her English language skills and seem intent on having extended conversations with her. She has kids and grandkids back in the Philippines who she sends money to regularly. While she did have opportunity to access Hammond's office and a cart in which to hide tainted water, I don't sense any motive there. As for the rest of them, I couldn't get them to talk about anything of substance."

Not exactly shooters, rapists, or serial killers, but there was something odd about that group. They were highly dysfunctional at best. They crossed the line of moral standards at worst, lying, cheating to get ahead. Once one person stops playing by the rules, the rules are out the window. It's dog-eat-dog for survival. At least that's how it appeared to Smeg. In answer to his next question, about why they didn't leave, he suspected the problem personalities had been there so long they either couldn't envision themselves elsewhere or couldn't compete with younger, more vibrant individuals in a job competition. He needed a plan to crack the dynamic open. And while he knew it likely didn't involve plants, he did need to ask, given the ready access to Hammond's office.

"What about the person who waters the plants?"

"They, who identify as non-binary, similarly don't have motive. I chatted with them, but only noticed an endearing commitment to bonsai and snake plants. The staff were intent on discussing non-binary gender pronouns. Their biggest concern was worrying they might not use the pronouns correctly."

Smeg paused. He sensed this was another thing he needed to ask Paul about. He also was hearing confirmation of his earlier belief in the strangeness of Hammond's colleagues. Although he supposed there wasn't anything wrong with adopting the grandmotherly cleaning staff as an English as a Second Language project or learning about gender issues. Certainly, the latter was a class he should sit in on.

Byatt continued, "I asked Abercrombie about seeing Rodriguez in the office. Said he was picking up work for her. I'm getting used to Abercrombie's excited responses to any opportunity to help out. Sifting through all that, I saw a man wanting to shape the narrative about Hammond. After the meeting, I asked Golding about Abercrombie's sometimes bizarre answers."

"What did she say?"

"I don't think she sees anything off in his behaviour. She laughed and said he loves to meddle. Her own behaviour displays a consistent pattern: she doesn't have a lot of time for answering questions."

Smeg signed off. He didn't mind that traffic had ground to a halt; it gave him time to ponder the case, reflect on what they knew, and decide what questions still needed to be asked. His face creased as he recalled another homicide investigation he'd been involved with. A boss who had murdered her assistant in order to keep a Ponzi scheme afloat. The boss was well spoken, admired, and had no history of violence. He had noted, at the time, that she reflected an image matching other successful leaders in the workplace. She was credible, dedicated, competent, and likable. And, remarkably effective with a knife.

He had done his homework and found an interesting trend—red collar crime. Murder in the workplace. Homicides and attempted homicides related to accounting fraud, identity fraud, forgery. The case had stuck with him. It was bizarre to him to think people would go to such lengths for something so seemingly superficial. Studies suggested two traits correlated with workplace violence: narcissism and psychopathy, the latter surprisingly common in the business world. Researchers administered a test used to determine psychopathy to a large group of managers and executives and discovered that five percent scored at the serial killer level. Their excellent communication and convincing skills, which would have made them attractive hiring candidates, continued to serve them well in their day-to-day dealings and positioned them for advancement.

Smeg thought that if he were a psychopath, he still wouldn't have chosen to work in either the public service or the corporate world. Endlessly more interesting possibilities were imaginable once moral standards were off the table. Counterfeiting came to mind. But what about his current case? Psychopathy was common in the business and corporate world. So what? Any number of Hammond's colleagues could be psychopaths, but he still didn't have a clear murder he could point to. Red collar crime was a partial argument he could use in support of his theory, but not enough to convince anyone that they should infiltrate the workplace. He needed more information. He unloaded his jacket onto the back of his chair and headed for the elevator. Time to see what Paul had discovered from the tips line.

Paul removed his earbuds upon Charlie's arrival.

"Hey, Paul," Charlie said. "How's it going down here?"

"Great, great," Paul said. "Just thinking about lunch."

"Lunch? What about breakfast?"

"Been there, done that, hungry again." He pulled on the arms of his too-short, long-sleeved T-shirt and checked his phone. "Okay, I guess it's too soon, but do you want to get lunch in a while? That chicken place?"

"Sure." He wasn't familiar with 'that chicken place' but liked having the opportunity to spend more time with Paul.

A smile spread across his stepson's face, splitting the patchy beard that hadn't firmly established itself. The smile, on the other hand, had. The smile that, genetically speaking, was his mother's. Charlie, aware he didn't share DNA with the boy, sensed the shared experience of solving crime was bringing them closer. Or else Paul was spending too much time alone in the windowless basement and latched onto anyone who stopped by.

"Just checking on the tips line," Charlie said. "Had a chance to sift through much of it yet?"

"Yeah, yeah." Paul was practically vibrating. "Listen to this. A woman called with information on a recent poisoning: a doctor who was convicted of the cyanide poisoning of his wife. The doctor had bought cyanide allegedly for stem cell experiments related to his research into Lou Gehrig's disease."

"Yeah," Charlie said. "Meaghan mentioned that one."

"The doctor covered his tracks well, including documenting all the experiments that included the use of cyanide. All vials accounted for, and no evidence that it had entered the family home. Numerous interviews led nowhere, beyond circumstantial evidence. The caller said the wife wanted another child and had threatened to leave if he went through with a vasectomy. Not much of a motive, but the suspect was cold, detached, never displayed emotion in relation to his dead wife."

"Sounds like you heard more information on the call than what was in the file. We didn't see an immediate connection, but that bit about the wife wanting another child is interesting. Investigators had assumed an affair. Killing your wife over her desire to have a baby is really cold."

"The caller said he had an exaggerated sense of self-importance and believed he was destined for a great breakthrough, maybe even a cure for ALS. The world needed his knowledge and expertise, and he couldn't be sidetracked by a baby. He also needed to appear flawless and that apparently included having a beautiful wife. Her threatening to leave was a problem."

"So, he killed her?"

"I think it was supposed to look like cancer. In that way, he would garner sympathy from the outside world."

"Who was the caller?"

"She wouldn't say. She only said that she should have been called as a witness at the trial but they turned her down."

"Hmm, so we have to question her credibility. That could be why the legal team didn't want her to testify."

Paul's shoulders slumped. "She sounded credible on the phone."

"She may well be. There are lots of reasons for rejecting a witness. She might not have seen the poisoning first-hand, so her testimony would be circumstantial. The version of events may be inconsistent with the testimony of other witnesses. That is, it doesn't fit the narrative the lawyers have created. There may have been stronger evidence of an affair. Who knows, at this point? Did you get a sense of how or if she knew the victim?"

"She seemed to know her well, like maybe a close friend."

"Any thoughts on why she's calling now? Does it have any connection to the current case?"

"I think she just thought her theory about poisoning might be useful." Paul looked at Charlie. "But I think they might be connected."

"This is great, Paul." Charlie stroked his imaginary beard. "Access to poison is another aspect we've considered but don't yet have a handle on. A doctor, especially one with a research lab, may have many poisonous substances to choose from. The case you're presenting highlights the possibilities related to access."

"Any doctors on your list of suspects?" Paul asked.

"No." Charlie sighed. "Not at the moment." But Abercrombie came close in terms of proximity to doctors.

Chapter Eighteen

He stared at the dull, moss green partition that separated him from his former partner, inspired as always by her tireless dedication; she was back from medical leave and arguing with the tenacity of a backhoe with a ridiculously high IQ. He had wisely learned to get out of the way and let her dig—into backgrounds of suspects, causes of death, or how to win over a particularly obstinate judge. Her health, often a challenge, Smeg knew, had proved once again not to be an obstacle given how quickly she had returned to work. His own reticence to come back after the incident that sidelined her could have been resolved quicker had he thought about how Usmani would have handled it—get back on the horse and ride. He was glad he had. Her arrival might have caused him internal conflict if she had been physically ready for active duty and he'd been offered up as her partner, but she wasn't ready for that. And he knew Singer wouldn't pull him away from Byatt. He was also glad about that. Byatt had many of Usmani's qualities: insight, intelligence, work ethic, and enthusiasm. And Byatt needed his mentorship.

Usmani was presently on what sounded like a three-way call with a judge and crown prosecutor, arguing effectively for a search warrant. He pulled himself back to his own case and his thoughts about baiting Hammond's colleagues to see how far they would go. An undercover officer posing as a new employee, Hammond's replacement, could provide an opportunity to see what was going on in the office, especially if that person came highly qualified and threatened the advancement of the current members of the branch. He knew he wouldn't be able to convince Singer that undercover was warranted, at least not until they had narrowed the suspect list to someone in the workplace. Usmani could provide advice. She had an uncanny ability to see into the minds of criminals, and an otherworldly skill at getting what she wanted.

When she got off the call, Smeg raised himself from his armchair and poked his head around the partition. "Got time for a chat?"

She swivelled her chair around to face him. "Of course, Smeg, Any time."

She'd accumulated a few grey hairs during her convalescence, highlighting the recalcitrant black ones that refused to be contained in a headband. Her dark eyes, offset by small crow's feet—also new—still shone with intensity as they locked onto Smeg's. The last few months had been difficult for her, but adversity wasn't in her vocabulary, and she looked none the worse for it all.

"Settling back in?" he asked.

She flashed him a smile. "You know me. Sitting at home was a killer."

"And that leg?"

"It's about ninety percent."

He wanted to believe that, but the way her hand reached down to rub her knee made him think otherwise. She saw his gaze and grasped her coffee mug instead.

"So really, seventy-five percent? Did you exaggerate to get back to work?"

"Not me," she said with feigned innocence. "What can I do for you?"

"Advice," he said. "I'm working on the Hammond case. Are you familiar with it?"

"I've followed it a bit." Which really meant: yes.

"I want to set up a sting but I don't know how to convince the sergeant." He rubbed his hands together as if they were cold.

Her eyebrows raised at the word sting. "Do you have enough evidence?"

"That's the line I'm hovering. Circumstantially, the source of the arsenic comes from within the office. We do have a suspect and had a number of conversations with him but we aren't getting much. There are others who had opportunity but we need the undercover to find out who."

"Have you ruled out the husband?" She tilted her head to one side in a familiar look of skepticism.

"No, but even if it was him, the tainted water seemed to have been planted in her water bottle in the office," he said.

It would have been audacious, he knew, for Rodriguez to go out of his way to carry out such a deed in her workplace. Surely there were more accessible ways to get to her. Unless he'd wanted to pin it on one of her colleagues.

"But if it was him, you won't catch him with a sting."

Smeg persisted. "Somebody knows something."

"Not enough of an argument. You'd have to be fairly sure you'd get the evidence to prosecute. That's the argument you need to make to Singer."

"Yeah. You're right." He looked at the floor.

Usmani glanced over his shoulder. "Hey, where's Byatt today? You two are usually together."

"She's off sick. Stomach problems."

"Really? She was complaining to me last week about a similar issue. Unusual for her."

"Oh shit," Smeg said. "She was at Hammond's office yesterday for most of the afternoon. Come to think of it, she was there last week, too. She's been given tainted water."

"There's your smoking gun, as it were. Now you've got an argument for Singer."

"Yes," Smeg thanked her as Paul arrived to go for lunch.

"Hey, Galloway," Usmani said. "I was glad to hear you'd joined the team."

"Yeah, Smeg mentioned that Agarwal was hiring, so I jumped at it," Paul said.

"Smeg?" Smeg asked.

Paul shrugged.

"Okay then, *Galloway*," Smeg said. "You buying lunch?"

Byatt was back early the next morning, pumped up about the things she'd learned of Rodriguez's foray into logging on Meares Island off the B.C. coast. She followed Smeg to his desk, her story moving faster than her legs as though she sought a position in the industry and he was hiring. He was pretty sure he'd just learned more about logging in five minutes than he'd ever known. It turned out that Rodriguez's business was beginning to thrive in the early nineties when government support of private resource extraction encouraged growth in the industry. Clear-cutting was highly profitable. When Smeg had been out that way, on a rare vacation in Tofino with Nancy, he'd barely given a thought to the felling of trees. He was much more attentive to the old-growth cedars that shaded the boardwalk from the blazing heat. Rodriguez's company, one that hadn't had a chance to establish itself firmly, tanked as the Clayoquot protests picked up steam. Blockades prevented timber from moving off the island, a particular target for protestors because the island was the main source of drinking water for the area.

Smeg hung his coat on the back of his chair and turned to her. "Explains why things didn't pan out for him."

"But listen to this," she continued. "The protest that had the most effect on Rodriguez's company slowly fizzled as a number of the protestors became sick. Drinking water turned out to be the source, blamed on logging companies' practices. At that point, however, Rodriquez and his partner could not turn the company back to profit."

"Speaking of drinking water." Smeg put a hand on Byatt's arm. "There's something I need to talk to you about."

"Oh?"

"The other day, when you were at Hammond's office, did you drink any water?"

"I had my own water bottle with me."

"Did you leave it unattended at any point?"

Byatt was silent for a moment. "Once, mid-afternoon. We took a break and I went to the washroom."

"Enough time for someone to replace the water in your bottle?"

Byatt took a sharp breath. She nodded, then hugged her chest. Smeg reached a thick arm around her, recognizing she felt violated. He knew the feeling, and it strengthened his resolve. He recalled the time he'd come home to the obvious signs of a house break-in; that feeling of something crawling on you. His privacy had been invaded; for Byatt, if the water had been tainted, it was worse than that.

"We need to get into that office," he said. "I've been thinking about an undercover operation."

"A Mr. Big?" Byatt's reaction mirrored Usmani's.

"We plant a new employee in the branch to replace Hammond. We'd profile Abercrombie as our most likely suspect and use what we know about his habits and personality to identify an undercover officer he'd likely bond with."

It would need to be an appointment. A hiring process would be too slow and too difficult to control. An appointment could be passed off as political; someone who is given the job because of their connections.

"Abercrombie seems to love bantering, especially about sports," Byatt said. "Someone who works out and has connections to high-profile athletes would be a good choice."

"It would also be important that the person comes highly qualified and is seen to be ripe for advancement. A threat to anyone in the branch who might have ambition."

"Singer will argue we're playing on vulnerabilities, pressuring folks into saying something in an environment that should be safe from outsiders," Byatt said. "Government employees sign an oath that includes not revealing information that is confidential. This might be seen as entrapment."

Smeg's head bobbed slightly as he thought about that dilemma. The Supreme Court had ruled that the value of evidence collected has to outweigh the harm. What that would mean in this case is that any confidential information obtained would be inadmissible in court.

"Best case scenario for us would be a confession. That way, other evidence wouldn't be needed."

"What about Rodriguez?" Byatt asked. "Are we ruling him out? Because there's more to what I found about his logging venture."

"What's that?"

"The chemicals found in the water supply were traced to his company and contained a slightly different mix from the chemical compounds that were a by-product of the other logging companies in the area." Her voice was steady, like it was locked onto something.

"And more toxic?"

"Yes. The difference was given a cursory look at the time but the conclusion was that the process they were using was slightly different and accounted for the different chemical mix."

"Seems odd they let it go."

Although he knew, back then, companies had free rein. Still did, really. Business was welcomed and environmental or human health took a back seat.

Byatt said, "Bottom line, Rodriguez has a history of harming people with tainted water."

Smeg sat down. "We definitely can't rule him out. But we're certain that the water was added to Hammond's bottle in the office. So even if it's Rodriguez, he took it there when she wasn't in. We saw him there a number of times. And he talked to Abercrombie. So getting into the office and targeting Abercrombie is still our best bet."

"If Abercrombie gives us something about Rodriguez we'd have grounds for a search warrant of his house," Byatt said.

"None of this is helping our argument with Singer. We're going off in two directions."

"Since Abercrombie is still our most likely suspect, we'll focus on him when we present our case to Singer."

He looked up at Byatt. "And the fact that you are likely now a target suggests we are getting too close for someone's comfort."

And so Smeg found himself in Singer's office, Byatt at his side, presenting a case for something his rational mind knew was a long shot at best—a covert operation. With the recent ruling of a provincial court judge that ultimately stayed proceedings against a drug trafficker because police hadn't engaged in a bona fide undercover investigation, he knew it had to be above board. The reasoning needed to be solid, and Smeg knew his argument wasn't. He pulled his shoulders back and tried to project confidence as he launched into his analysis. When he'd finished, Singer stared at him for an interminable length of time in which he could see her weighing the possibilities associated with his mental state. Had he considered that Singer might support their plan, he would have anticipated her first question and been prepared.

"The cost?"

He had to think fast; not his strong point. "$150,000," he said. "Give or take."

Take, for instance, the fact that he didn't have a clue what a sting operation would cost.

But on he went. "We'd need half a dozen officers; the undercover person and support team. Maybe more for overtime costs given Abercrombie's propensity to work on weekends."

"Seems low," she said. "And there's a high risk you won't get anything usable." She looked over at Byatt. "But given officer safety is a factor, I'll send it up the line for approval."

He wasn't sure what had just transpired, and having not used up all his arguments, stood firmly rooted. Byatt nudged him toward the door. Smeg thanked Singer and quickly led the way out before she had time to reconsider. And ask more questions he couldn't answer.

"Let's head across the street for coffee," he said to Byatt. "That way we can start planning the operation without listening ears." He motioned with his chin toward the bullpen. "Until we have approval, we should keep this thing under wraps."

Once seated, Smeg popped the lid off his cup and took a sip before setting it down. He hadn't expected a positive outcome from the meeting with Singer and now felt the pressure of his bold move. They'd have to produce. Byatt unzipped her coat but didn't take it off. She enclosed her cup with her hands and looked out the window. She was likely having similar thoughts, but she could turn to Smeg's leadership. He'd have to ante up. He had a small bit of practice at such an operation and thought back to lessons learned. The project had started well but the target had proved too good at keeping secrets. The male undercover bonded with the target, but the friendship formed didn't require the breaking of silences. The case had involved the death of a young woman and, eventually, they added a young female operative to the mix. It was her, on the pretext of a sexual relationship, who won his confidence and got him to talk.

"Who are our options for operative?" Byatt pulled a notepad from her pocket. "Who do we have who'd connect with Abercrombie?"

"I'm wondering about a woman, given Abercrombie's proclivity to attach himself and then dominate." It wasn't Smeg's first inclination, but now he considered. "What do you think?"

"He did seem to bond with Hammond." Byatt coughed and Smeg was reminded of her health, dismayed anew at the possibility she'd been given tainted drinking water. "At first, it seemed he wanted to give her guidance and generally micromanage her workday. Then he seemed to relish her health problems. A woman with similar characteristics might set up well as a target for him."

Smeg nodded. "It's a good thought. Although Abercrombie, while small in stature and seemingly gentle in nature, seems to respond well to males with strong personalities. He'd be impressed with the attentions of someone personable, self-confident, and on top of his game, especially if that person had connections to sports personalities. Those traits would need to balance with a desire to get ahead. Sports first, in order to connect with Abercrombie, but with enough ambition to be a threat to the hierarchical balance in the branch."

"That sounds like most of the cops I know," Byatt said.

Smeg frowned. "Gets a bit hard to take some days, doesn't it?"

"It is what it is," Byatt said and looked past him.

Smeg tried to read the look that wasn't directed at him. Resignation didn't seem like her style; maybe it was about being valued. Byatt's strengths were recognized by those who mattered at work, and maybe the male chauvinists with their misogynist comments weren't worth the time of day. True, but still. She wasn't including him in her analysis, but he vowed to be better, to speak up more in meetings, to not zone out to what wasn't directly relevant to him. While he might not have been interested in the coffee fund, he knew discussion of it provided many opportunities for rude comments about who should be making the coffee.

Byatt continued, "Given the plethora of options, even if we narrow to undercover officers, we may be in over our heads. We should start with identifying an undercover coordinator." She paused. "And maybe waiting for approval of the operation."

Chapter Nineteen

The gym was small, the lighting poor, and in a venue as run-down as its neighbourhood, the one where Charlie had started out his career. He struggled to reconcile the wealthy city he lived in with the many who made those streets their home. Not much had changed in the ensuing years, although redevelopment threatened to engulf the space and push the street folks northward. The little boxing club had resisted the land grab of redevelopers, but its membership was dropping amid struggles to pay the rent.

Whatever challenges faced the boxers in the ring, few could argue that it was the bleachers which rose sharply in front of him that were insurmountable for Charlie. He questioned the logic of his decision to accept Meaghan's invitation to her match. He wouldn't climb Mount Norquay at this point in his life. High school gym class had nothing on this; back then, it was just adolescent boys who hadn't mastered hygiene that posed the biggest difficulty in a gymnasium. He was in shape back then. In fact, he'd been a decent basketball player. Halfway up the stands,

Charlie, his bum knee throbbing, pulled the back of Paul's shirt to keep him from going all the way to the top.

Meaghan bounded up the well-worn stairs to the ring and slid between the ropes. She'd told them her participation was at the non-competitive level; she boxed in Basement Wars, the club's house league. Charlie hadn't been to a boxing match in years, professional or otherwise, and was looking forward to it. Meaghan had warned them that this one fell firmly into the otherwise category. But she assured them it would be amusing. Charlie was pleased to see the boxers wearing headgear, even for a match. A blow to the head could be career-limiting. Or at least put you on a management track. Meaghan's coach smeared goop from a Vaseline tub onto her cheeks, forehead, and chin. Paul looked questioningly at Charlie.

"To avoid cuts," Charlie said. "It makes the skin more elastic and slippery."

Meaghan pulled her headgear into place and snapped the strap together. She inserted her mouth guard and checked her pulse. Without thinking, Charlie checked his too. Meaghan barely had her gloves in place and, *ding*, the fight was on. He watched with interest as she and her opponent tested each other with jabs and blocks, impressed but not surprised by Meaghan's skill. He cringed when her opponent feinted, then landed a solid blow to the ribs with a thud like meat being tenderized. Meaghan buckled, then bounced back.

"You got this, Meaghan!" Paul shouted between handfuls of popcorn.

Charlie noticed the beads of sweat on the other woman's face melding into a smooth sheen and wondered if she was giving all she had too early in the fight. He was exhausted just watching. At the end of three rounds, the only points awarded were for that jab to Meaghan's ribs. The smattering of people in the stands was more interested in their phones than the fight. Paul checked his, too, and sent a quick reply. Finally, in the fifth round, the action picked up. At least Meaghan's did.

"Get out a three-punch combination!" her coach yelled, accompanied by a spray of saliva that landed in the ring. Charlie was now glad they'd climbed the bleachers.

"Why is he giving away her strategy?" Paul asked.

"He knows her opponent can't counter it anyway."

And true enough, she was slowing visibly. Then, she made a mistake. Meaghan pulsed left, then right, bobbing and weaving. She threw a straight right jab followed by a hard uppercut. Her opponent went down, and that was that.

Paul's cheering rose above the polite clapping in the room.

"What do you have planned for the rest of your Saturday?" Charlie asked him.

"Eloise is home for the weekend." Paul's face lit up like the LED lighting surrounding the boxing ring. "Maybe catch a movie."

"Sounds like fun." Charlie countered with a genuine smile of his own. "A date?"

Paul shrugged. "Guess so." His shoulders slumped. "She's awfully pretty, though."

"Is that a problem?"

"Don't know what she's doing with *me*."

Charlie thought about that one for a minute and decided against the usual platitudes. "Always punch above your weight." He gave Paul a jab to the shoulder.

Paul's smile returned. "She's so much fun. Maybe it's that drama training." He glanced at the time on his phone. "I better get going. What are you up to?"

"I'll wait for Meaghan."

Charlie was happy to chill for a while. A Saturday afternoon away from the office was never really free from thinking about a case, though, and he could spend the time running over their next steps. He thought about the strategy of the boxing match, wearing down an opponent. That had been the strategy used on Hammond; first wear her down by throwing roadblocks in the path of her advancement, then continue the process by chipping away at her health. A slow win over time. He blinked down at the bleacher below him and started his descent.

"Well done, Muhammad Ali," Charlie said as Meaghan approached.

"Don't you mean Laila Ali?" Meaghan jabbed at the air in front of him.

Charlie, reminded again of his need for sensitivity training, pulled his jacket on. Although, in all fairness, that gaffe was at least as much about his inability to get with the times as it was about sexism. Meaghan, on the other hand, was already in tune with the times. In some ways, boxing was like an extension of police training and she had developed an interest in the sport shortly after starting her career, she told him. She could take down an opponent and had the instinct to do so. He knew that as a detective, gender had nothing to do with it. On the streets, you didn't choose an opponent based on weight class either. She just knew how to handle herself. And she was young enough to do it.

"Do you want to grab a drink?" Meaghan said.

"Sure, that'd be great. Is there somewhere around here?"

"There's a bar across the street. Beer's not great, but the atmosphere is authentic."

"You mean in relation to this place?" Charlie looked around as they headed for the door.

"Yes. It's a dive."

"Perfect." Charlie beamed. "I'll feel right at home."

The day outside stung Charlie's cheeks and he figured they were now dotted with bright red circles as though warning off low-flying aircraft. Or warning people not to be out based on how quiet the street was. He breathed in the fresh air and was disinclined to step back inside when they reached the bar. He soon forgot the stale indoor air as they approached the counter and ordered drinks. The beer, Lucky Lager, was bad, even to his unrefined palette.

"This appears to be a neighbourhood kind of place, regulars mostly," he said. "A contrast to the white-collar atmosphere we've been frequenting lately."

"No red collar crime here," Meaghan agreed. "Any murders would be straight-up drunken knife fights."

"Which are generally easier to solve. Just go after the person covered in blood."

"Arsenic is invisible and more difficult to find. But it's the same principle. Go after the person who has arsenic."

"Doesn't narrow it down much. Even the cleaning staff aren't ruled out if we're considering who might have arsenic." Charlie peered into the dusty corners of the room. "Traditionally, it was used as rat poison."

Meaghan followed his gaze. "If we had rats in Alberta, they'd certainly be in this place."

Then he was clear of it, had chopped through the clinging rottenness of fetid breath and stinking clothes. Perhaps Meghan had also read *The Last Crossing*. Although, that seemed unlikely.

She did, however, have insights. "Maybe we should talk more about accidental poisoning. What if Hammond was using some type of cleaning product to wash her water bottle? I'll Google cleaning products that contain arsenic." Meaghan reached for her phone. "Wallpaper, paint, weed killer, pesticides, taxidermy, chicken feed."

"None of which are cleaning supplies."

"Here's something," Meaghan said. "Many fruit juices, including apple, grape, and juice blends, contain concerning levels of arsenic."

"Which could, of course, be consumed from a water bottle. It seems unlikely she would have consumed enough juice for that to be the source, but I'll make a note to ask Rodriguez about her juice consumption." Charlie pulled his notebook from his shirt pocket.

He told Meaghan about Paul's research and the case of the doctor who killed his wife. The choice of murder weapon was based on access to poison.

"Crime of opportunity."

"Back to that." Charlie waved for another beer. "Who had access?"

"Back to rats. Might there be someone in the office who knows something and is willing to inform?"

"We've talked to all the members of the branch."

"Hopefully, we'll have an undercover who might be able to get close enough to get some folks to let their guard down."

At work the next day, Smeg planned where to go next if the operation wasn't approved. Other options were less likely to be effective. They'd have to tail Abercrombie outside of work and be careful not to cross the line into entrapment. The loud shrill of the desk phone interrupted his thoughts. The call display indicated it was Singer. It was too soon for a positive answer but, then again, a quick jury deliberation didn't necessarily mean the defendant was in trouble. Her message that the undercover operation had been approved both surprised and thrilled him. After hanging up, he sat at his desk and wondered where to begin.

As luck would have it, the undercover coordinator showed up. In truth, more of a business manager, Buzz, whose real name escaped Charlie, was known for efficiency. And a very short buzz cut. He wondered how Buzz had gotten there so quickly and how many others had been informed before Smeg.

"Got a shortlist of candidates for you to review," he said and plunked a file folder down on the desk.

"Wasn't this operation just approved?"

"I heard it was in the works and got a jump on it. We haven't had an undercover in awhile, and the unit is itching to get started."

"Hmm."

"You can only sit around eating donuts for so long."

How long is that? Smeg wondered as he opened the file folder. Leafing through, he noted all the candidates were experienced and loosely fit the criteria. Buzz had already consulted with the police psychologist on the sort of person Abercrombie would be most likely to bond with. Following her advice, they selected all males, none of whom would threaten Abercrombie's self-image, but were alpha enough to impress him. They chose a male because Abercrombie displayed micro-aggressions toward women and would be less likely to bond with a female operative. Buzz had really done his homework.

"Some impressive folks here," Smeg said.

"I've ranked them top to bottom. The ones on top would be my recommendations."

"So, Aaftab is your first choice?"

"Yes, sir." Buzz was all business.

"Might Abercrombie respond negatively to someone from a minority?"

"Don't think so," the coordinator said. "Aaftab is easygoing and sociable. Abercrombie doesn't harbour any tendencies toward racial discrimination that we are aware of. Aaftab should be able to win him over. He's built like a soccer player. Black hair, light brown skin tone. He looks like Gurpreet Singh Sandhu, you know? Plays for Bengal." Smeg wondered who'd told him that. It was likely Buzz didn't know any more about soccer than he did.

"Let's do it then," Smeg handed back the file.

"We'll put together a surveillance team who have worked with Aaftab in the past. Can you guys handle affidavits for court orders and warrants?"

"Yeah, we'll do that. Byatt and I will need to stay away from the site. We'll be able to take care of the paperwork." Smeg couldn't believe those words had come out of his mouth; he could not recall ever having volunteered to do paperwork.

Smeg ran his hand through his hair. His wife had called him a silver fox; he wondered if his hair was still his best feature. She had first noticed him from across an open foyer and walked over to introduce herself. At least that's what she told him later on. At the time, her ruse was to join him in line at McDonald's. She'd also said, recalling the moment, that she didn't eat fast food and threw her purchase in the garbage on her way back to her office. Smeg decided that must be true love. And a waste of a perfectly good hamburger. He called Byatt with an update.

The coordinator had been in touch with the head of Human Resources at Environment, who agreed to the operation. Someone in their office would be assigned to work confidentially with Aaftab to create a suitable resume and then bring him up to speed on the work of the ministry. The resume would be shared with Golding. Aaftab had taken a couple of environmental science courses at university, which would help him speak credibly on the topic even without a background in animal diseases. HR would be in close contact with him throughout the operation in order to answer questions and help craft his responses.

"Will he need an online presence?" Byatt asked. "I'd say Facebook for sure and maybe Instagram. A thirty-something individual would have some sort of presence."

"I hadn't thought of that," Smeg said. "Abercrombie wouldn't likely search him online, would he?"

"No," Byatt said. "But others in the office will and would be surprised if they didn't find anything. We'll need to create accounts using his persona."

"Okay, I'll leave that bit to you." Probably went without saying that Smeg couldn't figure that one out.

"We'll have to pull back, you and I," Byatt said, her voice earnest. "So we don't get in Aaftab's way or risk blowing his cover. I'll let Golding know we've had all our questions answered at this point. That way, they will think our investigation has moved elsewhere."

Surveillance would be set up once Aaftab was assigned an office and the team could get in to install a camera, in there, as well as in the hallway. The cameras would transmit a live feed to the intercept office in a rented space on the floor below, as well as to an undercover officer posing as a security desk guard in the main floor lobby. That person would let the team know when everyone had left the office so installation of cameras could occur. It would also alert the team when Abercrombie entered the building.

"Aaftab will wear a mic at all times," Smeg said. "Our staff will watch and listen to the recording live and make notes, which they will pass along to us. We will decide which recordings to transcribe in full. We'll also analyze the wire worn by Aaftab."

"Looks like we're set," Byatt said. "And with an impressive team."

The moment Aaftab walked into the bull pen and pulled up a chair beside Byatt, Smeg knew he was exactly what they were looking for: boisterous, easy-going, chatty. He launched right in outlining how he moonlighted as a talent scout for a university hockey team and played a minor coaching role with the Edmonton Oil Kings.

"Just with the alternate goalies," he said. "I'm not at the calibre of the big leagues, the goalies that are actually in the line-up."

Smeg sat up straight in his chair. "Edmonton has some high-ranked goalies at its disposal. It must be gratifying, involvement on the ground with a junior hockey team."

"You must be a hockey fan," Aaftab said. "You're very informed."

"Absolutely." Smeg appreciated the recognition of that fact. "Have you thought about pursuing your sports prowess as a career?"

"What I love is the gratification of helping athletes. I think that aspect might be lost in the struggle to make a living at it. Besides, my true love is the environment."

Byatt's eyebrows rose. "I thought the environment bit was part of your character, not your real life."

Aaftab grinned. "All that about hockey is also fabricated. I thought I'd demonstrate my character as a way of introducing myself."

Smeg laughed. "Well done. Abercrombie will love you."

"Have you chosen a name?" Byatt asked.

"Matt Patel."

"Pleased to meet you, Patel." Smeg extended his hand, which Patel shook firmly.

"I'll be working with you on your social media platform," Byatt said, extending her hand as well. "We'll need to take some photos and develop a background story, including a wife so you can commiserate with Abercrombie about her health. Then we'll work with IT to backdate your accounts by a few years. You'll also need to take down any current accounts you have and you'll need to look different. Maybe facial hair?"

"I don't have any accounts. They aren't helpful in my line of work." Patel rose to leave. "And yes, I'll start the hair growth now."

It looked to Smeg like Patel had already started; he himself couldn't produce that much facial hair in a week, let alone a day.

Chapter Twenty

Smeg positioned himself at the kitchen window as he answered the phone, yet again. An endless array of urgent calls from the office threatened his morning. Although, it had already been derailed by an argument with his stepson, who hadn't managed to get the trash cans to the curb before the garbage truck arrived. Now the bins overflowed in the alley, and he'd have to deal with the mess for two weeks until their next pickup day. Already the magpies were helping themselves—banana peels, Mega Bowls wrappers, empty chip bags. Then there was the chaos from the office that also wasn't of his making. And it wasn't really chaos or urgent. They could reorganize the furniture just fine without his input. He was preparing to tell them so when he heard Byatt's voice on the line. His mood improved.

"Unless you're calling about office furniture?" he asked cautiously.

"What do you think about colour coding? Choosing a desk tone that reflects your personality?"

Smeg laughed. "Don't want to consider what my colour would be."

"Definitely red. A mover and shaker."

"The only place I'm moving is out of the line of fire while they get the job done. Don't know why we need to change things anyway."

"I'm steering clear of the process by hiding out in a back hallway."

"Maybe we can move our desks back there," he said. "We could avoid many problems that way."

Byatt relayed what she'd found on Rodriguez's Facebook account. Mostly mundane stuff, he thought, as he watched a hearty soul reach into the trash can, sending the scavenger birds scuttling for safety. The cigarette hanging from his mouth gave an illusion of warmth, the smoke curling around his face. The man wore many layers of clothing and could certainly compete with the birds in a struggle for survival in the frigid temperatures. Smeg marvelled at the tenacity needed to endure such conditions. He preferred to have the bottles beside the can so the unhoused people didn't have to dig through the bags, but Paul hadn't got that part done either. He knew the neighbour across the back alley didn't like him encouraging bottle pickers, or "scum" as he called them. "We don't need that type of person in our neighbourhood," he said.

But scum, Smeg knew, was a different character altogether, and he returned his focus to Byatt's telling of Rodriguez's posts. You'd think the guy's life was a whirlwind of social engagements. But even Smeg knew social media encouraged such presentation. Byatt moved on to the woman Rodriguez had the affair with, Ylva Erikksen. Her account proved very interesting, she said. The profile picture featured heavy-rimmed glasses, more sexy than bookish, with wavy hair dyed an Anime red. The overall schoolgirl image was not consistent with Erikksen's age.

"And Rodriguez took the bait," Smeg said.

"For a short time anyway, then she disappeared from his account."

"What did she do at that point?"

"She appears to have spent time outside Rodriguez's house. She posted a picture of his family taken through the front window from across the street with the caption, 'should have been mine.'"

"Did Rodriguez respond?"

"No, he'd un-friended her by that point."

"Did anyone respond?"

"A few likes but no comments. It's over the top. People would want to distance themselves from such an invasive post. She's clearly stalking him."

"Make a note of the people who liked the comment in case we need to talk to them later on." Smeg looked at the steam rising from houses that lined the back alley. "Anything else?"

"Once she was jilted, she moves on to anger. At that point, she suddenly feels she was cheated out of her share when the business collapsed. And she thinks it's the failure of the business that came between her and Rodriguez. She believes that he loves her but wanted to distance himself from her for financial reasons."

"I wonder if there's anything to the theory that he cheated her out of money?"

"They both seem sleazy to me. I can't read Rodriguez, he's both hot and cold and this Erikksen woman is delusional."

"We should talk to her," Smeg said.

"I'll set it up." Byatt ended the call.

Erikksen lived in an aging downtown high-rise whose prime units overlooked the river valley. Smeg recalled the building's developers proposing the project in the late 60s. Many Edmontonians weren't pleased with the idea of its multiple stories casting a shadow on the period homes of the neighbourhood. He was one of them. The area had a long history of building displacement. Surely the Indigenous people in Treaty Six, whose structures had been replaced by examples of various and highly touted architectural styles, were also displeased with what was positioned as progress. As predicted, that first high-rise was just the beginning, as soon after came an onslaught of tall buildings, each one lacking imagination, along the north side of the river and the old homes disappeared one by one.

Fading late afternoon sun glided toward the horizon on a brilliant orange carpet and snuffed out the light from the parking lot behind the building. Byatt turned her headlights on to park. They took the path through the snow around to the main entrance, quickly followed someone who had unlocked the front door, and found the elevator to the third floor. They walked the length of the musty, poorly lit hallway to Erikksen's condo, a northeast corner unit that would see the morning sun but predominantly faced the back. Out her window would be a view of Byatt's car tucked between a Chevrolet Spark and a Ford Fiesta. Erikksen opened the door and gave an exaggerated sigh.

"How did you get into the building? Soliciting isn't allowed in here."

In that case, Smeg thought, *her thickly applied makeup isn't an indication of what she does for a living.*

"We're not selling." Byatt introduced herself and Smeg.

"Oh, I'm sorry. I forgot you were coming." She ushered them in with a brusque wave.

Byatt stepped in ahead of Smeg. Peering past her, he saw a fifty-something woman with deep golden skin that looked like she'd spent time on a beach. Given it was January, he doubted that was so. Byatt hadn't mentioned any Facebook posts about recent travel. And on second thought, the look was more tanning bed rash.

"You've caught me in the middle of applying massage oil." She, too, sized him up, the parts she likely saw that extended on either side of Byatt, who still stood in front of him.

They were looking for information, but the image of her applying massage oil was too much and the wrong kind.

"We have a few questions," Smeg said.

"Officer Byatt mentioned something about Rodriguez. Is he finally being investigated about the logging company?" She led them into the living room without waiting for an answer and sat on the edge of a long, plush, emerald-green couch. "I'd love to get my money back."

Byatt and Smeg took the two chairs opposite. Byatt chose the hard-backed chair, and Smeg was left to sink into the depths of an overly soft armchair. The room smelled of eucalyptus and peppermint.

"No," Byatt said and shifted forward. "It's about his wife. You heard that she recently died?"

"Oh," she said, with a shaky smile. "What happened?"

Smeg scrutinized her and wondered if he had seen her before. There was something familiar about her eyes, like they'd watched him.

"Have you seen him recently?" Byatt asked.

Smeg tried to mirror Byatt's shift forward but couldn't manage it. He wondered if he would be able to remove himself from the chair when the time came.

"No." Her eyes narrowed to a point where the sculpted eyebrows almost came together. "Why?"

"We're looking into the circumstances surrounding Hammond's death. We want to talk to anyone who might have knowledge of her in the days and weeks leading up to her death." Smeg watched to see which way the eyebrows would go this time. They stayed pasted in place.

She folded her arms firmly across her chest, and her voice tightened. "I didn't know the woman, never met her, so there's not much I can tell you."

"But you knew Rodriguez," Smeg said.

"Like I said. I haven't seen him in a while."

"When exactly?" he asked.

"We bumped into each other a couple of months ago. He was in a hurry, so we didn't talk long."

"Did you try to contact him after that?" Byatt said.

"Sure." She looked down. "Once or twice."

It was impossible to warm to the woman, and Smeg was beginning to feel for Rodriguez. Certainly, they had intruded upon her day, but did she understand they were investigating a murder? And that she might be implicated?

"What was his response?" he asked.

"I think he's mad at me. It likely has to do with the money."

"What do you mean?" Byatt asked.

"You already know about the failed logging company."

"It went bankrupt," Smeg said. "No one walked away with money. How does Rodriguez owe you?" The mad-at-me routine seemed contrived. He chose not to engage, although that might be a gamble that wouldn't pay off if she were looking for allies.

"He made a promise to me. We were going to get married. The company was our livelihood."

"You feel betrayed." Byatt assumed her air of the caring cop.

"I think there's money involved. He took his share and didn't want to split it with me, so he bolted."

"Do you have evidence of that?" Smeg said. Finding evidence of missing money might be a motivation for stalking.

"Nothing concrete. But I know him. He loved me. Still does. So why is he avoiding me?"

Yikes. "He doesn't seem to want you in his life. Is it possible you misread the situation?" Smeg, the unsympathetic cop, asked.

"The only thing I misread is the depth of his ability to lie. To me. To himself. Maybe now that his wife is gone, he'll get back to what's important to him."

"Did you hope for a day when he'd come back to you?"

"I didn't want her or anyone else to get sick and die. I'm just saying he may change his tune now that he's single."

"How did you know she was sick?" Byatt asked.

"You said."

"No. I just said she died." The caring cop had left the room.

"Well, I assumed she was sick. What else do middle-aged women die from?"

Byatt raised her eyebrows, but didn't say anything. Smeg wasn't sure if Erikksen was a suspect, but he knew they needed her onside—there'd be more questions for her later on.

He changed tack. "You settled into life in Edmonton?"

"I've got a good job now as a customer service rep for a heavy equipment company," Erikksen said. "Alberta's oil and gas economy seems able to survive protests. People just aren't as passionate here, don't try to take down companies who are just trying to make ends meet."

"Make ends meet? Oil and gas companies set the bar higher than that," Byatt said.

"But Albertans understand how the economy works. You don't have a socialist government."

Byatt raised her eyebrows again. Smeg began the process of raising himself out of the chair. Politics was not something he wanted to discuss with her. Once on his feet he said, "We'll be in touch if we have more questions."

On the way back down the elevator, Smeg said, "What do you make of her saying she didn't know about Hammond's death?"

"I'd be surprised if she didn't know. On her Facebook feed, there's evidence of stalking Rodriguez beyond watching his house from her car. There's recent photos of him that he may not know she took."

Smeg nodded. "She looked familiar to me. I think I've seen her in the lobby of Rodriguez's office building. Just standing, as if she was waiting for someone."

Byatt turned toward him. "You know, I think you're right."

Erikksen was an excellent candidate for psychiatric intervention. Although Smeg could have assumed that based on what he'd known, prior to their meeting, about her recent obsessive behaviour. The Rodriguez they knew was coloured by investigating him as a potential killer, but Erikksen's interpretation seemed to peg Rodriguez as a thief and a liar. He wondered if her fixation had been there in their early years together and if Rodriguez had ever been concerned that he was her prey. Or had that been a recent addition to her personality? Smeg had pored over the business's documents that were in the public record, and everything was in order. Setting up the business was clearly a mutual act. The dissolution was filed by Rodriguez, but she had signed in all the appropriate places. Something had gone off the rails for Erikksen in the intervening years.

Where to begin. Erikksen was stalking Rodriguez, Abercrombie's wife was an irritant, and some yet-to-be-identified person had targeted Byatt. A surveillance unit followed Abercrombie for most of a day prior to launching the sting operation in hopes of establishing his comings and goings. With that initiative already in the works, Smeg committed firmly to going in that direction.

He had known the pair of stakeout officers for years and appreciated their unlikely chemistry: one was a clearheaded, feminist activist who neither drank nor smoked; the other, a chain-smoking borderline alcoholic known as a man's man. Smeg liked them both. He himself had done some surveillance work when he was younger, but only until he discovered that it was far less interesting than it sounded. He could neither cope with the clock ticking in slow motion on the dashboard nor could he stare at a spot for hours and maintain any degree of focus without eating nonstop. And meditating was just not within his genetic makeup.

Weariness overwhelmed him, dropped his head heavily against the horse's flank. He let it rest there. Just a minute. Guy Vanderhaeghe seemed to sum up surveillance work nicely.

The unit reported to Smeg that they followed Abercrombie from when he left his house at five a.m. He stopped at Tim Hortons, then continued on to work. They followed him into the parkade, through the mall, across a pedway, and under a staircase all the way to the lobby of his office tower. *Clearly, he doesn't have seniority based on the location of his parking stall*, Smeg thought. Abercrombie left his office at eight a.m. and drove to the stadium fitness centre, where he entered with a gym bag. He came out an hour later, tossed the gym bag on the passenger seat and drove back to work. He stayed there until 11:30 a.m. when he drove home and took the dog for a walk. After a short stint in the house, he returned to work. He left again at 2:30 p.m., picked up his wife, and took her to a doctor's office.

From where the officers were located in the parking lot, it appeared that Abercrombie went into the appointment with his wife. Smeg knew that only in the movies could operatives park right outside the window and watch without being noticed. Some of what the officers reported had been surmised. Abercrombie then took his wife back home, stopped at a drugstore, then went back to work where he stayed until six p.m. All in all, the activities sounded tedious to Smeg. The most interesting part of the day had apparently been the squirrels, who clearly living in the attic, ran up and down the exterior walls of Abercrombie's house bringing food and other bits. Much like Abercrombie did for his wife.

"Unless there's something other than gym clothes in that bag there doesn't appear to be much here," Smeg said.

"Although, it wouldn't be the first time drugs were trafficked from a fitness centre," the teetotaler said. "You'll recall a couple years back when Power Fitness was charged with trafficking in steroids." She turned to her partner. "But you'd know more about that."

The boozy cop appeared unfazed by his reputation. "The drugstore could also be moving illicit drugs. The one he stopped at is a small independent in a strip mall."

"Okay," Smeg said. "We'll check out both of those places."

They weren't yet done with Abercrombie. Smeg was relieved to have new leads. After all, he had convinced Singer to set up a sting based on Abercrombie's behaviour. Being completely wrong might have hastened his next launch into retirement. Just as he'd changed his mind about that.

Chapter Twenty-One

As they'd agreed in the pre-launch meeting, Golding was briefed on Patel's arrival. She was told his position in the Minister's office had ended, and he needed to be placed in the department. It came as no surprise to Smeg that such an appointment was made without the raising of eyebrows. In his own experience, a so-called fair hiring policy could be abandoned at the drop of a commissioner's Stetson. Eager to please her superiors, Golding accepted the decision without question. It also saved her the lengthy time required to post and interview, she later told Patel. Smeg recognized her quick acquiescence had value to them as well; no questions asked meant no delving into Patel's background. She apparently gushed to him upon his arrival that the position open in her sector was ideal, as it suited his background and experience perfectly. No surprise there, given they had created his portfolio to do just that.

Reading over the transcript from Patel's first day, the tedious meetings and interactions on the surface made the public service as a career about as appealing to Smeg as eating sawdust. But something lurked below, something that had harmed Hammond and threatened Byatt. Knowing

Byatt may have been put at risk during her visits to that place made his blood boil. His hands shook. The thought of another partner coming to harm was more than he could bear. He stopped reading; it hit him that his trembling hands were due to fear. He'd become attached again, a good thing from a policing perspective, but not so good for his blood pressure.

From the outset of the transcript, Smeg felt Patel displayed commendable interest, particularly in relation to Golding's self-aggrandizement. Smeg instructed the team to transcribe the entire first day in full, as it included introductions to all the key members of the unit. It was also a rare occasion when Golding was fully engaged in her team.

Golding: I came from the University of Alberta on secondment. The government was interested in my work with the French language community and, of course, my leadership skills.

Patel: Do you do a lot of work with the French community?

Golding: Oh yes. Because I speak fluent French, I'm an asset in dealing with environmental issues with French-speaking populations like the Métis in the north. Resource development is accused of producing toxic by-products and polluting lands that are crucial for endangered species. Indigenous populations rely on some of those species: bison, caribou, grouse.

Patel: And, of course, Indigenous communities are often left out in the cold in terms of the wealth created.

Golding: But our position is to support the government.

Patel: Of course.

[pause]

Patel: Do you travel throughout the province a lot?

Golding: Not so much anymore. Now I'm needed in the office to respond whenever the Minister needs something.
Patel: The woman I replaced. Was her name Deena? What can you tell me about her work? I assume I'll be picking up those threads?
Golding: Some of her work I've handed off to other staff who have more experience. We'll ease you in slowly. You'll be paired up with Delbert Abercrombie to get to know the ropes. There's a project you'll work on with him that I think you'll enjoy. It's related to the wildfire situation. Reduction in forests and the relationship to endangered species. Let's go see if he's in his office.

Smeg switched from the transcript to the recording in order to get the nuance of voice tones. Abercrombie was jovial upon meeting Patel.

"Happy to have another male on board," he said. "I'm a bit overrun here."

Patel said, "I know what you mean, mate."

"You have an impressive background," Abercrombie said. "I can see why they've offered you to us."

"Hope I can be of assistance. How about you? What's your background? I've been told you're very experienced."

Abercrombie laughed. "If you mean old, then yes. I have a diploma from NAIT and a few university courses, but I started here way back when you didn't need those sorts of things. A high school diploma got you in the door."

Patel reported to the team, in the debrief meeting in the precinct boardroom, that he spent the remainder of the morning reviewing policies and procedures while waiting for his email account to be activated. He asked if they'd like a rundown. Smeg declined. What he did want was something concrete to report to Singer, but knowing that these operations take time, he was pleased with day one. They now had a better sense of the personalities Hammond had worked most closely with, from the egoist to the control freak, with some genuine oddities in between. It was hard to imagine which of them was not capable of poisoning a colleague. What was truly baffling was the motive behind targeting Byatt. Had she been getting too close to discovering something? He needed to take another look at her notes from those visits.

"I signed a confidentiality agreement. That's a first for me." Patel grinned. "Lying under oath, since I'm reporting literally everything."

"It's Patel who lied, not you personally. Aaftab can still sleep at night. Anyway, your whole job is lying," the coordinator said.

"I do understand the need for confidentiality in some respects. Like if the ministry recommends a course of action that the government then rejects for political reasons. But the material and conversations I've encountered so far would put most cocktail party attendees to sleep. Even in the office, those conversations result in a lot of checking one's phone and pretending to have important emails to answer."

"Overall, how did the team function as a unit?" Smeg asked.

"They're personable. We all had lunch together. I let it be known that I'd met the Deputy Minister a few times. That resulted in a collective furrowing of brows. I also hinted that my plan is to climb the corporate ladder."

Back at his desk, Smeg reviewed Byatt's notes from her last visit to Hammond's place of work. He spent the better part of an hour, while waiting for Byatt to finish up paperwork, reading and rereading. Each pass through raised his suspicions further. He recalled, when Byatt used the term dysfunctional, that he had interpreted the collective behaviours of the staff as having crossed the line of moral standards. He saw an opening in her notes where her water bottle could have been tampered with and remembered the day he'd been offered coffee that he subsequently dumped in the sink because it was revolting. At the time, he hadn't questioned beyond the thought it had been made by someone who was coffee maker challenged. But now he wondered. And his mind wandered. To Alisha Acharya, the former colleague who had become ill before leaving the work unit for another job. Beyond lying and cheating to get ahead, there were many examples of elaborate stories and unsolicited details on each other's backgrounds designed to shape the narrative. Unfortunately, all of it was circumstantial.

Smeg rubbed the bridge of his nose. A nap would be a welcome interlude in his day. Byatt was rapidly approaching; he reached for his parka. They'd agreed to go check out Abercrombie's fitness centre.

Smeg settled for a parking spot by the back fence. Litter laced the perimeter of the large stadium lot like the remnants of a tailgate party, frozen in the snow that had blown to the edges. People moving to and from the light rail transit station came into focus as he and Byatt got closer, a diverse drove more representative of the working-class community than the downtown office crowd that beelined toward the fitness centre. What was also illuminated by the afternoon sun was street art that lined the walls of the station, paintings that told a story of those neighbourhood people. Even to Smeg's untrained eye, the murals were thoughtfully rendered and inspiring. They joined the uninspiring crowd, clad in shades of grey and brown, and headed to the gym.

"Did you notice some of that art has been tagged?" Byatt asked.

Smeg stared at her.

"Graffiti. Someone has spray-painted over parts of the mural," she said. "Why would someone cover the art? Wouldn't they see unity with different street art forms and want to respect it?"

Smeg watched his feet. He didn't want to trip over snow piles or slip on the ice. It wasn't a good look heading into a gym. This was the first he'd heard of respecting street art. But now that the subject had been introduced, he appreciated the concept.

"I don't know," he said. "It's just another form of expression. From a policing perspective, we see it as vandalism, but the kid with the spray paint might see it as personal space that doesn't exist anywhere else for them."

Now Byatt stared straight ahead. "Maybe I should have gotten myself a spray can as a teenager. Personal space in defiance of my mother."

"She would have loved that." He smiled at her. "To go along with your rugby playing."

He held the door open and followed her in. The stadium fitness centre had a funky smell, much like Byatt's gym, and sort of like his stepson's laundry basket.

"You must feel right at home here," Smeg said as the door closed behind them with a soft thud.

"We have bodybuilder types. This place is more selfie-obsessed millennials and insanely fit seniors," Byatt said.

In that moment, Smeg realized his presence in the place would need to be explained. "How do you want to play this?" he asked. "I'm clearly not here for a Pilates class."

Byatt turned toward him and, after seemingly considering her options, said. "Why don't you observe from the door? If anyone asks, you're waiting for me. I'll go inquire about a membership and see if I can get a tour of the place."

First thing Smeg noticed was a guy in a glass-enclosed office using a pager. A pager, a relic of 1992. Oddly out of place in the city-run facility, that, while not exactly modern, had been state of the art at a time more recent than that pager. Clearly, the entire municipal enterprise didn't exist for moving drugs or laundering drug money, but that guy in the office could be making a little on the side.

When Byatt returned, he said, "Next time you're here, ask that guy in the glass office if he knows where you can get a painkiller. Something strong."

"Why?"

"He has a pager."

"Ah."

"What did you discover in your travels?"

"I discovered that it's time for lunch. Even watching exercise makes me hungry." She held the door, then followed Smeg back outside. "Seriously, though, I didn't see much that was amiss. We should put a tail on Abercrombie and have them follow him in next time. I wonder who he talks to?"

Smeg agreed. Although he hadn't lost focus on that lunch idea.

Next stop, following the pizza place in the strip mall, was the drugstore. The place was dusty, much like the restaurant, where sparse offerings on the shelves were carefully spaced apart, rather than the kind of place where items flew off the shelves on sale days. The pharmacist, or what passed for one, was the only person visible in the shop. He didn't look up when they entered, which gave them time to look around. Smeg noticed the pharmacist's framed license on the wall, although no guarantee the person they saw in front of them was actually the person with the license; but the name tag did match. As Smeg stepped up to the 'order here' window, he noticed two boarding passes to Bariloche, Argentina, sitting on the counter. He envisioned a secret compound behind high gates.

"Nice," Smeg said and pointed to the tickets. "Winter getaway?"

"Can I help you?" the pharmacist asked.

"My wife is looking for pain medication for her migraines," Smeg said and cocked his head toward Byatt, who stood pasted to his side.

"Are these ongoing migraines?" the pharmacist asked, giving Byatt a piercing look.

Byatt tugged on the stray strands of hair that lay limp against her face. She'd created the look with her greasy fingers after eating what was arguably a very good pepperoni, mushroom, and green pepper pizza. The blank stare she gave could have made him wonder if a soul resided within.

Smeg reached an arm around her shoulders. "She's had migraines for many years. We've tried a lot of things, but nothing seems to work. My friend said you helped him out with his headaches."

The pharmacist spoke slowly to Byatt. "What was it you wanted?"

"Not the run-of-the-mill stuff. We've tried all that." Smeg gave Byatt a loving look.

"Have you tried tinted glasses?"

"Tinted glasses?"

"Yes, precision-tinted eyeglasses help normalize brain activity." He looked again at Byatt. "For those that have it."

"Brain activity?"

This time he looked at Smeg. "Sorry. I meant whose visual cortex gets overstimulated." Then back at Byatt. "Although I don't suppose over-stimulation is a problem here."

"We were hoping for medication," Smeg said.

"There are many possibilities. We'd need a diagnosis in order to know which medication is right for her. Perhaps she can answer a few questions." The pharmacist turned away from Smeg.

Byatt let her head drop as though she was hoping for inspiration from a phone opened to Google.

"Have you tried over-the-counter pain relievers?"

She looked past him. "Don't work. Even when I take a handful of them."

"Have you had an MRI or CT scan?"

"No."

"Prescription drugs such as sumatriptan or rizatriptan?"

"No."

"Dihydroergotamine?"

"What?"

"Lasmiditan?"

"No."

"Have you had your blood pressure checked? Are you on anti-depressants?"

Byatt stared at him.

"Botox injections?"

"No."

"I don't think I can help you."

Returning to the truck, Byatt said. "I think our performance was a big fail."

Smeg agreed. "I think it might have worked better if you hadn't answered his questions honestly. I see why we engaged real undercover cops for our operation. Ones with training."

"I did have time to notice a few things while giving the place a blank stare. There were two cash registers. One possibly for cash-only transactions? The shelves looked like those in a zombie apocalypse: dental floss but no toothpaste, hair conditioner but no shampoo, Aleve was the only pain killer, and I didn't bother to check the expiry date on the packaged cakes. Also, no other customers. How would a place like that stay in business?"

"How indeed," Smeg said. "We'll have to come at this another way. Maybe Patel can find out what Abercrombie picks up here. You know, for his own wife's supposed health issues."

"And how does this get us to arsenic? We seem to have shifted our focus to drug dealing."

"I did notice arsenic trioxide on the shelf behind the pharmacist. My wife took it; it's a cancer drug. Low doses could easily cause Abercrombie's wife's symptoms. Higher doses could lead to death following the type of illness Hammond had."

"He could have taken care of both of them at once. One-stop shopping."

"Win-win."

As Smeg reached for the driver's side door handle, he noticed someone had written in the dirt on the hood, *nothing to see here*. The lettering was childlike and oddly neat.

He scanned the outer perimeter of the parking lot and, seeing no one, he peered closer at the pathway leading out of the lot to the north through the trees. Nothing. The sidewalk leading south was also quiet.

No real surprise. The strip mall was out of the way, located just off Strathearn Drive. Most of the shops were vacant. The few cars at the edge the lot may have been left there by residents of the nearby walk-up apartment.

Byatt looked confused. She stepped back to get perspective on the lettering, then circled the truck, looking at the ground.

"There are a couple of footprints here that look recent and are too small to be either of us."

"It's not much of a threat," he said. "Someone just wants us to know we're being followed."

"Why, though? We need to figure out who did that." Byatt pulled out her phone and took a photo of the lettering and the ground around the truck.

"What does it mean?" Smeg asked.

"Maybe that you should wash your truck?"

"I'm afraid to. Dirt may be all that's holding it together."

"I wonder if Abercrombie had something to do with it?" Smeg asked. "Although I thought he was at the office this morning."

Byatt clicked an app on her phone. "Yeah, Patel just posted a selfie on Instagram of him and Abercrombie. Although it could have been taken earlier."

Smeg's mind would have gone to the surveillance tape. But he wasn't a Millennial.

What about his wife?" he asked.

"She's too afraid to leave the house. Although the footprints could be those of a smaller woman."

Day two, and the intercept office reported Patel's early arrival. The job had flexible hours but the team had agreed it would be best if he matched Abercrombie's start and end times. Abercrombie would be impressed, and it would provide an opportunity for conversation.

"What's it been like working here all these years?" Patel asked.

"Honestly, I love it. There's always a new challenge."

"I'm looking forward to that," Patel said. "My last job was dull as ditch water. Literally. I was monitoring agrichemical contamination in irrigation ditches to understand the threat to farmland. But I felt like I was becoming more stagnant than the water."

Smeg, who had opted to listen to the early morning interaction through the live feed, thought Patel might be laying it on a bit thick.

Abercrombie laughed. "Well, I don't think you'll find that here."

"I may not be here too long anyway," Patel said. "My plan is to move up the chain as quickly as possible."

"I had those ambitions once, too, but my wife requires a lot of care, so that has become my focus."

"I understand totally, mate. My wife is also ill. A bit of a burden at times, eh?"

"Sometimes. But I love her dearly. Mostly, I feel bad for her. She really is incapacitated."

"Is that a signed photo of Tim Horton?" Patel asked.

"Yeah, I met him once at the opening of one of his doughnut shops. I was a teenager at the time, and he stopped to talk to me. He was such a great guy."

"That's impressive. Does that explain the paper cup collection?'

Abercrombie laughed. "No, the explanation there is I haven't got around to walking them to the garbage. You have the advantage of a fresh, clean office."

Now Patel laughed. "I'm sure it won't stay that way. So, are you into hockey?"

"I listen to it on the radio, but my true love is football. Too small to play but not too small to be a big fan. Actually, watching sports is likely my downfall. A person can get out of shape in a hurry, sitting on the couch eating doughnuts."

"But you work out at the stadium regularly?"

"Yes, I have a really good trainer over there, Trevor MacIntyre. He works with the Edmonton Wildcats and Edmonton Huskies. He also worked with San Francisco 49ers players."

"Cool. I'd love to get in with a guy like that."

"I can talk to him if you like. See if he has room for a new client."

"Awesome," Patel said.

All in all, Smeg thought it had been a good day. Abercrombie seemed to be taking a shine to Patel, who responded by sharing himself. He told Abercrombie that he'd met his wife, Olivia, at college in the States. She was an American, beautiful and active in campus club environment groups. She happily followed him back to Canada when they graduated and they'd had some laughs before she got sick. She'd become a Canadian citizen by then, so health care covered most of her medical expenses. But Patel complained to Abercrombie, there were still bills to pay, and it didn't help that she could no longer work. Abercrombie, of course, commiserated.

Chapter Twenty-Two

Meanwhile, back at the precinct, Paul had a report from his review of the tips line and was waiting for Smeg at his desk. There was stuff about Erikksen he felt the detectives should know right away. He had that fire in his eyes, and Smeg was proud to watch it burn. Byatt was on her way to join them.

"Hiya," Paul called out as Byatt approached.

He was sitting on the edge of the desk, swinging one leg, and his mouth hung slightly open.

Byatt reached out and clasped his wrist. "You're on trend this morning. Nice shoes."

They were new, dark forest green sneakers with black laces. They offset his khaki pants and a grey dress shirt. Smeg had twigged onto a general sense of growing professionalism in the boy, but couldn't have pinpointed it to the shoes.

Paul's head bobbed up and down a few times before he launched in. "One caller said Erikksen was obsessed with Rodriguez. She bought groceries at a bulk foods store he was known to frequent and lattes at his favourite coffee shop, in the hopes of running into him. She knew what time he left the house in the morning and when he took his lunch break. The caller identified herself as a friend of hers. Apparently, Erikksen is extremely bright and capable of weaponizing her talents. She came to Alberta with the intent of winning Rodriguez back. She believed if she hovered around him long enough, he would announce his love for her."

"She's in love?" Smeg asked.

"The caller seemed to think her motivation stems from being jilted, not from actual love. Erikksen's an obsessed overachiever and feels her failed relationship with Rodriguez reflects badly on her. Something she couldn't control and it eats at her."

"I wonder if Rodriguez knows. And what his role might have been in her downfall. Does she have reason to be pissed at him?" Byatt asked.

"The caller seemed to think it was all on Erikksen. The two of them had consumed a couple of bottles of Prosecco one night and, based on what Erikksen shared, the caller became concerned. Erikksen felt betrayed. She'd worked twice as hard as Rodriguez to keep the logging business afloat while he got all the credit. *Logging and Sawmilling Journal* ran a feature citing their company as the best new start-up of the year. It featured Rodriguez."

"He may not be completely innocent in all this," Smeg said.

"He may not be aware," Byatt said. "Some men have always been pampered, given credit when it wasn't their due. Women tend to eat a lot of that shit, especially in the workplace."

"That shouldn't let him off the hook." Paul's brow had furrowed. "He was the one who ended the relationship, both professional and personal, but the severance wasn't necessarily vindictive. She rolled it into a madness, a doubting of reason, or so it would appear."

“We know the business failed, but why did he end their love affair?” Smeg asked.

“Maybe just didn’t view it in the same way she did.” Byatt reached down to retrieve a silver garland that had fallen from its perch. “Someone should put this stuff away. Christmas is done gone.”

Smeg looked at the gaudy plastic balls that clung to the artificial tree and had to agree it was sad. He wondered why the tree was flat on one side. His grandma had decorated their Douglas fir with handmade paper snowflakes and spiders. In the later years, when her stiff fingers no longer allowed her to make those things, she bought tinsel. He always got to hang it on the tree.

“What should we do about Erikksen?” he said.

“Maybe we should follow her,” Byatt said. “Or send a trained surveillance team.”

Smeg smiled broadly. “We can likely do it ourselves. This task is simpler than our drugstore caper—we won’t need to talk to anyone.”

He turned to Paul. “Thanks for the update. This is great stuff.”

Paul checked his Apple watch, ruffled his hair and jumped off the desk. Smeg watched him lope back toward the stairwell.

Smeg swung by Byatt’s place to pick her up. She texted to say she’d be right out. Wind blew snow off the ground and swirled it around the large tree trunks on the boulevard and across the road to abut the bank on the other side. Visibility was poor. It was maybe not the best day for tailing Erikksen, but it would have to do. The undercover team at Hammond’s office was gaining traction, but slowly. Smeg still believed their suspect was in that office, but they did need to wrap up other loose ends. Erikksen and Rodriguez were the two prominent ones. He heard the truck door open before he saw Byatt. The crunch of ice breaking the seal was an unmistakable sign of the freeze-thaw cycle of winter.

"Sorry," she said, sliding into her seat. "I was trying to map where Erikksen would likely go today. As a customer service rep, her job takes her out of the office, often multiple times a day, so she could be heading in a variety of directions."

Smeg pulled out into traffic toward Erikksen's apartment, hoping to be early so as not to miss her leaving, and almost sideswiped a delivery van. The driver yelled something he didn't need to hear to grasp the meaning of. Nodding an apology that didn't help much, he slowed down and let the van get well ahead. Likely a better speed for road conditions anyway. Arriving at Erikksen's place, they remained across the street from her parking lot exit.

The blizzard was strengthening, slapping at horse and rider; he could feel the gelding's mane fluttering against his hands clamped to the reins.

He turned the lights off but left the engine running and meagre heat on. Smeg would rather have been reading the novel he had shoved in the glovebox. If he'd been alone, he might have been tempted. He'd become quite adept at reading during long surveillance duties, glancing up every few words.

"At least with the blowing snow our presence is less likely to be noticed," Byatt said.

He also thought he was starting to hone his skills at reading Byatt, one sentence at a time. He was confident she could have done the surveillance alone.

"That will help our talents nicely." Smeg turned toward her and smiled, wondering if he wasn't the handicap.

Byatt pointed. "There she is, turning onto the road."

And just like that, Smeg closed his thoughts about Byatt as tightly as the novel in the glovebox. It was time to get to work.

They followed her to a strip mall in the west end. First stop was a flower shop. Smeg peered through the gloom at the TD Bank and gift shop before his eyes came to rest on Burger Bar. Recognizing it wasn't open, he had almost nodded off when Byatt nudged him and pointed. Erikksen was coming out with a paper-covered arrangement of some sort. Under clearing skies, they could now see Erikksen stride sharply on chunky-heeled boots with flared pants and a belted overcoat that she flipped out of the way as she got into her car. Schoolgirl apparently wasn't her work image.

"Dressed for success," Byatt said.

"Might say power dressed."

"Flowers are an odd thing for a heavy equipment company. Doesn't seem like a sales call." Byatt jotted down the name and address of the shop.

"Could be personal. A fox is a wolf who sends flowers."

"Personal experience?"

"Ruth Brown. 1950s R & B singer."

Reminded of R & B, Smeg hit the start button on his CD player. Paul had told him there were way more music options on his phone. That seemed out of reach to him.

Interest was piqued when Erikksen travelled into Rodriguez's neighbourhood. She pulled up in front of the house and went to the door, package in hand. Rodriguez's son answered, then after a brief conversation, took the flowers from her and closed the door. Erikksen stood for a moment, looking around, and then peered down the side of the house before returning to her car. When she drove into the alley behind the house, Smeg hesitated. It would be too easy to notice them following in the alley. He looped around the block and waited for her to exit.

"She's really scouting the place," Byatt said.

"And not even carefully. She's counting on the son being absorbed in a video game."

From there, they trailed her to a house in Mill Creek. While Erikksen sat watching the house, Byatt used her iPad to search the address of the house in the police database.

"Hilaria Golding's." There was a note of surprise in her voice.

Smeg matched it. "Really? What could be the connection there?"

"Given her interest in Rodriguez, the question might be what's Golding's interest in him?"

The waiting game was short. Golding left the house through the back door and pulled her minivan out of the garage. Erikksen followed her down the street and then to a coffee shop on the east edge of downtown. Golding entered the shop. As Smeg parked across the street from where they'd have a clear view of the interior through the large front windows, Byatt was already reporting what she saw.

"She's joining Rodriguez," Byatt said. "He's reached across the table and taken her hands in his."

"Can you tell if it's a romantic gesture? Or comforting?"

"Why would Rodriguez be comforting Golding? It would be the other way around."

He peered over at Erikksen, who was parked out front. She pounded her fist on the steering wheel. From what he could tell, she appeared to seethe.

He looked over at Byatt, who was now watching Erikksen. After a few minutes, Erikksen sped off, fishtailing on the icy road.

Smeg watched her for a moment before remembering they were following her. Golding would have to wait. Byatt was scribbling in her notebook. They followed Erikksen back to her office, where she remained for the next two hours.

"We should have tailed Golding instead. She might have done something more interesting," Byatt said.

"Let's get lunch," Smeg said.

Byatt took the afternoon surveillance shift alone, while Smeg went back to the office. She promised to call if Erikksen went anywhere of interest. He proceeded to the monitoring room to catch up on recordings from Hammond's office. As he listened, he made notes and tried to draw connections to Hammond's death. The hallway feed showed Golding march swiftly into the office, her coat hanging neatly open, her arms occupied with thick folders and a handbag. She called a cheery greeting to those she passed on the way. In her office, at the end of the hall, Smeg could see her hang her coat and place her things neatly in a row on the shelf, then run her hand along the spines of the books, pushing some back into place. A large pile of folders on the table was straightened, along with the tissues at the back of the desk. She touched up her lipstick and sat down at her computer.

Shortly, she left her office. From there, Patel's mic picked up the thread as he, Golding, and the rest of the team joined a meeting which revealed itself to be about their social media presence, particularly LinkedIn and Twitter. Smeg knew Patel would struggle with the topic. At least he could fall back on being the new guy and keep his mouth shut. The meeting was chaired by three young-sounding consultants who outlined the proposed strategy. Golding cut in.

"If I may, your goal is well thought out and could certainly enhance our engagement. Leadership has often talked about ways to bring individual stakeholders, not just groups, into the conversation. I would suggest we can measure our success by following the comments posted as well as the number of likes and mentions by other users."

"True, and vanity metrics can be helpful," one of the female leads said. "But what we ideally want to see is click-throughs and conversion rates. For example, if we're using LinkedIn, we want to see high numbers of click-throughs to our website."

"Of course," Golding said. "Please continue."

Smeg sensed Golding didn't like being revealed for her lack of social media knowledge. When they moved on to Facebook, she tried again.

"You're targeting millennials with Facebook? That seems unwise," she said. "Boomers might be a better target here."

The male guide jumped up. "Millennials still outnumber baby boomers on Facebook, with 84% saying they use the platform. Even Gen X are on Facebook at higher rates than Boomers. Young people like to say they're not on, but they are." He chuckled. "It's a thing they do."

On the way out, Patel engaged his colleagues in conversation.

"You seem to know quite a bit about social media, Hilaria. More than me for sure."

"And way more than me," Abercrombie said. "I'm a Luddite."

"I have teenagers," Golding said. "And my husband Randy spends a lot of time on X, so I hear a lot about it."

"What does your husband do?"

"He's a researcher at the university. His current role is in the department of veterinary medicine, mainly applying for grants. He's not super stoked about his role. He'd rather be more hands-on."

"Yes," Patel said. "That does sound tedious."

"Grants are the essence of boredom," Abercrombie said. "I worked in grants for a while. Until I could get out."

A phone rang in the background, and Abercrombie said, "That's mine."

After a brief pause, he answered. "Hi Amelia. What's up?"

Smeg scanned his crib sheet. Abercrombie's daughter.

"Just leave it, Amelia."

Pause.

"No. You can't follow them. Let them do their jobs."

At that point, Smeg's phone rang. He paused the recording.

"Erikksen's back at Rodriguez's house," Byatt said. "The house looks quiet, and with the sun going down, she may be making a move of some sort."

"I'm on my way," Smeg said. "I'll park around the corner and hop in with you."

Up and down the block, blinds were closing and drapes pulled shut as the streetlights flickered to life. Erikksen sat in her car until the sun set, which conveniently gave Smeg enough time to get there. The house was dark when she climbed the steps to the front door. He saw her glance up while inserting a key in the lock. Save for this small gesture, her entrance was as someone who lived there. For reasons known only to her, it appeared she had missed her calling. There's a lot of money to be had as a cat burglar. Although, this cat burglar had a key. Once the door closed behind her, a dim light, as from a penlight, bounced ahead of her into Rodriguez's office. The last time he'd visited, the door to the office had been ajar and he'd seen the mess of papers on the desk. He'd itched to flip through the documents and now even more so. Perhaps Erikksen was on to something.

"I'll try and get a closer look." Byatt got out and softly shut the car door.

Smeg watched Byatt's dark form move along the side of the house, slip on the ice, and disappear from view. He held his breath; she rose quickly to her feet. He shifted his attention to the muted light within and its corresponding shadow that now had its back to the front-facing part of the corner window, as she hunched over the desk. Erikksen stayed in the office for a short time before gliding back to the front entrance. Smeg's breath stalled as Erikksen locked the front door and went to the edge of the porch. She glanced in Byatt's direction, but seemed to decide all was in order and headed back to her car. Byatt stayed in place until Erikksen drove off.

"Fortunately, she wasn't faced in my direction, so I was able to get close. She inserted a USB into his computer," Byatt said. "Then seemed to install something."

"Likely a keylogger. Then she can see everything without having to sign in. It has to be activated on his computer and then she can see everything he's typed."

Byatt started the car. "Devious. And he won't notice it because it's buried in the background, hidden among other files. I wonder why she didn't install it remotely? She could have sent an email with the keylogger embedded in a Word document."

"She may have tried, but Rodriguez would have had to open the attachment," Smeg said.

"Is she looking for something to help win him back? Is she seeking revenge?"

"Maybe after the money she feels is owed her. Something to blackmail him with?"

"But how would that feed her undying love?" Byatt asked.

"I don't know. Maybe she's looking for evidence that he loves her. A new angle to play."

"Or evidence he's having an affair with Golding."

"How did she get a house key?" Byatt's brow creased. "And how did she get to a state where she would commit break and enter?"

"And what, if anything, does this have to do with his dead wife?" Smeg clucked his tongue.

He remembered his grade eight math teacher peering down at him with enormous eyes of coal. Focus on the problem, Charlie. It doesn't matter if you want to go to Calgary or not, the question is about distance. He also remembered her saying that grade eight students, being at a particular phase of development, should be homeschooled.

"Possibly nothing," she said. "Soon we will need to turn this over to Cyber Crimes if we don't find any evidence of harm to Hammond."

Byatt dropped him off at his truck. "Let's meet back at the office and go talk to them. If this is going in the wrong direction for us, we'll need to unload it before Singer gets wind of what we're up to."

It was late when they arrived at the detachment, but Smeg knew someone would be on duty. Cyber Crimes doesn't take the night off.

Smeg thought about how easy it was to obtain a keylogger, most being legal and having legitimate uses. Erikksen's own company could be using them to track non-work-related use of their computers.

They did indeed find someone: the night operations manager, Officer Leigh. She appeared to be playing some kind of game on her phone, long legs stretched out in front of her.

"What can I do for you?" she asked.

Smeg gave a brief background of their case and how it had led to following Erikksen. "Where do we go from here?" he asked her.

"We'll need to find out what information Erikksen has in order to determine what she's doing with it. She's likely using an internet café in order to hide her IP address," Leigh said. "We'll put a tail on her to see where she's accessing the internet. Then we can get a warrant."

"What should we do? She's still a suspect in our investigation," Byatt said.

Leigh shook her head. "As soon as she inserted that USB, she entered Cyber Crimes jurisdiction. We'll take it from here and let you know if her activity points to your case. Most cybercrimes are extortion-related, so Rodriguez is her likely target."

"We've already got access to Rodriguez's account, so his end should be easy," Byatt said.

"How so?" Leigh asked. "This only transpired this evening."

"He's a suspect in his wife's murder," Smeg said. "The warrant was just approved."

Leigh pulled up his email account on her computer. "We'll go over this with a fine-toothed comb tomorrow but let's take a quick look."

"Can't we intercept his emails to Erikksen? Get at her that way?"

"No, that's considered wiretapping. It's even harder to get a warrant for that. We're better off following her and identifying the source location."

Smeg pulled up a chair and leaned in to see her screen as she scrolled slowly through Rodriguez's email. "There's something." He pointed. "Amelia Pelham. That's Abercrombie's daughter. Why would she be in touch with Rodriguez?"

"I do recall her approaching him at Hammond's funeral," Byatt said. "He seemed annoyed with the intrusion."

Leigh narrowed in on the emails from her, the first one from the day after the funeral.

Amelia Pelham: *Hey Jay. I wanted to talk more with you yesterday but obvs not the right time. I'm impressed with your work. Can we meet up for coffee?*

Two days later, she followed up.

Amelia Pelham: *You are dope. I think you can help me. Please respond.*

Jay Rodriguez: *I don't know what your game is but I'm not interested.*

Amelia Pelham: *I'm not talking about sex. I think you can help me with my mother. I need to do something. My dad's going off dealing with her all day. He's real salty.*

Another two-day delay.

Amelia Pelham: *Obvs we'd keep it on the downlow. I have access just need your know-how.*

Jay Rodriguez: *Don't contact me again or I'll have to report you.*

Smeg reread the exchange slowly. Just to be clear.

On the way back to the parking lot, he said, "It's too much of a coincidence that Erikksen's targeting him now. I still think there could be a connection to Hammond's death. It's too soon to rule her out."

"Leigh didn't say we had to take her off our list of suspects, just stop targeting the internet activity."

Smeg's head bobbed slightly. There was something about both Erikksen and Rodriguez that irked him. The self-satisfied smiles, the evasive answers to questions, the snippiness, made Smeg hope something could be pinned on them.

"But the big news here is Amelia. What's her game?"

"Do you suppose it was her tailing us to the drug store?" Byatt asked.

It was certainly plausible. They'd already ruled out Abercrombie and his wife as having done the writing on his truck. Now they needed to rule out the daughter. Or find evidence of a crime.

Chapter Twenty-Three

Smeg was starting to feel the strains of a familiar exhaustion. The kind that came weeks into a case of relentless focus, day and night. Doubt, pushed aside with each new lead, nipped at him. Did they have a case here? He rubbed his eyes and refocused on the meeting with Patel and the project coordinator to discuss ways to ramp up the undercover operation. Patel walked into the boardroom looking dapper with his hair beginning to curl over his collar and his beard neatly trimmed, the look of success, like a guy on the rise, promotion only a matter of time. But things were moving too slowly since he'd entered Hammond's workplace, and Singer would soon expect a report. For this reason, they needed Patel to be more assertive about his wife's health and how she was in the way of his ambition to advance quickly.

"How's the assignment you're working on with Abercrombie going?" Smeg asked.

Patel set his keys on the table, leaned back and crossed his legs.

"The wildfires? We haven't really gotten into it. Abercrombie is busy with other projects. It's difficult to match his erratic schedule without a lot to keep me busy. Hanging around after hours looks odd."

"Press him," the coordinator said. "Suggest you'd be happy to come in on Saturday when it's quiet in order to get that one going. Tell him Golding is after action on the file."

"He'll say that's her nature, she presses for action on everything," Patel said. "I've tried that one. But I could mention it's a top priority for the Deputy Minister. Remind him of my relationship there."

"Great. Without other people around, you may also be able to get him to share personal stuff," Smeg said. "What about others in the office who might be inclined to spill information?"

"There's a woman named Russo. She loves to gossip. She often pops into my office and chats in a conspiratorial, flirting kind of way. She has family members with health issues. I can chat her up about that."

"And what about Golding?" the coordinator asked. "How's your relationship with her?"

"Pleasant, but she's hard to pin down. Another reason to get going on the wildfire project. She's happy to talk, but it has to be about a work issue that furthers her own interests. She's definitely a climber." Patel grimaced and put a hand briefly on his stomach.

"What's that about?" Smeg motioned toward Patel's stomach.

"Nothing," he said. "It'll pass."

"How long's it been going on?"

"A couple days."

Smeg was more than suspicious. "We need to get you in for a blood test. And we'll need to take samples in your office. Have you been careful with your water bottle? Anything else someone could have slipped tainted water into?"

Realization landed firmly on Patel's face. "I've been really careful, but maybe coffee? I pick up takeout at Starbucks. Maybe I left it on my desk."

"Okay." Smeg nodded. "Pick up a coffee again today and leave it on your desk. Bring it out with you at lunchtime and pass it to the team at the front desk. We'll have it analyzed."

The next morning, Patel's mic picked up the sound of giggling followed by Russo's voice.

"Look at these German Shepherd puppies," she said.

Her voice was elevated in both excitement and proximity. Smeg imagined shaggy hair and a quick grin.

"Cute picture," Patel said.

"Want to take one home?"

"My wife would love it, but no, not until her health improves."

"A puppy might help. My dogs are what get me through the day. After dealing with my mom's dementia and my brother's craziness, I can't wait to get home to my dogs. They calm me."

"Dementia's difficult," Patel said. "Is she in a care facility?"

"No, she's at home and is still legal guardian to my brother. Which means that I'm responsible for both of them."

"Are you getting assistance? I mean from our employer? Are there programs like flex time or leave that can help out?"

"Yes, but Hilaria won't approve anything like that. She thinks I'm making it up to get out of work."

"That must be annoying."

"She treats us like her personal servants. If we weren't here, she'd have to do all that shit herself. And she doesn't have the background knowledge that people like Delbert and I have."

"What about Deena? She approved her leave."

"But not until the very end, when it was obvious Deena couldn't continue. An earlier leave might have saved her."

Patel's voice lowered. "I heard Deena was killed. Have you heard that rumour?"

"I've heard a million rumours."

"Would anyone here be capable of that?"

"There are jealousies, but that's going too far."

The team in the workplace lobby noted Patel's arrival at the office at 8:00 a.m. Saturday, and when the camera caught up with him, his head was stuck into Abercrombie's office.

"You're here already," Patel said.

"Been here for an hour."

"Impressive. How was your evening?"

"Quiet," Abercrombie said. "My wife was having one of her regular headaches, not a migraine, but enough to wind her up on the couch. We watched three episodes of The Queen.*"*

Smeg wondered what sort of queen as he scanned through the video footage. Paul used to watch one called *RuPaul's Drag Race* featuring a trio of drag queens. Smeg was of a generation where he wasn't sure if he should laugh at the antics or not.

"I haven't watched that, but I'm sure my wife has," Patel said and scoffed. "She spends a lot of time watching movies and television. We used to walk down Whyte Avenue on a Friday night and stop in at whatever restaurant was hopping with activity before meandering through the park and maybe a nightcap on the way home. Now our evenings are pretty boring."

"I know what you mean. For us, you know, we're old, so sitting on the couch suits us. But maybe more difficult for you?"

"Yeah, I mean, I understand she's sick and all. And if it was just interfering with our social life, it would be one thing, but there's also my career." Patel paused. "I should be more sympathetic and I feel guilty about that. You're an inspiration the way you handle things."

"I really don't mind. My wife has always been dependent on me and I like that. It makes me feel as if she needs me," Abercrombie said. "Any hope of improvement for your wife?"

"If we could just find the right medication."

"We've had a bit of luck with a particular drugstore where I know the pharmacist. He's willing to sell me a painkiller that isn't approved by Health Canada. If you're interested, I can tell him you'll stop by."

"That'd be awesome. I'd love to get my life back on track," Patel said. "Hey, I'll get rid of my coat and then we can start on that forest fire project. I've done some research and I think we may want to highlight the woodland caribou and how forest fires have led to their endangerment. I know the Deputy Minister is keen on a profile of resource management that shows it to be a balance between the economic interests of logging and the economic interests of environmental concerns such as caribou cultivation."

"Always economic interests front and centre." Abercrombie laughed. "You'll get used to that."

"Works for me," Patel said. "And Hilaria too seems keen on advancing the economy."

"Hilaria is keen on advancing her own interests. She'd kill to get ahead."

"Oh?"

Smeg hoped Patel would leave that little question hanging and not try to elaborate. It was easy to slip into interrogation, which led people to get defensive and clam up.

"Well, not literally if that's what you're thinking." Abercrombie snorted.

Byatt stuck her head into the viewing room and asked Smeg how it was going. She didn't look hopeful. Smeg welcomed the break; his eyes were starting to blur from staring at the dim images on the screen.

"Watch this clip," he said and skipped back to the bits about Golding. "Both Abercrombie and Russo make reference to Golding's desire to get ahead, seemingly joking, but I wonder if it warrants a closer look."

Byatt watched the conversations; Smeg watched Byatt for her reaction. Could cheerful, golden girl Golding be hiding something under that smooth surface?

"Hmm," Byatt said. "Maybe we should go back through the footage and focus in on Golding."

Smeg hit the back button and started the feed over.

"Here's something," he said. "Abercrombie and Patel leave together at the end of the day. They both call out a goodnight to Golding as they walk by her office. The feed doesn't show anything after that but there's still audio."

"She must be on the phone as we didn't see anyone enter her office," Byatt said.

"An email from the Assistant Deputy Minister just came so I'll be late getting home," Golding said. "He's looking for updated budget numbers for the technology proposals. He's copied the folks in grants management. As usual, he doesn't know who to ask so he's fired it out shotgun style. He needs to learn I'm his go-to."

Pause.

"It'll take me a few hours, babe. Oh, I almost forgot. We were going to go to a movie."

Pause.

"Yes, but I want it in his inbox when he arrives in the morning. I can work up a few budget scenarios and have this done before grants even see that email in the morning."

Pause.

"They appreciate my attention to detail for sure," she said. "What do you have going for dinner?"

Pause.

"The kids will be happy. They love French onion soup."

There was another pause, and then Golding ended the call.

"Not much there beyond evidence of commitment to work," Smeg said.

"Maybe over family, although we'd need to see more of a pattern to confirm that."

Smeg fast-forwarded through the next morning when the entire branch left for a meeting and started watching again upon their return. The hallway was quiet as they all returned to their offices and they were able to hear Golding on the phone again.

"The meeting with her teacher." Golding sighed. "I know it's my turn, but can you go? I'm just heading into a meeting."

Golding thanked him and hung up.

"So, what do we have?" Byatt asked. "Beyond the workaholic bit?"

"Russo talked about Golding's father, a marshmallow with the grandkids, a contrast to how he was with his own kids. Apparently, his health had been bad when Golding was growing up but improved once he retired. A pattern of psychotic episodes meant her father was unable to hold a job for long. They moved north for work when Golding was eight. She was close to him, in part because he valued her intelligence and hard work. Even in his worst hallucinogenic states, he still knew she was gifted, and told her just so she would know, Golding apparently told Russo. He wanted her to continue to believe in herself. Golding told her she couldn't connect with other kids; they seemed whiny but she didn't need them anyway. They got in the way of her goals."

"That's a lot to share given we've seen Golding keep pretty much to herself," Byatt said.

"Russo said she wasn't always like that. She changed when she became hyper ambitious."

"Any idea when that was?" Byatt asked.

"No, but Golding's father apparently had mapped out a plan for her future, which started with her leaving home early to finish high school in Edmonton. She loves discussing work with him at Sunday dinners now that her parents have moved to the city."

"I wonder how much of that is true—Russo is an unreliable narrator."

"Agreed. But I think I'll ask Agarwal for research into veterinary labs. Golding's husband works at one."

After Byatt left, Smeg stared at the wall. Spots of dirt made him think of a Rorschach test, which made him remember the research report on personality disorders found on the front seat of Hammond's car after the accident, bookmarked to alexithymia. He recalled he'd looked it up—dysfunction in emotional awareness, social attachment and interpersonal relating. Caused by childhood trauma. Hammond must have had suspicions about Golding.

He'd need to get Agarwal's team to delve further into that one. And more on psychopathy wouldn't hurt either, given that a salient feature is a focus that's so strong, it can exclude other stimuli, such as ethics. Or pesky colleagues who get in the way of one's career advancement. It was well documented that psychopaths functioned well in high-stress situations, and then there's the charm, which Golding had in abundance. At least, when she had time for it.

Singer had requested their presence and it didn't sound like an invitation to tea. It was a bit of misfortune that Smeg and Byatt bumped into her heading to the cafeteria. To the best of Smeg's knowledge, Singer didn't frequent such places. Lunch to her was a power bar eaten standing up. Had opportunity not presented itself, they might have gotten away with the whole surveillance on Erikksen thing and extended their chance to dig into connections to their case. Had they presented a plan to her, rather than being caught without one, the temperature in her office might not have been so chilly. The corners of her lips twitched and her head shook slightly as she ordered them to take a seat, her voice more forceful than usual. Smeg sat up straight in his chair, aware that what was coming would make his high school gym teacher look timorous.

"You set up surveillance on Erikksen?" Her eyes managed to fix firmly on both of them at once as she continued, the question clearly not requiring an answer. "Without permission. The reason these operations require forethought is so that harms can be weighed against possible benefits."

That basic bit of police procedure they, of course, knew.

"We turned it over to Cyber Crimes as soon as we had evidence of computer tampering," Smeg said.

"Yes, but you didn't stop there, did you?" This time, she waited for a response.

"We've stopped." Smeg drew in a deep breath. "We're closing in on Golding. We've got results from Patel's blood test and his coffee. Both show higher-than-normal levels of arsenic. The video feed shows her entering Patel's office when he isn't there and after hours."

He didn't mention Abercrombie's daughter. They still needed to figure out what her game was, but Singer didn't need to know that. It weakened their case against Golding. They'd brought Pelham in for questioning, which had revealed an attention-seeking young woman who seemed unable to get her life started in any meaningful direction. Not surprising. But he still wondered how far she'd go.

"Where would she be getting arsenic?" Singer's voice had returned to a reasonable decibel.

"Her husband works in a veterinary lab at the university," Byatt said. "We think we have enough for a search warrant."

"Okay. Move forward," Singer ordered.

They'd been dismissed. Relatively unscathed.

Chapter Twenty-Four

Smeg leaned up against his truck, parked at the back of the research station parking lot, and appraised the sprawling University of Alberta south campus. He knew the university farm was a source of pride as one of the best agricultural research and teaching facilities in North America. Recently, two world-class athletic facilities were added to the site. Paul's friend Femi had been in a volleyball tournament a few years back and Smeg had dropped by. Beyond that, he hadn't paid much attention, over the years, to the small farm plot in the middle of the city, except when the wind was blowing in the wrong direction. Then he was reminded of the cows, pigs, and chickens housed in the cleanly laid out barns. The odour wafting on the breeze was reminiscent of the warm summer days of his boyhood. But today it was his breath that hung in the air, in the form of ice crystals. He didn't mind. Things were about to heat up.

He brought his attention back to the parking lot, where he waited for the rest of the team to arrive. His battered vehicle didn't stand out like a marked police car would, but it was still best to stay out of the way until the search was officially launched. Then absolutely he'd be in the thick of it. Randy Lavoie, Golding's husband, had the misfortune of working in the poultry research centre. Applying for grants was a job that could be conducted anywhere, Smeg would have thought, so why down here on the farm? Although the obvious connection to a role that was mind-numbing enough to require a certain holding of one's nose meant Lavoie was likely suited to the location. And if the state-of-the-art facilities and equipment were any indication, he was adept at bringing in money.

Smeg had done his research as well—arsenic was used in chicken production. Tiny doses cause the chickens to gain weight faster and also protect them from parasitic infection. The addition of arsenic to chicken feed needed government approval and this lab was involved in research and safety studies toward that end. The form of arsenic was organic, but unfortunately, carcinogenic. In North America, trace amounts were deemed safe. The same had not been determined in relation to manure produced by chickens that had been fed arsenic, so more research was needed—it seemed likely the poison was being used on the premises.

Smeg was not so interested in chicken poop and had followed Google to chicken McNuggets. McDonald's, while not needing to be redeemed in his eyes, apparently only bought chicken meat from producers that didn't use arsenic. Trans fats would take a lot longer to kill you, he reasoned. He stepped away from his truck as Byatt pulled up and got out of her car. She'd had to wait for the search warrant but was still ahead of the forensic team.

“All quiet?” she asked and placed a gloved hand on his arm.

"Yes," Smeg said. "Lavoie's vehicle is parked by the front door." He pointed to a late-model, cobalt SUV. "Not a lot of other vehicles, so hopefully we won't encounter too many people when we enter."

Byatt appraised the site. "Peaceful little spot in the middle of the city. A bit like an urban park. I come in the summer and fall to buy vegetables from the community garden."

"Seriously? They grow vegetables?" Smeg stared at the snow and tried to fathom what was underneath. Considering his mixed farm experience, he now saw steak *and* baked potatoes. "Any problems getting the warrant?"

"They were busy this morning so a bit slow, but the judge didn't have any questions. With pretty clear evidence that an undercover officer was poisoned, they were anxious to put a stamp on it."

"Excellent," Smeg said. "We've got a tail on Golding. Once we enter this building and her husband knows we're sniffing around, he may call her. She could start cleaning things in the office or head home to get rid of evidence there."

"Then what?"

"If we have evidence here, we'll have to get a warrant for the home. If there's something there, we'll find it even if she tries to cover her tracks."

The two officers who made up the search team pulled into the lot. They were in a marked car that they parked adjacent to the front door. Show time. Smeg and Byatt walked over.

"Let's go," Smeg said. "Before there are too many eyes on us."

They entered the building and were met with glittering machines, Petri dishes, test tubes, and computers. Smeg had no idea who to present the search warrant to. Foghorn Leghorn didn't seem to be around. Conveniently, a bell had rung as they entered and shortly, a man in a white lab coat, likely tall if not stooped, wearing safety glasses, entered from the chicken coop. Smeg supposed the area that housed the chickens had a more formal name, but he couldn't imagine what it was.

"We're looking for the person in charge," Smeg said.

"I'm the lab supervisor," he said. "What can I do for you?"

"We have a search warrant for the premises." Smeg showed it to him. "It allows us to collect specific evidence of a crime."

"You are in the wrong place," he said. "This is a research lab. We deal with chickens."

Smeg waited for him to review the warrant. To say the man was surprised would be an understatement; his eyes widened and his mouth fell open as if it were feeding time and a bucket of hot wings had just arrived.

"What crime?" he asked. "We do research into chicken feed. Does someone think we're stealing it by taking handfuls out each night in our backpacks? I can guarantee there's no missing equipment. Or plots to overthrow the poultry industry."

"We know that." Smeg motioned for the team to move in. "The crime is specific to chemicals you use for research."

The man frowned. He had a burn on his forehead that reminded Smeg of an incident in his high school chemistry class that resulted in the building being evacuated. He hadn't been directly involved, but his grandma had given him a safety lecture anyway.

"We'll need everyone out while we collect evidence," he said.

The frown turned to outrage. "We're in the middle of sensitive experiments."

"The active researchers can continue working for now. We'll start with the storage units. Can you show us where the chemicals are kept?"

The man pointed to a large, yellow, metal cabinet with glass doors.

"We'll need that unlocked," Smeg said.

He noticed a fire extinguisher beside the cabinet. The room was neat and tidy with no obvious hazards. At a quick glance, it appeared to be compliant with safety codes.

"And," Byatt interjected. "We'll need to talk to Randy Lavoie. Can you direct us to him?"

"Lavoie is in the administration office." He pointed to the back corner.

Smeg and Byatt made their way directly to him as the other two officers headed for the supply cabinet.

"Randy Lavoie?" Byatt asked as she stepped up to a desk with his nameplate on it.

"Yes?"

He was a nice-looking man, handsome rather than striking, in his mid-forties. He wore jeans with an untucked grey button-down shirt, sleeves rolled up. Dressing casual was one perk of an office located on the farm. His pleasant demeanour matched his wife's.

"We're detectives and we're here with a search warrant. We're going to need to look at your workspace."

"What?" Like Golding, his quick smile flickered off and then back on.

"We're investigating a crime," Byatt said. "You can go for a walk."

"I assume you're looking at everyone?"

Neither of them responded.

"Fine," he said and unplugged his laptop from the docking station. "I'll go work in my car."

Byatt reached for the laptop. "The computer stays with us."

Smeg followed Lavoie out the door. When Lavoie got outside, he pulled a cell phone from his pocket. Byatt had his work phone, but apparently, he also had a personal cell. He made a call as he walked slowly around the perimeter of the parking lot. Smeg stayed out of sight, close enough to hear his conversation.

"Yeah, babe, they've taken my computer. Can't imagine they'll find anything there. We really didn't talk about it electronically." After a pause, he said, "If you can head home and have a look around that'd be a good idea."

Smeg walked back toward the door, pulled his own phone out of his pocket and called the officer in charge of the surveillance on Golding. "She's headed home to seek and destroy evidence. Have the unit follow her there."

Like Lavoie, he forgot to look behind him.

"What the hell?" Lavoie said. "You're tailing my wife? That's bullshit. If you've got some beef with this place fine but what do you want with her?"

"Seems like you've pulled her into it, given the call you just made to her."

"Just because I made a phone call doesn't mean it was to her."

"'Babe' is your pet pig?"

"Only in Alberta would you go after university researchers," Lavoie said. "I doubt you watch the oil patch this closely. This is a shit show."

Smeg watched him storm off, slam his car door, and spray gravel all the way out of the parking lot. Smeg went back to the shit show. Or was it manure?

He crossed back over to where Byatt was hunched over Lavoie's computer. "We managed to get in before it timed out, so we don't even need his password."

"Have you checked his deleted emails yet?"

"Yeah, just scanning through. Listen to this one he sent to Golding. *You're going to have to stop now. Boss is starting to ask questions*. That email was sent six months ago, so he may not have known she continued to administer the poison."

"Did she reply?"

"Doesn't look like it. She likely knew better. I think she's the more devious one."

Smeg pulled out his phone and called the surveillance officer again. "Where are you?"

"Parked across the street from Golding's house. She just pulled into the garage."

"Okay, hang tight, I'm on my way. We have enough to arrest her."

"Fuck, Smeg, there are kids heading up the front sidewalk."

"Her husband's on his way. We'll get them out of the house before we take her in."

"What about him? An undercover officer has been poisoned."

"He's an accessory but we'll deal with that later. My guess is he didn't know the extent to which Golding was using the arsenic."

The house was on a cozy, tree-lined street across from a colourful playground. Smeg tucked his truck in behind the officer's car, got out, and tapped on his window. The officer stepped from his car, and they walked to the front door. Lavoie answered. It appeared to take him a moment to register the meaning of their presence.

He gave Smeg a dagger of a look. "You get the hell away from my family."

Smeg said, "How about you take your kids out for a bit while we chat with your wife."

"She's told you everything she knows already. You're not coming in here."

"We can wait for the warrant before we come in. As long as your wife comes out."

He didn't move.

Smeg said. "Gotta wonder what she's afraid of. Avoiding us doesn't look good."

"I'll get her, but you stay here." He closed the door.

Shortly, it was reopened by Golding. She had a winning smile for them both as she gazed at a spot somewhere between them. She'd found time to put on fluffy pink slippers since racing in the side door.

"What can I do to help? Although I'm sure there's nothing more I can offer, I'd dearly love to assist Deena's poor family answer their questions so they can rest easy. Obviously, no one did anything to harm the unfortunate woman, but I do understand people look to blame when bad things happen."

"How about we step in out of the doorway. We're letting cold air into your lovely house," Smeg said.

"Sorry." She stepped back and waved them in. "Where are my manners?"

She glanced into the living room. Smeg followed her gaze to where everything was, presumably, in its place. Flawlessness met him, elegant pieces of furniture, cushions chosen for aesthetics, not comfort, and a few expensive art pieces on the mantle. Everything matched, consistent with the perfection of her office. Perfect harmony, at least on the surface. He wondered what it took to maintain that equilibrium. Or if maintaining it caused her to crack, a dissonance between the need to have such order and what it took to control it.

The surveillance officer removed his hat. "You should know there's a search team on their way. We have evidence that you gave Deena Hammond trace amounts of arsenic over a period of time."

Golding laughed. "Oh god," she said. "Are you still on that theme?" The officer stared at her, and she met his eyes. "Sometimes people do things they aren't proud of to get ahead in the world," she said. "I mean, everyone does it. Takes credit for someone else's work, doesn't tell them about an important meeting, and withholds documents. It's all part of the game."

"Knowingly causing harm to another person is called assault. When that person dies as a result, it's murder," the officer said.

Golding radiated condemnation as she replied, "I've never intended to hurt anyone. If folks got sick, that's on them."

Smeg said, "I am arresting you for the murder of Deena Hammond. You have the right to retain and instruct counsel without delay. Do you understand?"

Golding laughed again. "You're crazy. This will never stick."

"You'll need to come with us. We'd be happy to do this without cuffs. I notice your husband didn't take our advice to get the kids out of the house. We don't want to make it difficult."

"You're arresting me and you don't want to make it difficult?"

"Get your coat."

Chapter Twenty-Five

The interview room was cold and smelled like the drunk who had just been questioned in it—a pungent aroma of yesterday's alcohol sweating through pores. Smeg was used to the odour, but Golding clearly wasn't. She held a scarf over her nose and inspected the chair before carefully sitting down. During the drive from her house to the station, she had reconstituted her features and, on arrival, presented her public persona. Calm, cool, collected. Byatt, meeting up with them in the hallway, face to face with Golding's perfect smile, rolled her eyes at Smeg. By this point, the evidence of Golding's disconnect with reality was mounting. Entering the building, she had confidently stated her belief that things could be straightened up quickly. Any evidence to the contrary didn't stick. Smeg and Byatt took the chairs opposite her and her lawyer. He turned on the recorder, hoping to pre-empt small talk.

Byatt stated the date and time for the recording. "You are not obligated to say anything, but anything you do say may be given in evidence."

Golding laughed. "No problem. I have nothing to hide. I'll need to get home for dinner. It's my daughter's birthday. Randy doesn't like it when I'm late on special occasion days."

"You know you're under arrest. For murder." Smeg wondered—not for the first time—if they should be requesting a psychiatric evaluation.

"That's a false claim. I'm trained to recognize those. The Minister can't do his job without facts, and my job is to provide them in order to support the government. Like when the closing of provincial parks was to be debated in the legislature. Deena Hammond helped me with the research on that one. Her report said biodiversity is in decline globally and especially in Alberta, where wildlife and wildlands require more space, not less. Pushing animals into reduced tracts of land increases the possibility of disease transmission. But that was false. The Minister was looking for support to close the parks and it is my job to provide it."

And that was the real false narrative. The one Golding told herself every day. He wondered how long it had taken her to reach such a view of the world. Did it come with the job, or did she generally believe she had a grandiose purpose?

Byatt leaned her elbows on the table. "Did that make you mad? When Hammond provided you with information that didn't help your purposes?"

"Yes," she said. "You get it. The department relies on me. That is how I rose so quickly in the organization. I put in the hours and I produce detailed documents to perfection."

Her lawyer turned toward her. "You don't need to talk about that."

Golding looked confused. Momentarily.

"Tell us about Hammond," Byatt said.

"She was a good worker."

"Good enough to advance?"

"Maybe eventually, but she wasn't ready. She needed to be slowed down a bit. You know, until she was ready."

"How did you slow her down?"

"You don't need to answer," her lawyer said.

Again, Golding appeared bewildered and gave her lawyer a blank stare before turning back to Byatt. "I didn't recommend her for management positions. Like I said, she wasn't ready. Randy thought I was a bit rough on her but her health was a hindrance, too."

"How were you rough on her?" Byatt asked.

"What happened wasn't my fault. The accident was caused by bad weather."

The lawyer glared at her.

Smeg took over. "Tell us about the day you found out she had died."

Golding took in a deep breath and tilted her chin upward. "I called a meeting of the staff to inform them of the news. I knew the day would be lost, work-wise, while they talked about Deena and the details of her death. That's an expectation of the healing process. I planned to take care of deadlines personally that day, to get us through. Leadership needed to know the work was being done so as not to deflect it elsewhere out of misguided sympathy."

Talk about a toxic boss. Golding had a sense of satisfaction about her. She was pleased to have managed the whole affair so well. But other stuff came back to Smeg. Russo talking about Golding's euphoria when she was praised by her bosses. Like she'd won a spelling bee or got the best mark in the class on her science test. Daddy would be so proud. *I wonder what he'd think of this mess. Or was he also deluded?*

"And you talked with Randy about the situation?" Smeg said.

"Oh yes, Randy and I have managed my career together. He's supportive, like my father. They both talk about breaking the glass ceiling, but ultimately, my success is about talent. I'm an influencer."

And hopped up on ego. Golding's colleagues had said many things about her, but talent wasn't one of them. They said she wasn't around for her kids. Smeg wasn't sure they would have said that about a man, but the message of her single-minded determination to reach the top was presented by everyone they interviewed. So was the flash of something dark that crossed her brow when things didn't go her way.

"And of course there are jealousies when someone rises in the organization quickly," Golding said.

"Was Hammond jealous of your success?" he asked.

"Probably. I mean, anyone who wants to advance would be jealous."

"How did you deal with that?"

"I kept my distance, didn't get too close. I'm very professional. I made the mistake earlier in my career of getting too friendly with someone. When I pulled back, she accused me of being cold. When she sought employment in a different division, in a different building, she even suggested I'd caused her mysterious illness. It just isn't worth it to get close to people."

"No comment is the answer you're looking for," the lawyer said, shaking his head at her.

"Tell us about these mysterious illnesses," Smeg said. "Hammond's was caused by arsenic poisoning."

"I don't believe that."

Smeg leaned in. "Supplied to you by your husband."

"Why would he risk his job by taking unauthorized chemicals?"

"You tell me."

"I wouldn't ask that of him. I love him and wouldn't want to get him into trouble."

"I submit the real issue is that he loves you," Smeg said. "Enough to get you anything your heart desires. Including your dream job. Hammond was a threat; she was too talented. You got her out of the way."

"She needed to be slowed down a bit."

"By giving her trace amounts of arsenic in tainted water?"

"You don't need to answer that," her lawyer said.

Smeg ordered out for coffee. It was going to be a long night. He'd suggested food as well, but Golding still thought she was going to be home in time for dinner.

"Okay," Smeg said. "Let's get to it." He'd noticed she wasn't even sweating despite the rising temperature in the room. He wiped his brow.

"You mentioned my dream job." Golding sat straight and jabbed herself in the chest with her forefinger. "It's true. I've worked hard to get to where I am. Both Randy and I have. You've seen our lovely home, the result of him supporting me in my career path." She paused. "I'm still not sure what you want from me. Although, I should thank you for profiling me. Not that I need it, but I come out rosy on this one."

"Oh?" Smeg leaned in and raised his eyebrows. This should be good.

"We've fleshed out a problem with staff and these abuses of medical leaves. My branch doesn't tolerate malingerers and that's appreciated by management."

"What we uncovered is a superior undertaking that deftly resulted in one person ill and likely two. Not to mention two recent half-hearted attempts." Smeg tapped the table. "Impressive."

Golding took in a sharp breath. The first slip Smeg had noticed. He felt a lightness in his chest. They were making headway.

"Superior undertaking?"

Smeg nodded. "It was *very* clever, the use of small bits of poison in a water bottle. Who would ever know?"

"Surely you don't know then?"

"We know it was arsenic that killed Hammond," Byatt said." You slowed her down by not promoting her, but the real genius was the person who wielded the poison. That's what truly hampered her progress."

A crease formed across her brow. "There's no one who's smarter than me. I was the one who slowed Hammond's progress. She simply wasn't ready to move into a higher-level position."

"You're the one who poisoned her?" Smeg asked.

Golding shook her head. Smeg's shoulders dropped, then hitched back up.

"I've known all along that you're the clever one." Smeg, a bit breathless, consciously leaned back in his chair. "I could tell from the moment I first met you in your office. Do you remember? You provided so much assistance to us, even detailed notes on each employee. You understood them at a very high level. You must have great emotional intelligence."

He didn't look at Byatt. They both knew Golding's emotional intelligence was zero.

Golding sat very still. She appeared not to know how to respond. Smeg knew she'd lap up the praise, but was also smart enough to know she was walking into something. Sweat formed on her upper lip.

"But Abercrombie is smarter," Smeg's breath came easier. "He even put trace amounts of arsenic in Patel's coffee so that we'd find it and think someone was targeting him. He's very ambitious."

"No," Golding said. "He's not that smart. I only took him on because HR wanted me to. He's been shuffled around the department for years. My boss likes it when I'm agreeable."

"What he managed to accomplish was incredible. I interviewed him. He saw himself as your equal. It's remarkable."

"No." Her voice wavered. "He wasn't smart at all. He's taking credit for my work."

"He said you take credit that isn't rightly yours. In fact, many of your colleagues said the same thing."

Golding looked at the door. "Are they coming with the coffee? Can I have water?"

Smeg ignored her. "There are rumours Abercrombie will get promoted with you in prison."

"He's not the smart one. I am," she asserted.

"No one can top that bit of work with the arsenic."

"He's a moron. You'd know that if you had half a brain."

Smeg waited.

"Did you even talk to him?"

Smeg waited.

"It was me, you idiot. I'm the one who figured that out."

"For god's sake," her lawyer said.

"You poisoned Hammond."

"I just said that I figured it out. I'm the clever one."

Not so clever. You certainly walked right into that one, Smeg thought.

"Do you want food now?" he asked. "Since you're not going home for dinner."

"I'm not hungry." She glared at her lawyer. "Do something."

Her lawyer stared back. "We'll look at bail but I won't be able to arrange it until morning."

We got her, he thought. The butterflies that had been nesting in his stomach abruptly left.

Out in the parking lot, he turned to Byatt. "Great job," he said. And he meant it.

"Thanks. We made a great team." She beamed at him. "Fancy a burger?"

Smeg and Byatt were already seated when Paul walked confidently into the boardroom with a file tucked under his arm. It was one of those blustery blizzard days known only to northerners. The kind that had cancelled school when Smeg lived on the farm, leading to a day of building a fort with bed sheets and reading inside. But today he'd been up and out the door early. The heater in his truck was on the fritz again; fortunately, there was heat in the boardroom for once.

"What do you have for us?" Smeg asked.

"I googled alexithymia," Paul said. "I had no idea this condition even existed. One in ten people has it and likely don't even know that they lack emotions. Some realize they're feeling an emotion but don't know which one it is. Like they might misinterpret butterflies in the stomach as hunger pangs."

"Maybe I have it." Smeg patted his stomach.

"Listen to this from the transcript of Golding's statement," Byatt said. *"I don't spend a lot of time on personal relationships. I've been told I'm very good at maintaining a honeymoon period for longer than expected.*

But after a while, it takes a turn. People don't do what they're supposed to do. I react cognitively mostly, but apparently that's not what people want. Randy's the only person who understands me."

"That fits," Paul said. "People think they should react a certain way, that particular behaviours are expected of them. They can read the social cues. But it isn't emotions making them react, and so it isn't real. It seems fake, because it is fake. A person can only pretend for so long."

"Golding has words for emotions but doesn't seem to know if they're the right words for the right emotion," Smeg said. "She's consistently happy even when the situation doesn't call for cheeriness. Like when Hammond died and she maintained the façade throughout. People thought it was weird. Or heartless."

"What about her kids?" Byatt asked. "She seems to love them."

"Lavoie was adamant that she loves them but did concede she rarely says so. He said she has difficulty saying the words but that doesn't mean anything about the way she feels."

Smeg understood that on a certain level.

Paul scanned through his pages. "The theory says an individual with the condition might recognize a situation that is highly emotional but feels it as a rush of adrenaline, a racing heart, which is scary to them. The reaction is to run away or become verbally aggressive."

Byatt nodded. "In Golding's case, she backed off from anything emotional."

"What are the causes of the condition?" Smeg asked. "Is it genetic?"

"Emotional neglect is a big part of it," Paul said. "Did something happen to her?"

"Her father," Byatt said. "Trauma at a young age. Her father had a psychotic episode when she was eight. There was really no support for her as a child."

Smeg considered what he had read about the condition in the book found in Hammond's car. And whether there was a connection to violent crime. It seemed alexithymia alone wouldn't lead a person to kill a colleague. Nor would it lead to a desire to cause harm if one believed Golding only intended to make Hammond sick. On the other hand, not a lot was known about the condition and its possible connections to past trauma. Golding had likely experienced psychological distress in childhood, the results of which could have triggered post-traumatic stress disorder, even homicidal thoughts.

A psychiatric evaluation was definitely in order. Agarwal's team had also supplied interesting research findings on psychopathy. Primary traits were associated with over-focused attention and reduced processing of information peripheral to the goal. Golding might not have even considered the elimination of things that were in her way, as wrong, only necessary.

Smeg rang Rodriguez's doorbell and waited. He had called to say he was coming, but didn't sense his visit was welcome. It might be because Rodriguez had told him to get lost. Smeg now knew Rodriguez wasn't guilty of the murder and also knew he was definitely an asshole. The door opened with a creak.

"May I come in?" Smeg drew on all his limited charm.

Rodriguez sighed. "Sure."

Smeg didn't wait to be invited to sit down. "Just wanted to let you know an arrest has been made in relation to your wife's death."

The façade softened. "Oh?"

"We've charged Hilaria Golding with second-degree murder. She's admitted to supplying Deena with water tainted with Roxarsone, a type of arsenic."

Smeg waited for a reaction. If he was having an affair with Golding, he wasn't letting on.

Rodriguez let out a long, slow breath. "Why would she do that?"

"She thought she could make Deena sick enough that she'd lose focus on her career goals. She saw your wife as a threat. Apparently, she had done the same thing to another woman a few years back and that woman ended up transferring to a different job. She may have hoped for a similar outcome with Deena."

"That's demented," Rodriguez said. "How did she come by the poison?"

"Her husband brought it home from work."

He thought about the search of Golding's house which had found Roxarsone, a specific type of arsenic compound used in poultry production. It had been mixed with water in a glass bottle found on a shelf in the garage. An empty vial was tucked in behind it on the shelf, dusty and forgotten. She'd dumped the remains from the bottle into the back alley drain when the search team arrived, but trace amounts were still in the bottle. A similar bottle, recently emptied and rinsed, was found in her office.

Smeg was frustrated that a search of Lavoie's lab found none. But then he learned that the drug was no longer approved in Canada and the lab had moved on to other compounds. The logbook showed two vials unaccounted for. The missing Roxarsone was not followed up on, the supervisor said, because it was no longer used and it was assumed someone had simply disposed of it. That someone was Lavoie.

"Did you know either of them on a personal level?" Smeg asked.

He received a blank stare. "No, why would I?"

"We saw you with Golding. In a café."

Recognition dawned. "Oh, that. She wanted to meet. Said she was thinking about Deena and just wanted to talk. I thought she was upset so agreed to coffee. It was weird. She tried to convince me that Deena had mental health problems."

That sounded about right. Golding, trying to shape the narrative.

Charlie had just finished pouring Meaghan's Pilsner Urquell into a tall beer glass when Paul walked into the kitchen, hand in hand with Eloise. A dazzling smile brought out the bronze glow of her face, a contrast to the constant tinge of pink on Paul's ivory cheeks. Charlie had refrained from asking if they were now dating, or were 'a thing' as Paul would have said, but in the days before relationships needed verification by social media, holding hands was the official announcement. Charlie was thrilled. He'd only met Eloise a few times, but she was lovely and brought out the best in Paul. He'd rarely seen him animated in a social situations outside of role-playing video games. And now here he was happily introducing her to Meaghan, who wrapped her arm in Eloise's as if they'd grown up across the street from each other.

"It's so nice to meet you," Meaghan said. "What an outfit. The colours are gorgeous. Like sitting on the sand looking out to the ocean."

Eloise laughed. "Wishful thinking, although a winter vacation would be nice. Maybe Reading Week?" She looked at Paul.

"Don't think I have any holidays accumulated yet." He turned to Charlie.

Charlie clapped Paul on the arm. "Maybe next year. Raj will likely be tired of you by then."

Paul grinned. "Probably is already."

"What can I get you two to drink? Wine? Beer? Or I can mix something."

"Be careful of the mixed option," Paul said to Eloise. "It isn't based on sound bartending theory."

Eloise laughed. "I'd love a glass of white wine."

Charlie motioned for them to sit as he set a plate of appetizers on the table. Pineapple chicken meatballs, spring rolls, and mozzarella sticks, all chosen from the freezer aisle at Save-On Foods. Paul popped a couple of meatballs in his mouth. Meaghan turned to Eloise.

"Tell me about your drama involvement. I hear you were in a play recently."

"It was a version of the play *Twisted*, adapted for urban Edmonton life. The story's a bit cliché, but it was fun. There was a good turnout for it. I think it helped that people are looking for something to do in the winter."

"You were awesome," Paul said. "Although I prefer your non-drug addicted self."

"That was one of the cliché parts—that people of colour are the ones who are addicted." A line formed across her brow. "But events like that one are good for debunking the myths. There was a great discussion forum after, and the media included some highlights of that in their coverage."

Charlie set their drinks down in front of them.

Eloise took a sip. "That's a nice wine."

"Paul picked it out. Apparently, all wine doesn't come in boxes."

She laughed. "So, your case is all wrapped up?"

"There's enough evidence to hold the suspect," Charlie said. "Her husband has been charged as an accessory to murder, but because there are minor children involved, he may be granted leniency by the courts. And because he really was blind to his wife's cognitive issues and subsequent behaviours."

"So sad," Eloise said. "What can parents be thinking?"

"I thought my mother was bad," Meaghan said. "Apparently, she's just the thin edge of the wedge."

Paul looked over at Charlie. "On to the next case?"

Charlie looked at Meaghan. "Yeah." He nodded.

"I was hoping you'd say that." She gave him a warm smile.

Paul grinned. "Maybe the next one will be Abercrombie."

Charlie was warmed by the laughter as he walked over to the stove and removed the lid from the Dutch oven. Giving it a stir, a rich aroma filled the room.

"Irish stew." Paul smiled. "My favourite."

"Let's eat," Charlie said.

Acknowledgments

Detective Charlie Smeg was inspired by a slightly grouchy sixty-five year old silver-top who was a media darling in Edmonton. While not exactly as he seemed in interviews he inspired people for a living. So does Smeg. Only Smeg is sincere to the core—it is his strength as a detective, mentor and stepfather. Many people helped bring him to life.

First thanks goes to Tina and Alex of Rising Action Publishing. Tina for believing that Smeg was a story worth telling and Alex for recognizing that, while odd, the case held together. Both deserve credit for their insightful editing and tireless efforts at building an indie publishing house in Canada. The rest of the team at Rising Action helped bring the book to the public and I appreciate all their efforts.

Thank you to friends who helped edit along the way and in particular my writing group who have kept me moving forward over many years.

Thanks especially to my family for your love, support and enthusiasm for my writing efforts.

About the Author

Diane Wishart is the author of *The rose that grew from concrete: Teaching and learning with disenfranchised youth,* published by the University of Alberta Press. For this work Diane interviewed many at-risk students in an urban high school, young people who have fallen between the cracks in the public school system. What she discovered weren't statistics, but teens and their experiences, needs, and personalities. Diane's work with young people also informed the narrative published in *Case studies in educational foundations: Canadian perspectives,* published by Oxford University Press.

Diane has 20 years of experience in the field of education, including work with Alberta Advanced Education, consulting with post-secondary institutions. Her past teaching and academic publishing includes high school literacy programs for youth, as well as teacher education at the University of Alberta. Diane's first novel, *Smeg* was inspired by attendance at a creative writing workshop on villains, and their counterpart, the detective.

Diane has been a member of the Alberta Writer's Guild writing critique group since 2011, and in July 2014 attended Sage Hill Writing Experience in Lumsden, Saskatchewan where she worked with Merilyn Simonds and Wayne Grady. Diane has attended a variety of writing workshops put on by the Canadian Authors Association, University of Alberta, and MacEwan University. In January 2021 Diane took a writing course taught by Annabel Lyon and Nancy Lee through the University of British Columbia.